# HOUSE OF DEVOTION

# N. E. BUTCHER

Book Cover by Lucy M of Cover Ever After
Developmental Edit by Makenna Albert of On the Same Page Editing
2nd Developmental Edit by Beth Stedman
1st Line Edit by Sarah Lamb of Sarah Lamb Writing
First Edition: September 2025
Identifiers: ISBN 9798987991671 (paperback)

# ALSØ BY

**Contemporary Romance**

House of Deceit
House of Desire
House of Devotion

**<u>Paranormal Romance</u>**

Breaking, Gracefully
Breaking, Gracefully 2 (2026)

# TRIGGER WARNINGS

Graphic sexual acts, vulgar language, stalker, guns present, alcoholism, mention of drug additions, parental abandonment, mention of child sickness and death.

As always, your mental health comes first. This is not an all encompassing list. If you have a specific trigger, please reach out to N.E. Butcher on Instagram @nebutcher_author and she will verify if the trigger is present.

# DEDICATION

To Jessi.
Every sibling relationship I write will always have a bit of us in it.
I've had the time of my life fighting dragons with you.

# CHAPTER ONE

## DOMINIC

A waded up ball of tape sits on the bench next to me. Mocking me. Breaking my routine. The tape on my ankle is too tight. I've taped it every day since I twisted it during my sophomore year of high school. It's muscle memory, but today it's like my muscles have sudden onset amnesia.

I'm not a superstitious person by nature. Except when it comes to football. I've done the same warm up, listened to the same playlist, and gotten dressed in the exact same way every single game.

Taped my ankle the same, too.

Does that mean I've never lost a game?

No.

But I can say we didn't lose those games because I put my socks on in the wrong order.

Maybe it's crazy.

Maybe I need to be checked out by a doctor, but not for my lingering ankle injury.

Maybe I need to have my brain checked.

I rip the tape off my ankle for the fourth time, balling it up in frustration and throwing it behind me.

No one else seems to notice my inability to tape my ankle or the slow breakdown I'm having over something so minuscule. The team is dancing to the music, Ryan Jade's most recent hit blaring through the speakers.

I would dance too.

Normally.

But my ankle. And the tape. And the elephant taking up residence on my chest.

"Can someone *please* pick another song? I'm tired of this trash!" one of the guys yells out.

"Don't act like I haven't seen you doing leg day to "Break Away," Jones!" Tim, our kicker, says with a laugh. He was able to tape his own ankle just fine on the first try.

"I wasn't in charge of the radio!"

"That's what they all say," Scott jokes. "Have you seen her concert outfits? She's hot as shit."

"She's more than just hot," Tim grumbles, as if offended on her behalf.

I grind my teeth. Because of the tape. Not at all because they're talking about how attractive Ryan Jade is. And she is.

Attractive, that is.

She's beautiful, actually.

Ripping off the fifth hack job of a taping, the card she gave me when Anya and I dropped off the cake at her parents' vow renewal, comes to mind. Matte black with nothing but a glossy number. If it is possible to be intimidated by cardstock, this one has my knees quaking.

It's sitting on my bedside table, right beneath the light, the first thing I see every morning and the last thing I see every night.

I've dialed her phone number no less than a hundred and sixty-two times, always chickening out before pressing "call." Maybe my muscles got rid of the memory of how to tape up my ankle in favor of memorizing how to dial that phone number.

I wouldn't blame them if that were the case.

Or, I wouldn't if this wasn't the biggest game of my career.

Of my life.

My first Super Bowl. I can't have any distractions. Not even a beautiful pop star.

"Alright, men," Coach says, clapping as he enters the room, like always. Maybe we are all a little superstitious in different ways. "It's time. There is no tomorrow. This is it. Leave it all out on the field like this is the last game you'll ever play. Take care of the man beside you. Be the men I know you are."

I can't mess with my ankle any longer. The now too-loose tape is what I'm going to be dealing with for the rest of the game. I shove my feet into my cleats and throw on my pads and jersey.

Picking up my helmet, I move to the center of the room with my brothers.

"The sixty minutes on the clock are all there is. Let's make the most of every one. Fly high on three. One, two, three."

"Fly high."

Confetti rains down on me, but it's the wrong color. My helmet weighs a thousand pounds hanging from my fingertips as I trudge to the locker room, my teammates streaming around me. One of the trainers claps me on the back as he passes.

"Hell of a game, Reynier."

"Thanks, man," I answer, my voice empty.

As I reach the tunnel, I take a second and look back. The opposing team's fans remain in the stadium, unlike our own. Bright lights shine down on the stage where the quarterback is accepting the Super Bowl trophy, the score of 28-24 in the background. One score, all that stood between us and victory.

If I hadn't dropped that touchdown pass, we would be celebrating right now.

But the tape on my ankle was too loose and when I came down, it twisted out from under me, the ball falling from my fingers on a fourth and goal. A hail Mary of a last play.

If I had held on.

If I had just taped my *stupid, damn ankle* correctly, we would have won.

For a second, I breathe deep.

From the time I was seven, I have been working toward this goal. I gave up parties and girlfriends in school. My family gave up summer vacations for my camps and their nights and weekends for practices and games.

All for this.

All that sacrifice for this one moment. A moment I might never get again.

And we lost.

My eyes fill with tears as the realization it wasn't just being here I dreamed about my entire life. It was holding up the trophy. My cleats might have touched the biggest stage possible, but I came up short.

It wasn't enough.

*I* wasn't enough.

This was my chance to prove to all the people who told me this was a pipe dream that they were wrong. They weren't wrong enough, though. I made it to the league, but that isn't enough.

Not for me.

Not to silence the doubt deep inside.

"When you do this long enough, sometimes you forget even being here was everything you had ever hoped for." I look over at my coach and his bushy mustache. "It's good, win or lose, to take a moment and soak it in."

"Yes, sir," I say, and we continue staring out at the field for a disappointment-tinged moment.

"So long as you can stay healthy, one day, you're going to have a ring. This"—he waves his hand in front of him—"will be a blip in your career. Don't forget to soak it all in. Because careers in this league are short, and you never know when you'll put those pads on for the last time."

He's right, I may not see the end of it coming before it's here. All it takes is one hit, one move, one fall for it all to disappear like a mirage.

Football is a demanding sport. Physically. Mentally.

Emotionally.

We turn in unison back toward the tunnel, lined with various personnel, giving us this moment, and we head to the locker room where the rest of our team waits.

No one is changing their clothes or in the showers like they would be after a different game. Any other game. Everyone sits there, dejected and broken. Shattered.

"That was a hell of a game, team," Coach says, clapping his hands. Everyone but the players join in. "You all worked your asses off to be here. Sometimes it doesn't work out. This year I have seen you all grow as a team and, men, and I couldn't be prouder of every single one of you. Everything was left out on the field, and that's all I've ever asked.

"It doesn't feel good to lose, I know. I know there are no words I can give you to soothe this sting right now. Now you've seen it. You've seen the top of the mountain and you were a foot from the summit and next season? I know it'll drive you to push harder. Hands in."

He holds his hand in the air and we get up to crowd around, raising our hands as a team.

"Team on three. One, two, three."

"Team."

We stand there for a second before breaking our last huddle of the season. I make quick work of taking off all my clothes and wrapping a towel around my waist, and head toward the showers, wanting to get away from the disappointment I caused.

Our kicker, Tim, is standing with his hands pressed against the wall, head down, the water beating on his neck.

"Hey, man. You did a great job. We'll get it next time," I say, losing my towel and turning on the water.

He doesn't respond, so I leave him be. Losing affects everyone differently, and I don't want to encroach on his process. Especially since my dropped touchdown is the reason we are here right now instead of celebrating.

Walking back into the locker room, the head of public relations comes in and pulls a few guys to go to the interview room, giving me a look telling me I'll be next. I can't stop thinking about Coach's words as I get dressed.

Next year we'll be the ones out on the field celebrating. I'm going to make sure of it.

After my interview, we are shepherded onto the bus, heading for what should've been our celebration, and is now our consolation, the equipment team taking care of clearing out our lockers.

"We are going to have to trade for a new wide receiver," one of the assistant coaches says, unaware I'm walking by. "We need someone we can rely on."

*Trade.*

Just lost the Super Bowl and now I might be traded.

They're going to trade me. My heart races as I move up the aisle, taking a seat in an empty row.

Tank sits next to me, his leg stretched into the aisle. "Next time," he whispers. I nod. "You did good, kid. No matter what anyone says."

"Thanks."

"You'll get a ring. Don't worry."

"That's what Coach said, too. What's it like?" A touch of awe enters my voice. Tank was a part of the last Thunderhawk team that won a Super Bowl the year before I joined.

"It feels like nothing can touch you. Watching my wife walk down the aisle to me is the only thing I've found that was better."

I get that. Dad would say the same thing about Mom. It's something they always instilled in Anastasia and me. Any celebration is better with the right person by your side. And anything is survivable, too. The bus pulls into the hotel our party will be at, our family and friends shuttled over from the stadium.

The space is beautiful, but I don't see any of it. All I can do is look for my parents, a knot forming in my throat.

A part of me wishes Ryan was here. It'd be nice to be looking for a girlfriend or a wife like everyone else. Though, considering I lost us the biggest game of my entire life, I really don't need the distraction.

And then I see them. Dad's arm is around Mom's shoulders, her hands clasped in front of her chest bearing my number, and as she reaches for me, I feel my chin tremble.

"Mom," I say, becoming the fourteen-year-old that didn't make it on the varsity squad my freshman year. Her arms envelop me the way they always do, win or lose. Game of a lifetime or when I don't catch a single pass.

"I'm so proud of you, baby," she says into my neck and I silently cry.

My family is everything to me. There's no way I'm leaving this city. No way I'm going to let them trade me. I'm going to do everything I can to make sure I'm ready for next year.

No matter what.

# CHAPTER TWO

## RYAN

LYING ON THE COUCH in the small dressing room, my head is resting on the arm, bopping to a song on my ever growing hype playlist playing from my phone as I scroll social media. An ad pops up for some energy drink or food or something. I don't know, or really care, as I stare at a stylized shot of Dominic Reynier running down a football field.

When I gave him my card, I'd hoped he would call me. Not only for the tour I offered him, but maybe even for a date. There were sparks aplenty when we met, but it's been radio silence ever since. Maybe I need to host a charity gala for my friend Taylor and her non-profit so I could invite him or something? I know she'd let me, always needing funding for some new research.

Taylor is brilliant. She received a full ride to Harvard where she double majored in Biomedical Engineering and Kinesiology. She followed that up with Orthopedic Surgery at Johns Hopkins. A year into her program, her brother came back from a training exercise with the Marines without an arm. Pivoting, she focused everything she had on helping him and started making custom, high-tech prosthetics.

In the first few years of my career, I would perform at various benefits and fundraisers. If someone wanted to pay me to sing, I was there.

And Taylor was willing.

She had sent me an email, telling me about the foundation she was trying to launch and would I be willing to put my name behind it? After five minutes on the phone with her, I gave her almost every penny I had earned. It didn't amount to much, just a few million, but it was enough to get her started.

I've been on her board every year since, and ten percent of everything I make automatically goes to them. My financial planners love the tax write off, but that doesn't matter to me. I have so much money, I couldn't spend it in twenty lifetimes, and it seems pointless to let it sit there not doing anyone any good.

Thinking about my calendar, I know I don't have time to actually throw a gala. Plus, I wanted Dom to *want* to call me.

Even in the small interaction we had, he seemed so *different*. Kind.

With a sigh, I sit up, my long hair falling down my back. A white envelope under the counter I use as my makeup station catches my eye. Pausing the music, I move, pulling the chair out of my way before crouching down. Snatching it up, I rip it open.

The handwriting on the letter makes my stomach clench. How it ended up in my dressing room, I don't know. We have been screening my mail for over a year. When the letters started to get a little more aggressive.

Knowing it got past my team makes me sick, but there's nothing I can do now. I have exactly two minutes until a hand knocks on my dressing room door, a golf cart waiting to take me to the stage.

Despite the letter, I won't let myself be rattled. I check the clock on my phone.

Twelve minutes until I ride the lift into the middle of the stage to sing in front of seventy-five thousand people.

One hundred twenty-eight minutes until I am back in this room.

And two hundred forty-nine minutes until I'm on a plane home for a few days between shows.

The knock echoes through the dressing room, exactly on time. Like every night of this tour.

"Ryan? We are ready for you," my music manager and right-hand woman, Zoe, tells me through the door.

I push the letter from my mind. Every person out there spent their hard-earned money to be here. They deserve everything I can give them. Pasting my smile on my face, I look in the mirror one last time before making my way to the door.

Zoe's eagle eyes take me in, and I see them make note of the tightness I feel in every muscle. She also knows, after our decade of working together, that now is not the time to address it.

She slides onto the back seat of the golf cart first, and I take my seat quickly, drinking a bottle of water as our driver takes off. Zoe takes out her phone and shoots off a text.

"Ready?" she asks.

I nod, not wanting to use my voice. Other than the vocal exercises my voice coach has given me, I don't talk on concert nights. Especially when I have two shows back-to-back.

We come out of the tunnel and the split second my cart is visible sends those in the nearby seats into a frenzy. I start counting down the last few minutes in my head as people move around me, tugging at my clothes, making sure my hair is just so, checking the mic pack tucked into the back of my glittering dress. I put my monitors in, voices immediately filling my brain. One of the crew leads me under the stage, a flashlight beam helping me step over and through various supports until I'm crouching on the lift, my bedazzled microphone in my hand.

The opening chords of my first song take over in my ears, the guitar and drums faint but there. My lift begins moving as the lyrics are about to start.

"Five, four, three, two." The mechanical voice cuts off, click track taking over, my lift finishes its ascent, and I raise my microphone.

*Pulse of the party, with a groove so sweet,*
*Catching dreams like confetti, dancing on our feet.*

My voice joins the guitar and drums in my ears, and I know I'm on pitch. The crowd goes wild as I move around the stage, singing the first song of the set. Strutting across the stage, my sky-high heels hurt my feet, despite the wardrobe team doing their best to make them as comfortable as possible. My band flows seamlessly into the second song, the drilled choreography flowing out of me without thought. I'm a quarter of a second off the beat, and I quickly make an adjustment, syncing back up.

As our second song comes to a close, the crowd is filtered into my monitors. Hearing the crowd, feeding off their energy is incredibly important to me, so it's important to my audio engineers. The screams, the joy, the happiness brings a genuine smile to my face, and the letter fades from my mind.

"Indianapolis. Night two of two. Hundredth show," the robot tells me in my monitors.

"Hello, Indianapolis!" They scream even louder as I put my microphone in the stand a crew member placed in front of me. "Welcome to the Radiance tour!"

The crowd is electric. My team sent me pictures of their arrival as I was getting ready. Various outfits the color of the rainbow, t-shirts with my name and face. My fans are so creative and I love them all so deeply. Every move I make, I think of them.

They are mine and I am theirs.

"Thirty seconds until next song," I'm told by the mechanical voice.

"For those that don't know, tonight is the hundredth show of this tour and tonight, *tonight*, we have an amazing show for you." I make eye contact with as many of the crowd as I can, trying to memorize even a single detail of them. The glitter in their hair. The happiness on their faces.

The tears.

"Now, I know you know this next song since, as of today, you've made it my newest number one! Will you sing it with me?"

Guitar and drums start back up in my ears, the crowd noise is removed, and the mechanical voice is back.

"Five, four, three, two."

My dressing room is empty and blissfully quiet. I collapse on the small sofa, unzipping the boots from my last costume change. A deep, enthusiastic moan escapes me as I set my feet flat on the floor for the first time in almost two hours. The water in the unopened bottle on the table is lukewarm and tastes like heaven as I chug half of it in one go.

A sharp knock at the door interrupts my relaxing, and Zoe pushes into the room.

"Ryan? Are you almost ready? We have the groups waiting in the other room."

"Do you think they'll be disappointed if I wear my slippers?" I ask, desperate not to put my shoes back on. Her face is full of sympathy and even without words, I know the answer. My body is exhausted, pure grit keeping me from lying on the ground.

Some of my Jade Stones, the name my fans gave themselves, are waiting for me and that has me reaching for my rhinestone boots, shoving my swollen feet back into them. I check my face in the mirror, wanting to give them the best picture they can have, and turn on my smile.

"I'm ready," I tell Zoe, and we leave the room. She runs through the names of the fourteen people waiting for me, any pertinent details, and flicks through their pictures on her phone. Memory exercises are an important part of my day for exactly these types of situations.

Before I stepped on my first stage, sang under my first spotlight, had my first crowd cheer for me, Mom, technically my Aunt Margo, but she became 'mom' when she took me in after my parents abandoned me, told me every moment of my career would be decided by my fans. My payment for having every dream come true is to give them everything I have, and make them feel seen when they meet me.

And because I love it. I love making their experience the best I can. This industry is hard, and no one knows better than me what it can take from you, but whenever I get to hug my fans, when they tell me how much my songs mean to them and get them through their darkest of days, I know I would never want to do anything else.

So I take as much time as my highly regulated schedule allows.

Excited voices reach my ears and I push away my exhaustion and through every ache. Two of my security team stand outside the room. Seeing my approach, they grab the doors and open them for me like I'm the queen.

"Thank you so much, fellas," I say and make my way into the room. Snacks and drinks for the guests sit on a table against one wall. Various spots around the perimeter are set up as photo stations we will utilize together, shortly.

A scream meets my ears as the first guest catches sight of me, triggering the others, and I smile in welcome. They all rush me, and I hug all of them, greeting them by name in turn before I step back, taking a small amount of space for myself.

"Hi, everyone! Thank you so much for coming tonight to see me play. I think I might have one more song in me. Would y'all like to hear it?" One of my team brings my acoustic guitar, the same one I wrote my first song on, while another brings me my chair.

Everyone takes their seat, eyes on me. I swallow, my throat a little scratchy. Zoe hands me a bottle of water, anticipating my needs.

I strum the first chords and all of their faces light up, Sarah clapping the hardest. She had posted the other day about how this was her favorite song and my team had found it. Tonight was her first concert, a celebration of her father getting a new job after nearly a year of being laid off. They wanted to surprise her after all the sacrifices the family had made to limit their expenses. I smile at her, holding her gaze for a moment.

The lyrics come out perfectly and soon they are swaying to one of my favorites from my second album. As the song comes to a close, I hand Sarah the pick I was using while the others are given new ones.

Zoe steps up as I hand off my guitar.

"Alright, everyone. We are going to do pictures and autographs now. Each person will only have a few minutes, unfortunately, as we have a flight to catch, so only one item can be signed. Bethany, would you like to start us off?"

Each guest gets five minutes with me. In exactly seventy minutes, I'll be back in my dressing room, taking these shoes off my feet once more.

Youngest of all my guests, Bethany with the blue hair stands up. Her pigtails are full of silver tinsel and she's missing her front two teeth. My heart melts as she all but throws herself into my lap.

"Bethany, thank you so much for coming tonight! I'm so excited to meet you."

""Saving My Soul" was my favorite song. The dress was really pretty." Her little voice has the slightest lisp as I tuck my hair behind my ear, a parent with a cell phone trained on us moving around in my periphery.

"I'm going to tell you a secret," I say, leaning close and dropping my voice a little, "that's my favorite dress. When I first tried it on, I twirled in it. Do you like to twirl in dresses?"

Her eyes light up, like I knew they would. "Twirling is my favorite thing!"

"Mine too! Would you mind if we take a picture together?" I ask her, Zoe subtly signaling the end of our time. Bethany nods and we turn toward her parents, my smile perfect as they snap various shots. Zoe takes a few herself to add to my photo album before handing me the Sharpie to sign the picture Bethany's parents hold.

I stand from my chair, and move around the room, meeting the remainder of my Stones until, finally, the last one leaves, happy tears streaming down his face.

Exhausted, the smile falls from my face, but I don't regret the extra time.

"Let's get you changed and back to the house," Zoe says, saddling up to my side, and ushering me out of the room to the golf cart waiting to take us back to the dressing room.

I love concert nights, but nothing sounds better than my bed now.

# CHAPTER THREE

M Y HAND SLAPS OUT of my fluffy bedding, silencing my alarm. Knowing I set it for the last possible second, I press the button on my bedside table, pulling up the blackout shades. Sunlight filters in the floor to ceiling windows overlooking the small courtyard, a luxury in New York City.

The hardwood floor is cool beneath my feet, and I wonder, for what feels like the millionth time, if I should redo the floors and have heat added. But the thought of pulling out one of the few remaining original features in the hundred-year-old house makes me incredibly sad.

Just because you can afford to do something to a house doesn't mean you should. Some of the most beautiful character can be stripped out in favor of following new trends.

The bottoms of my feet ache as I walk into the bathroom. Thankfully, the masseur will be here later to help.

A soft pink clawfoot tub stands in front of a frosted picture window and is the first thing I see every time I walk into this bathroom. It's my favorite tub in the houses I own, and I promise myself I'll do a bubble bath this week. Moving to the double shower, I turn on one side, letting the water warm as I strip out of my clothes and put them in the hamper for the staff.

When I'm not on tour, I like to be self-sufficient. While I have housekeepers year-round, I don't like to have everything done for me. It doesn't matter I can afford the service. If the clothes can go in a washing machine, I'm going to take care of it. But with the crazy schedules and late nights, it's easier to have someone take care of those tasks for me. It's also when I'll hire a private chef, making sure my body is fueled to handle the increased demand so I can make it through the set without feeling like I'm going to pass out.

Stepping beneath the stream, the water pressure is perfect. There are a few things in this world that can make me feel like a new person, and taking a shower is one of them. Without a lot of time to linger, I get my hair and body washed before turning off the water and dry myself. My favorite fluffy robe is toasty from the towel warmer and I sigh at the decadence.

This really is my favorite bathroom.

The vanity is covered in various products meant to keep my porcelain skin hydrated, supple, and wrinkle free, because God forbid I age in any way. With the invention of high definition, my skincare is incredibly important and something I prioritize every morning and night, no matter what time I'm going to bed. I also make sure to coat my body in various lotions because America's pop star can't have dry elbows or knees. There would be bedlam.

The slow part of my day is always my favorite. No one asking me questions. No one pulling at my hair, or adjusting my clothes, or telling me where to stand. I can exist in peace.

No matter how much I love the fans and the music and performing, there are days when it can all be too much. If I wanted to, I could stop working tomorrow and have no one bother me ever again. Just quit. No more songs or concerts or interviews.

Only peace.

I think about it for a moment.

Every five years or so, I consider hanging everything up. Disappearing off the face of the Earth like I'd never been there to begin with, leaving only my music behind as proof of my existence.

Then, a song will work its way into my brain I know I have to share.

That will deserve to be sung on stage with my fans screaming the words back to me.

And I know I'll never be able to quit, the music too much a part of me.

At least, not now. Maybe in the future.

A future I can't see.

Knocking at the door startles me from my thoughts. The bottle of lotion hits the ground beside my foot.

"Ryan?" Zoe calls out. I must not have heard her letting herself into the house with the key I had made. "Hair and makeup are here. Please be out in five minutes." Footsteps move away from my door. She knows I won't keep people waiting.

A pet peeve of mine. Once I was kept waiting by a powerhouse I was going to collaborate with for two hours. Myself and six other people were there, ready to record the song, waiting on her. I vowed then and there no one would ever have to waste their time checking their watches for my arrival.

I bask in the final few moments of being alone. The voices of my newer hairdresser and Elaine, my longtime makeup artist, echo as my housekeeper shows them to the bedroom I have designated for these types of things.

Grabbing up my phone, I leave my bedroom, knowing the bed will be made long before I come back.

"Hey, y'all," I say, entering the room, as the team is unpacking their various tools.

"Ryan! It's so good to see you," Elaine says. Her tight coils bounce around her head as she comes over to kiss my cheek in hello. The light in the room catches her subtle highlighter, making her dark brown skin look like it's glowing from within.

"I've missed you! Your protege is doing *amazing* on the tour. I wish you could have come with us, though."

Her hands go to a small bump, a loving look coming over her face.

"I do, too, but you know my husband. I had to call my doctor and have them tell him it was okay for me to continue working before he'd let me even leave the bed. Traveling for months? He would have had a stroke."

"Well, as soon as you get your registry put together, make sure to send me a link."

"I will. So, what are you thinking today?" She takes my arm and leads me over to the chair, the hairdresser giving me a small wave as he continues to unpack his hair tools.

"Honestly, I'd like to let my skin breathe today. Could we"—I wave my hands in front of my face—"go bare?"

Her eyes melt in understanding. "Sweetie, we can do whatever you want." She takes my chin in her hand, moving my face this way and that as she studies me. While we have been working together for the better part of a decade, she always takes a moment to study her canvas. Everything from the amount of sleep I've had, water I've drunk, and products I've used can dictate her approach.

And she is nothing if not a master of her craft.

"How about some mascara, a small amount of blush to give you color, and a light pink gloss? Or would you like to go *bare* bare?"

"Whatever you think is best. I trust you," I tell her and she nods, moving to her various cases, grabbing the few products she needs.

The hairstylist stands, turning toward me. "If you're going simple on the makeup, we are going to go simple on your hair."

"Sounds great," I tell him. He joined the team in the past year. We have yet to get particularly close since I have a tour specific hair team and we haven't had much time together.

He grabs some products, working them through my wet strands.

"Good morning!" Zoe says, walking into the room, handing me my favorite iced chai latte.

"Bless you," I say, taking a drink.

"Anything for you. Now, let's go through the itinerary. You have thirteen interviews at fifteen minutes each." She runs through a list of the various radio stations, television shows, and podcasts I'm going to be meeting with today.

The stylist turns on the hairdryer, pulling my strands taut with a brush while he aims the hairdryer at my hair.

"Did you already do your skincare this morning?" Elaine asks.

"Yes, ma'am. Just like you taught me."

"That's my girl." She pulls out some little gel under-eye patches, placing them on my face. The cooling effect is almost immediate. "Tilt your head back a bit or they'll slide off."

"Cash has tried reaching out again. Do you want to respond?" Zoe asks.

My shoulders slump. "What was it about this time?"

"The usual. He's given up drinking and the models. He's ready to settle down and wants to get back together."

One thing about Cash is he is good at promising me everything will be different if I'd just give him a chance. Apparently, the five chances before this weren't enough. He was one of the first people I collaborated with on my debut album. He was so nice, lending me a sympathetic ear, and before long, it leaked we were dating.

He called me, outraged someone would tell the press about us.

Everywhere we went was stalked by photographers trying to catch a glimpse of us together. We would wear wigs and other various disguises to hide, yet they always seemed to find us. Him calling them to let them know where we were helped. I was so naïve, I didn't realize it was unusual for paparazzi to follow burgeoning artists.

And then both of our careers exploded. We were invited to every party and award show, and it was the beginning of the end.

At only sixteen, we were being offered anything we wanted. It started with a drink here or there, until his weekends would be spent in a drunken stupor. He started becoming entangled in various scandals culminating in a model being splashed across the cover of every magazine with "Cash's Other Woman."

That's when Zoe came into my life.

She was starting to gain traction in the industry, ten years my senior, when she approached me at an awards show a week after the cheating broke in the news.

"*Women are held to a different standard in this industry and that boy is going to tank your career before it can even take off. I'm going to stop it for you. Call me.*" She handed me a simple card with her name and phone number before walking off. I called her the next day, and she's been beside me every day since.

Normally music managers aren't as involved in the day to day like Zoe is, but she's meshed into my life. As her only client, she's become more my career manager. She and her team handle everything for me.

"Ignore him."

"Got it. Your mom called. She asked if you wanted her to meet up with you at the next leg? She's out of town this week, so she won't get to see you during your off days."

"If she's free, that'd be great."

My phone vibrates in my hand, one of my actress friends, Sky, inviting me to a gallery opening. I don't respond immediately, unsure how I'll feel after all these interviews. I also don't know if I want to be photographed today. One thing I can count on is if I leave my house, there's going to be craziness, and the last thing I want to do is take attention away from the artist having their show.

Zoe would also have to do research on the artist. Any time I go to an event in public, we have to make sure I want to support the person or business.

Because my mere presence tells the world I endorse them, we have to vet everything.

The chef comes into the room, carrying a full food tray and my favorite tumbler cup filled with iced water.

"I'll place this over here for you, Miss Jade," he says before backing out of the room.

"Miss Jade?" Justin, one of the security guys calls out from the hallway. "Where would you like the camera team to set up?"

"What do you think about blue mascara today?" Elaine asks at the same time.

"In the sunroom please," I call out to Justin before answering Elaine. "Sounds fun."

Zoe's assistant, Paige, walks into the room, talking in lowered tones. Ears filled with sounds, I miss the peace of my bathroom.

Before I know it, my hair is done. It's perfect for what Elaine will be doing with my makeup. It looks tamed but not sleek or overdone. Simple. A timer beeps on Elaine's phone and she removes the under-eye patches, and slathers my face in a moisturizer.

"That needs to set for about ten minutes. Why don't you go ahead and eat while you wait."

"This is why you're my favorite," I tell her, making my way over to the table and begin shoveling in my food. One thing I've learned over the years is I have to take every opportunity to eat when I can. Too many days have been so packed with various meetings, interviews, and award shows there wasn't a moment to eat.

She and Zoe come over to sit with me while the stylist starts packing up his various tools.

"How did your date go?" Elaine asks Zoe and I almost drop my fork.

"You went on a date?" I ask.

Zoe's cheeks pink with her blush, an expression I don't think I've ever seen on her face.

"It went okay. I don't have time to get into a relationship though, *which I told you*, so I probably won't see him again." Guilt eats away at my stomach. She doesn't have time to date because of me. She must feel me turn in on myself because she pats my hand, continuing to talk to Elaine. "You weren't lying on him looking like Michael B. Jordan. They could be twins."

"I told you!"

The ladies talk while I eat my food, my mind once again trying to wander to the different possibilities of why Dominic never called me. Stopping the thought in its tracks, I focus on the here and now. It's so nice when I'm not the center of attention. I live for the moments where I fade into the background and can just exist. But those moments never last. Elaine gets me back into the chair and in under five minutes, she has enhanced my features perfectly while keeping my skin bare but for the cream blush.

I say goodbye to my glam team, getting a promise out of Elaine to send her registry once more, and then head back to my bedroom and pull on a comfortable ice blue boat neck sweater and perfectly tailored jeans.

Taking a moment before I cross the threshold into the parlor, I settle into Ryan Jade, the pop star. Ready, I walk into the room, heading straight to the computer where my first interviewer waits.

# CHAPTER FOUR

## DOMINIC

"Hey, Reynier! You lost me a grand with that dropped catch!" some guy standing in line outside my sister's bakery yells as I cross the parking lot to the front door.

I nod but don't engage. Mostly, the fans have been forgiving in person, telling me we'll get them next time. Online, however, it feels like the entire world is calling for my transfer. Squeezing past a customer holding the door open while they wait their turn, I enter the best bakery in town.

The smell of sugar and chocolate greets and relaxes me. Bright blue and pink walls burn my retinas. When Anya rented this place, it was an ice cream shop. Without a lot of money, she focused on getting equipment instead of updating the store. It's been busy enough since Ryan Jade posted about it last year, they have sold out of everything every day regardless of how much they make.

Hopefully, she'll be able to redo the place soon. It could really use a facelift.

"Hey, Liam," I say, greeting the high schooler working the counter.

"Hi, Dom." He looks at the customer he's ringing up. "Your total is $29.76, ma'am." He swivels the tablet toward her. "You'll catch it next time."

"I'll make sure of it." My family has a deep soft spot for Liam and are going to be incredibly sad when he graduates high school and moves on. "Where's Anastasia?"

Once the woman has paid, he pulls the tablet back toward himself, thanks her, and begins ringing up the next customer.

"She's in the back. We ran out of one of the cookie flavors faster than we expected, and she wanted to get them baking before leaving with you."

I start making my way to the kitchen, but I pause, turning back toward my sister's employee. "Want to come to a game this season? Anastasia can bring you with her. We can get you on the field and everything."

Assuming I'm still here next year, but I leave that part out.

His smile is wide, the small gap between his front two teeth reminding me of my smile before I had braces. Granted, his gap is endearing whereas mine was as wide as a freeway.

"Seriously? That'd be amazing!" He runs over to me and throws his arms around me, trapping my arms at my side. One of my favorite things about this kid is his enthusiasm. I pat him on the back, and then he releases me, returning to ringing up his customers.

"When it gets closer, we'll figure out which games works for you. Make sure your parents are okay with it in the meantime."

"Okay! Thanks, Dom."

I give him a thumbs up before making my way into the kitchen. Anastasia is at a mixing bowl, her arm moving quickly, stirring whatever is in there. Courtney is pulling a pan of something amazing smelling from one of the ovens. When Ryan hired Anya, she brought Courtney on to help out. It's worked really well for the past few months and has given my sister some breathing room she didn't previously have.

"Hey, A. What did that dough do to you?"

"It insulted our mother, and now, it has to die." She looks up at me, wild eyes and disheveled hair. "What are you doing here?"

"House hunting, remember? You said you wanted to go with me." We had talked about it during the season, but I didn't have time. And now, I don't want to admit I might be traded. Like, maybe if I buy a house, it won't be real.

I reach my hand out for one of the cooling cookies and she delivers a sharp smack to the back of it before pointing to a plate at the end on another counter, a giant cookie waiting.

I take a bite as she begins weighing out cookie balls.

Courtney moves over to me, another pan of desserts in her hands. She leans in.

"Gimme a bite," she says, holding her mouth open. With a laugh, I hold the cookie out to her and she takes a huge chunk.

"Holy shit!" I gasp, laughing as she chews and walks to the ovens. It's like having two sisters in the kitchen now.

"I'll be ready in ten minutes. Give me a hand?" Anya says, ignoring our antics.

I give her a salute, shoving the last chunk of cookie into my mouth, Anya rolling her eyes at my chipmunk cheeks.

"How has your week been?" She rolls a cookie dough ball before setting it on the awaiting tray. "Have you started working with your trainer yet?"

"Nah, she gave me the week off to rest. Then we are going to start working. I want to improve my explosiveness this year."

"Did one of your coaches mention that?"

Opening my mouth to tell her what I overheard, I really look at her. She's not only disheveled, she looks exhausted. Deciding to put off telling her again, I move to help her.

I grab gloves from the box of extra larges Anya keeps for when I help. Slipping them on, I begin moving the cookies in the way Anya taught me when she first started the bakery.

"I haven't met with them yet. That'll come, but it's something we discussed throughout the season."

She nods and we get to work, cranking out the cookies as fast as possible. Dad walks in to help Courtney, kissing Anya's cheek, who's calling out instructions even after the door has shut behind us.

Within twenty minutes, I'm standing in a house I'm not sure I should even be buying.

Not with possibly being traded.

Our bonuses for making it to the Super Bowl were more than I anticipated. Added to the sizable savings I've accumulated over the past few seasons, I decided back in November I wanted to buy a house at the end of the season.

Now I wonder if the coaches are in process of negotiating my transfer to another team. The Hawks could pay me half of what I was making and I'd accept it to stay here near my family and on this team.

One thing that's been difficult about being a professional athlete is the instability. I could be cut or traded and have to pick up my entire life in a flash, so I've been renting an apartment this entire time. It was nerve wracking my first year. Any time I dropped a pass or ran the wrong route, I thought for sure I was going to be let go.

But I wasn't.

My coaches worked with me tirelessly, and this past year I feel like I finally settled into the team. All those roots I was planting might get pulled out all because I couldn't catch the most meaningful pass of my career.

"This house is 4,600 square feet. It's a little outside your price range, but it's a new build. Apparently, the person who had it built passed away about six months after it was done. I know the price tag is high at seven million, but Hightower Homes is one of the best builders in the state," my realtor tells me as I look through the glass wall and out over the pool.

"Hightower Homes? They made this?" I ask, turning to look at her.

She looks up from her notes. "Yes, you know it?"

I smile. Parker's company. "I've heard a thing or two."

"Apparently, the business has blown up after he was on *House of Desire*, the dating show? Other than this one, only one of the other homes built by them has ever gone on the market. It went for two million over asking because of the quality. I think the extra half a million is worth it."

It's a beautiful house. Perfect in every way. Plus, I know Parker would never cut a single corner. Wouldn't it be funny if I ended up in a house my sister's boyfriend built?

But what does a single guy, whose family lives in the same city, need with five bedrooms?

Randomly, the thought of Ryan Jade comes to mind and I wonder if she'd ever live in a house like this. I feel like she'd want something homier. Then again, maybe she expects extravagance in every facet of her life. It's not like she can't afford it.

"Did you know your boyfriend built this house?" I ask my sister, walking into the kitchen, pushing thoughts of Ryan from my mind.

"No wonder it's such high quality. What do you think of this one?"

"I'm not sure I should be buying a house," I say, leaning my forearms on the counter.

She pauses and looks down at her phone. "I think you're wrong."

My gut twists at the thought of possibly being traded and I switch topics.

"You remember Ryan Jade?"

"The global pop sensation one Tony away from an EGOT?" She makes an exaggerated thinking face. "The name sounds familiar."

"You're such a smartass."

"Don't ask questions you know the answer to then, dum-dum. What about the incomparable Ryan Jade?"

"I never called her, but I want to."

"You *still* haven't called her? Dom! It's been like four months!"

"Three months."

She smacks her forehead with her palm, before giving me the most exasperated expression I've ever seen.

"Why, you absolute jackass, the hell haven't you called her? You should and beg for her forgiveness for not doing so earlier." She talks slowly, enunciating every word.

Looking down, I trace the marbling on the countertop.

"I think I might get traded." Maybe I'm not too worried about her exhaustion to unload on her.

"You know she like, owns planes, right? She can see you in whatever city you live in." I look at her and she must finally see something in my face. "Okay, what's really going on?"

"Is it dumb to be looking at a house to buy in a city I might not live in for much longer? They might *trade me*, A. I'd have to move away from you and Dad and Mom. I've never lived in another city. I *love* this team. I've never wanted to play for anyone else."

"I don't think it's dumb. You could always keep the house here and when you retire, move back in it. Rent it in the meantime or something. And you'll see us plenty. In the off season you could come visit. But I don't think they are going to trade you, Dom. You fit in this team. You had a bad game."

"I had a bad game at the most important game of the season."

"You'll do better."

We fall into silence. I can hear the realtor moving about, but she gives us our space and I appreciate it.

"Ryan would be a distraction and I have to focus."

Anya sighs. "Dom, you're allowed to have a life outside of football."

Annoyance sours my mood. I know it'll pass quickly, I can never stay mad at Anya, but my words are sharp.

"This is what I've always been working for. If my career is long, we are only talking about possibly ten more years. I'll be retired before I'm forty. I don't have time to fuck around. I'll have a life when I'm done."

"You can do both."

"And that's what you did while you were trying to get the bakery to take off? Until you went on *House of Desire* you were basically a nun."

Indignation lights her face, her hands going to her hips and suddenly, I'm looking at Mom.

"I was not a nun!"

"The laundromat on the corner with the guy who pees in the machines saw more action than you did." I can feel how wide my grin is as her jaw drops and I laugh. "What if she doesn't remember me?" I ask, voicing a very real concern.

"She meets a lot of people, Dom. But something tells me she doesn't give just anyone her number. And if she doesn't remember you? Well, that's her loss."

And that's why I asked my sister instead of one of my friends on the team. Because she has the ability to make me feel like I have something to offer to someone so accomplished.

My phone sits on the coffee table. I stand in the kitchen, staring at it. It's been a week since my conversation with Anya and every day my will breaks down more and more. Decided, I walk toward the living room.

Spinning around, I head back to the kitchen.

"This is insane. I'm not *afraid* of texting Ryan," I say to myself. I stare at the phone for a bit longer before exploding into movement.

"This is stupid. Just text her." I snatch up my phone and type out a text.

**Dom: Hi Ryan. You might not remember me, but this is Dominic. I met you at your parents' vow renewal thing with my sister Anastasia. We were dropping off the cake?**

My thumb pauses, but before I can second guess, I hit send and then throw my phone to the other end of the couch so I can't check it obsessively. When it vibrates, I know there's no way she's responding already and assume it's someone else.

**Ryan Jade: Did the doctors get you all fixed up?**

I read her text four times, certain she has confused me for someone else.

**Dom: Doctors? I haven't been to any doctors recently.**

**Ryan Jade: My mistake. I assumed you were in a coma considering I never heard from you.**

My head falls to the back of my couch, relief washing over me. She does remember me.

**Dom: No coma. Thankfully. Just a general fear of rejection.**

**Ryan Jade: So you rejected yourself for me?**

**Dom: I didn't actually think of it that way. I'm really sorry for the delay. I was in season and was trying to stay focused.**

**Dom: I knew if I texted a beautiful woman, the last thing I would be is focused.**

My screen lights up with a video call. Swiping my thumb across the screen, I'm hoping I don't throw up from nerves.

"Are you trying to flirt with me so I won't be annoyed I thought you were ghosting me?" she asks, her voice joking. Her hair is in a bun on top of her head, much like Anya wears when she's relaxing. Escaped tendrils frame her completely bare face.

She's beautiful when she done up for shows and interviews, but seeing her like this, I almost feel like I'm being let in on a secret.

"I was only stating a fact. I didn't figure flirting would be appreciated when I'm trying to grovel." Shifting back into the couch, my stomach settles. There's an unexpected ease to the conversation I've never felt with anyone else.

She laughs, her eyes sparkling. "Flirting is always appreciated."

"I'll keep it in mind. That painting behind you is beautiful." An abstract painting hangs on the wall behind her. There's something about the soft reds and pinks and yellows coming through the blacks and blues that makes me feel hopeful.

She turns around, almost as if she needs to remind herself what's back there.

"Thank you. It's one of my favorites."

"Who painted it, if you don't mind me asking?" Art was one of my unexpected favorite classes in college and I have a deep love for it. Something almost no one knows about me.

"Um, I did, actually." A blush spreads across the piece of her chest not covered by her oversized shirt, and creeps up her neck.

"It's stunning. It makes me feel like coming out of depression."

She stares at me for a moment and I clear my throat, embarrassed. Art can be incredibly personal and here I am commenting on hers, when it's obviously a secret she keeps from the world.

"That was exactly what I was trying to convey," she whispers, something like surprise in her voice.

"I think you nailed it."

She gives me a smile and it raises slightly higher on one side. It's not the one I've seen in numerous magazines. It's better for it's imperfection.

"What an incredible compliment. Thank you. So, what did I do to finally receive the honor of your call?" She cocks her head to the side and I can tell she doesn't mean for the question to be snarky, merely curious.

"You had mentioned taking me on a tour backstage and I'm currently in off-season. If your offer is still on the table, I was hoping to take you up on it."

My heart is racing in my chest and I hope she can't hear how loud it's pounding through the phone. If I didn't know the signs of a heart attack, I'd be concerned I was having one while I waited on her answer. She looks toward something off screen and my stomach drops.

She's not alone.

She gives a thumbs up and then focuses back on the screen again.

"Is there a specific show that'd work better for you?" I see the change in her eyes. This is Ryan Jade, the businesswoman.

"I'm pretty free until April. If there's a city that's better for you, I can make it work."

She looks off to the side again. This time, I hear another woman's voice in the background. It's faint, so I can't make out the words; the tone sounds no nonsense.

"Want to meet me in Dallas? It's two weekends from now. Zoe thinks that'd be the best one."

"Zoe?" I ask.

"My music manager." Her mouth quirks like she's trying to suppress a smile.

"Dallas would be perfect."

"Great! If you could text me your manager's phone number, Zoe and her assistant, Paige, will get everything taken care of."

"Oh, I don't have a manager like that. They can call me directly," I say, a little embarrassed. She probably has entire teams at her disposal for anything she needs, since she's such a mega star.

"Even better. It'll go faster that way," she says, assuaging my fears.

I can feel the conversation coming to a close and a seed of disappointment plants itself inside my chest. I want to keep talking to this woman who likes to paint and has a slightly crooked smile.

"Sounds good. Thanks, Ryan."

"Of course. And Dominic? I'm looking forward to seeing you." She shoots me a wink and my insides turn to mush.

I think I might have a date with Ryan Jade.

# CHAPTER FIVE

## RYAN

"Has the jet landed yet?" I ask Zoe, checking my outfit in the mirror one last time. The goal is to look casually cute. Not like I'm trying.

"Like I told you six seconds ago, he'll be landing in the next ten minutes and then it'll take twenty for him to get here. It's cute you're nervous."

I turn away from the mirror.

"I'm not nervous," I tell her, straightening my clothes one last time.

"You woke up early and you're breaking your no talking stance for the day."

"It'd be rude to use a whiteboard during our tour. And time consuming."

"Just remember seventy-four thousand people paid to hear you sing tonight, and wearing your voice out for a boy isn't worth doing a substandard show."

Embarrassment turns to anger at her assessment. Not only do I know she's right, I hate she's right.

"You don't need to remind me what my job is. I've been doing this for over a decade."

She holds her hands up in front of her in surrender, her phone screen flashing with a text. Checking it, she nods.

"He landed. Do you want to start with breakfast?"

I nod and she starts to move out of my bedroom, pausing one foot over the threshold.

"Not everyone deserves your time," she says, her voice softening. "Remember that."

I cross my arms over my chest, raising an eyebrow.

"I'm looking out for you. The last three guys you dated used you as a stepping stone for their career."

My facial muscles move into a scowl, but I can't keep from answering out loud.

"Aware. Thanks."

I sit down on my bed, head in my hands.

Zoe acts like it wasn't my heart that was broken when things ended. Like I wasn't the one crying on the bathroom floor. My twenty-first birthday flashes through my mind. How I looked more at my watch than paid attention to my guests.

But he had landed a part in a potential blockbuster and apparently he didn't need me anymore.

And despite everything, all the bad dates, all the fake friendships, every time I met someone I hoped.

Hoped they could see me past the lights.

Past the fame.

The door opens downstairs, and I shut the emotions away in a locked chest in my mind.

Dominic stands in the foyer, a backpack slung over one shoulder, taking in the vast space. His chiseled jaw could cut glass, yet there's something boyish about him. His eyes land on me and he smiles, a single dimple appearing, and my heart flutters.

"I hope you know you didn't need to send a jet for me," he tells me, his eyes never leaving me as I walk down the stairs. Even though I'm tall, in my flat shoes, I don't even come up to his chin.

"Next time I'll leave you to fight through TSA at LAX." I smile up at him. "Hi."

"Hi. Thank you, for the plane." He seems perfectly at ease, while I want to vomit with nerves.

"Thank you for finally texting me. Why don't you leave your bag on the stairs here. Someone will take care of it for you."

"I don't mind handling it," he tells me, and already he's different from Cash and the others before him. "If you could point me to my room?"

Once the plans were made, we had decided it made the most sense for him to stay here with me, in a separate room, to keep everything as low-key as possible. It's not like there's not plenty of room. We always make sure to rent a big enough space so Zoe and a few others can stay close by in the cities I tour.

We might have gone a little overboard once it was determined Dom would be joining us at this stop.

"It's okay. We need to head to the stadium soon." We stand there for a second smiling at each other and then Paige moves, catching my attention. "Are you hungry?"

"I could eat." He puts his backpack on the stairs where I indicated.

"Then follow me." I lead him to the kitchen, signaling Zoe and Paige to give us some space. "How was the flight?"

"I spent most of it looking at everything. Your plane is a lot nicer than the ones I've rented with teammates before for trips. That bed must make red-eye flights way easier than the tiny chairs."

"A lot of times I have to hit the ground running when I get wherever I'm going, and I might only catch a few hours of sleep on the plane." I indicate he should sit on one of the stools around the island and head to the giant stove, pulling the lid off the breakfast the chef made.

"That must be hard," he says, his voice sympathetic.

"It's all part of the job." I give him a smile over my shoulder before grabbing up one plate and spooning all the dishes on it, then repeating with the other. "Do you want something to drink?"

"Ryan, you don't have to wait on me." He stands from the stool. "I'll get it. What would you like?"

I expected for there to be a bit of awkwardness, but there is none. Just like when we had talked on the phone the first time. "Some tea would be great. The blend I drink is by the kettle over there." I nod toward the drink station in the kitchen and he grabs the kettle, filling it with water at the sink. He puts the kettle back on the heating pad and flips the switch, turning it on before moving to the refrigerator and coming out with a bottle of orange juice.

Grabbing up the plates, I move to the island, setting his at his place. Dominic tears two paper towels off the roll and then looks through the various drawers until he finds the utensils, picking up two of all of them and bringing them to me.

"Thanks," I say and he gives me a wink, sending butterflies through my stomach.

"Don't wait for me. Go ahead and eat it while it's hot." The kettle goes off, the water done. "I'll get your tea."

I take a bite of my food and watch him. My favorite mug in the house's collection sits on the counter of the drink station and Dominic pulls it toward himself. He fills the tea infuser ball, puts it in the mug, and then pours the hot water over it and walks it to me. With a click, he sets the mug in front of me.

"Do you need any milk or sugar or anything?" he asks, remaining standing, waiting for my answer.

"No, it's perfect as is. Thank you."

He takes a seat and looks down at his plate. His eyelashes are so long they distract me for a moment. Fork in hand, he takes his first bite and moans a bit, which distracts me even more. My phone vibrates a few times in quick succession. I check it, making sure it's not an emergency.

**Karter: OMG have you guys been to the new club, Vixen??**

**Sky: No! I've tried to get in but haven't been able to score a reservation. It's super exclusive, gotta know someone who knows someone.**

**Karter: Ryan? Do you think you could get us in?**

**Taylor: Y'all, Ryan is busy with her show tonight.**

**Sky: She could just call them. Please, Ryan?**

**Ryan: I'll have Zoe call them**

"Is everything okay?" Dom says, taking a bite of eggs.

I look at him, feeling like the biggest jackass of all time, typing out a text to Zoe.

"I'm so sorry," I say, tucking my phone back into my pocket. "Some friends were texting, needing me to get them into a club."

"No problem. So, what's the itinerary for today?" He's so earnest and relaxed. Cash always got pissed if I texted someone anytime we were together.

"I thought we'd have breakfast, then head to the stadium. I can show you around the stage and things like the costume room. Stuff like that."

"Sounds awesome. Do I get to see you do a sound check or anything?" He shovels some eggs into his mouth, chewing with a hopeful look on his face.

"Oh, I normally only do sound checks on the first night in a new city. If you want to see one, I could do a song or two."

Something in me wants to show him everything a show entails. To impress him.

"No, no. We'll stick to your routine. Don't want to mess with the luck."

"Luck?" I don't even taste the food I'm eating as nerves eat at me. I want him to have a good time while he's here.

"In sports, a lot of times, we have certain pregame rituals or superstitions. It might seem a little silly, but they believe it affects their play."

"I could see that. The ritual getting you into the right mindset. Telling your body you're about to play. It makes sense. I think there's something to those superstitions. There was one tour I did, every time I sound checked a specific song, we seemed to have issues during the show. Mics cutting out. My in-ears not working. Whatever.

When I stopped doing that song during sound check, all those problems went away. It was crazy."

"I can't imagine how stressful it must be when things stop working mid-show."

Standing from my stool, I grab up my empty plate and mug, setting them in the sink. He shovels in his last few bites and then follows my lead.

"Honestly, I'm at the point now where I know it's inevitable, so I just go with it. My team works incredibly hard to fix things as quickly as possible, and sometimes it seems like the audience actually enjoys it. Like it makes it special for them." He leans his hip against the counter, crossing his arms over his chest, and waits to see if there's anything further I want to say. Having his full attention makes me a little nervous. And a little rambly. "Are we ready to go?"

"Let's do it," he says and I call out to Paige letting her know we're ready.

Heading out of the house, Bradford, my head of security, goes to open my door, but Dominic steps forward.

"Is it alright if I open her door? My parents would die if they knew I didn't open the door for a date."

A date. My heart explodes at the words.

I don't think I've had my door opened for me by a date since I was being picked up for a movie date in junior high. And that was more because it was a two-door car and he had to push the seat forward for me. Instead of sitting with me in the back, he sat in the front next to his dad.

"Of course, sir. I'll let you know if there's ever a situation where security takes precedence."

"You can call me Dom, and I appreciate her safety will always come first. Thank you."

Brad gives him a nod and moves out of the way, wiggling his eyebrows at me behind Dom's back, as he opens the door. Smiling, I make my way past him.

"Thank you, Dom."

"You're welcome, Ry."

I've never had anyone call me 'Ry' before, and I find myself liking the way it sounds. My biological mom named me RyanJade Marie Collins. Quite the mouthful. When I started sending out demos, I decided to split my first name and create Ryan Jade.

Dom shuts the door behind me before making his way around the car and sliding in next to me. Once Brad is in the front seat, the car pulls away from the house, whisking us to the stadium.

"Have you ever played at Lone Star Stadium?" I ask Dom, not wanting him to feel ignored.

"Back in my rookie season. Dallas isn't in the same division as us, so we don't play them every year."

"Will I lose points if I tell you I don't watch football? Or know anything about football?" He lets out a small laugh, and for a second I'm worried he's laughing *at* me for my lack of knowledge. When he grabs my hand, the worry melts away.

"You'd never lose any points for something like that. I know about as much about putting on a concert and tour as you know about football, so I'd say we're even. Can you promise me something?"

"Anything," I find myself saying with no thought. It's true, though. I'd promise him anything so long as he's holding my hand.

"Promise you'll ask any questions you have? No matter how small or silly you might think they are?"

"I promise. Do you promise the same?"

His thumb sweeps over the back of my hand, setting the butterflies in my stomach aflutter. "I promise."

# CHAPTER SIX

## DOMINIC

R YAN'S TOUR IS PERFECT. She shows me everything. Costumes. Every angle of the stage. The sound booth. And in each area, a member of her team is there, ready to help. I can easily see how much they love her. Not only are they here early for us, they seem happy to do it. And she knows all of their names, their families, and all the things that are possible in her show thanks to them.

Her appreciation of all these people runs deep.

"What's your favorite part of all of it?" I ask Ryan as we make our way back to her dressing room.

"Is it going to sound cheesy if I say the fans?" She tucks her blonde hair behind her ear, peeking up at me.

"Maybe a little. Doesn't make it less true, I'm sure. What part of the show is your favorite? Like riding the shuttle below the stage? Or the pyrotechnics?"

"Easy. The costumes. These are the best ones I've ever had. I haven't had my skin zipped up in a single one!"

My mouth drops at her beaming grin.

"I'm sorry, your skin gets zipped up in them?" I ask. What kind of costume designer wouldn't want to keep the star from being accidentally *zipped up in their design*?

"Not every night or anything, but when we are changing in the dark and whatnot, it's basically inevitable. This time they've put in these panel things that go between me and the dress."

"It's nice they got that figured out for you," I say, still shocked. "That blue floor-length tiered dress, the one with the deep v in the front? That's my favorite."

"Really?" She blushes and it runs down her neck.

"Really. It's beautiful and you look beautiful in it."

Zoe gives a sharp knock on the door, breaking the spell. "Sorry to interrupt, you have to start getting ready, Ryan. Dominic, this is for the VIP section."

She hands me a laminated pass and I put the lanyard over my head. The pass is pretty cool. A holographic image of Ryan singing flashes in the bottom corner when I tip it back and forth.

"Thanks," I tell her, putting my hands in my pockets and wait. Zoe looks between Ryan and me, and the silence takes on a bit of awkwardness. "Oh, were you nicely kicking me out?"

Ryan and her music manager look at me, and they both let out little laughs.

"I have to get ready and there's a whole routine and I have to change. Don't be mad," Ryan says, her brow furrowing ever so slightly.

"Why would I be mad? This is your job. Alright," I say clapping my hands. "I guess I should go find some other place to be. Have a fantastic show and I'll see you after?"

She nods enthusiastically before surprising us both by throwing her arms around me.

"I have you to the left of the stage. If you come up to the side at the last number, security will lead you back here to me."

I pull back from her, putting some distance between her amazing body and me.

"Left side. Find security. Got it." I give her a wave and shut the door behind me. A golf cart is sitting right outside the door, the driver scrolling on his phone as I walk by.

"Hey, man. I'm supposed to take you where you want to go," he says.

"Oh, cool. Could you take me to the entrance? I want to walk around with the crowd." It's not every day I can be a part of the fans in a football stadium. We ride in silence and in a blink he drops me at the front gate.

Just like at the shows back in L.A., there is glitter and sparkles *everywhere*. Pinks. Purples. Blues. A living rainbow streams by me, their happiness infectious.

A light pressure at my elbow draws my eyes behind me and down, catching on a little girl no older than seven, her mom standing to the side watching us.

"Do you want to trade gemstones with me?" she asks, holding out a pin. The fans had taken to swapping different gems they create, adding to the exciting atmosphere.

"I don't have any gemstones on me. I'm sorry."

"That's okay. Everyone should have a gemstone." She thrusts it at me again and I take it, touched.

"Thank you. That's very generous of you." I affix the gemstone to my lanyard and she smiles up at me, grabs her mom's hand, and skips off.

Grabbing a drink, I stand at one of the tabletops watching the crowd. They trade gemstones. Take pictures. Talk about how much they love Ryan. It's obvious her music has touched all of their lives. It's amazing, really. To have such a lasting impact on so many people.

The opening act comes on stage, and I head down the stairs to the VIP tent, flashing my badge at each security person in my path. With each song, the crowd grows more and more restless until the lights go down and the real screaming begins.

My view is amazing. I clap for each dancer that comes out dressed in various shades of the rainbow with the crowd until finally, *finally* Ryan rises up mic raised to her mouth.

*Pulse of the party, with a groove so sweet,*
*Catching dreams like confetti, dancing on our feet.*

I find myself cheering along with everyone, singing every word of the first song. The final notes fade and Ryan takes a moment to greet the crowd.

"Dallas, welcome to the Radiance tour! Tonight is not only a special show because 74,000 of my closest friends are here, but because I have a very special friend out there with you tonight." The crowd cheers at her words. We lock eyes across the distance and my heart starts racing like I'm about to step out onto the field under the lights. "Let's show them how amazing my Jade Stones are! Will you all help me sing this next song? You might know it," Ryan says and the music starts again.

And I'm entranced for every single note.

Two hours later, the final song starts and I beeline to the security barrier on the side.

"Hi, I'm Dominic. Ryan sa—"

"This way," the security guard says before I can finish, moving the barrier out of my way. She wasn't kidding about them being prepared for me.

The tall man leads me through the visitors' tunnel we use when we play in this stadium. He drops me off in front of the dressing room door and tells me to wait. Even deep in the bowels of the stadium, I can hear the cheers of the crowd.

One thing about Ryan is she doesn't do encores. Every song she intends to perform is done as a part of the normal set. No forcing fans to cheer and pretending like it wasn't planned when the songs played are the most popular hits. I didn't realize how much encores annoyed me until the first time I went to her concert.

More and more people stream into the hall. Then the largest cluster arrives. Ryan, the queen bee, in the center of all her worker bees. I stand back, giving her time and space.

"Yes, I understand. I will be there in a minute. Thank you." The group disperses quickly. She rolls her eyes, walking toward me. "Follow me."

We walk into the dressing room, shutting the door, and for the first time in hours, there is no other noise.

"Thank fuck," she says dropping down on a chair, grabbing the waiting water bottle sitting beside it. "I can't feel my feet."

I eye her heeled boots. "That doesn't surprise me. You did amazing. The crowd was loving it."

She smiles. "Yes, they were amazing. They always are. Did you have a great time? I see you got a gemstone."

My hand goes to my keepsake and I stroke it for a second. The question is almost shy in its asking. Nervous. She busies herself with the water waiting for my critique.

"I had a fantastic time. The VIP tent was great, the people in it were so nice, and you were captivating. I don't think I sat once."

"Ryan?" Zoe calls out with a knock. "The kids are ready."

"Kids?"

Her facial expression is excited and giddy. "I meet some fans after every show. It's the best. You can come watch, if you want. Zoe can take you down there."

"I'd love to."

# CHAPTER SEVEN

## RYAN

MY HAIR IS TUCKED up into the wig cap and secured with quite a few bobby pins. I settle the wig on top of my head and shift it into place, like Elaine taught me, and secure it with the various clips. The piece is custom made to look as natural as possible and be easy for me to put on myself. There are plenty of times Elaine puts me in a wig for a show, like when we want a drastic, temporary change. But the lace front wigs require more skill to apply and are beyond my capability.

The shoulder-length brown hair looks good on me, though I prefer my natural blonde. I didn't believe Zoe, initially, when she said it would only take a wig to keep people from recognizing me, but she was right. Used to seeing me in more curated looks, most people don't give me a second glance in regular street clothes.

And that's the goal tonight. For no one to give me a second look. Except Dom.

I want him to give me a second, third, and fourth look.

I'm in a midnight blue maxi dress with a slit going almost indecently high. Something I'd never wear as Ryan Jade the pop star. It feels like I'm in another costume. It's worth it, though, to have this night of normalcy.

Dom is waiting for me outside the dressing room, his fingers flying over his phone screen, and I'm surprised to see he's changed clothes. The plain white t-shirt he's wearing looks painted on. His jeans hug his tree trunk like thighs and it makes my hormones go haywire. He looked hot earlier, but he looks downright sexy right now. I'm going to have to beat the other women off him with a stick.

I watch him for a second and smile. Keeping my eyes off of him during the show was hard. I was so used to Cash being bored and not even watching the show, I'd work extra hard to make it fun for him. Dom was different. Singing and dancing along with everyone else.

And maybe I threw in some of my sexier dance moves trying to impress him. Because, apparently, I'm fourteen again trying to attract the attention of the cute quarterback. Granted, Dom isn't a quarterback, but still. I wanted him to have a good time.

"You ready?" I ask. His eyes snap up and take me in starting at my feet and ending at the wig.

"Wow, you look so different."

"Bad different?" Cash always hated when I wore a wig. He would rather go to an exclusive restaurant that requires background checks and certain bank account levels than a popular local bar.

I always hated going to those places. Sure, they are nice and the service is great, but I just want to be Ryan out on a date with her boyfriend. Make friends with some drunk girls in the bathroom and dance to music that's a little too loud for the venue.

"Still beautiful, just different. Where are we going?" My stress melts at his words.

"It's a surprise, but you're going to love it."

"Are you serious?" he asks, as the car is pulling up in front of my favorite bar, the neon glowing.

"I am *very* serious. Where did Paige put the—"

"Right behind your seat," Brad mutters from the front seat as he clocks all the activity outside the bar.

I unhook my seat belt and look into the third row and squeal with excitement before passing Dom the various packages. Pulling one of the ribbons, I untie the bow and open the hatbox. Grabbing up the cowboy hat, I place it on Dom's head.

And decide this might not be a good choice, but we're here and it's too late to back out now.

"What do you think?" he asks, his eyes trying to see the top of his head.

I clear my throat trying to get my voice to start working again. "Looks good."

Understatement.

Of the.

Century.

Peeling my eyes off him like I want to peel off his shirt, I root around in the bag and pull out a belt and buckle, thrusting it at him. "Put this on, too."

"Do you think this is necessary? I'm not exactly a cowboy, Ry."

"It definitely is, thank you so much for asking though."

He rolls his eyes at me, but I can tell it's not out of annoyance. I untie my hatbox and pull out an equally impressive hat for myself. A horn blares behind us while I toss all the remnants of Paige's shopping back to the third row.

"Ready?" I ask and Dom nods. Brad moves to open his door, but I stop him with my hand. "Blending in, remember? No doors or anything."

I know I don't need to remind him how important this night is to me. I want Dom to know I can be a normal girl. Someone who can go to bars and drink and hang out with normal people just as well as all the stars in my other world.

Brad gives me a sharp nod and gets out of the car. I know he'll do his best, but between stalkers and normal rabid fans, my safety is more important to him than my ability to blend in. If anything goes sideways, he'll get me out of the building and back into this car if it's the last thing he does. And if Dominic gets left behind, so be it. When we discussed this plan before Dom arrived, it was a point Brad wouldn't budge on.

And I hate that part of this whole thing. That someone could be sacrificed for me. One of my team. My friends. Family. Boyfriends. They all come last to my security team.

I slide across the bench seat behind Dom once he's out of the car. He holds his hand out to me and it's warm and, surprisingly, soft when I take it. I don't drop it when he closes the door and I start pulling him toward the front.

"Free to go," Brad says to the driver via his earpiece. Once we are in the bar, that won't be possible.

The line is only fifteen people and we join at the end. I don't mind waiting. So often I'm rushed in and out of buildings, sometimes it's nice to relax and *wait*.

I open my mouth to ask Dom a question, but one of the girls in front of us says my name and I freeze, afraid they recognized me.

"Ryan Jade puts on amazing shows. Easily one of the best concerts I've ever been to," the redhead standing in front of Dom says. My heart swells at the praise.

"Worth every penny to come here. I'm glad we bit the bullet on those floor seats," the blonde in front of me says.

"I think my credit card is still crying, but it was once in a lifetime."

My heart sinks so low it's at the core of the Earth. I don't want them hurting financially because of me. Dom must feel the change in my mood and steps in.

"What was your favorite part of the concert?" Dom asks, getting the girls to turn around. "Sorry to interrupt. I went to the concert, too, and overheard you talking about it. How long have you been Jade Stones?"

"Oh my gosh, since I was in elementary school! Ryan Jade was my first concert and I fell in love with music because of her. I begged my parents for guitar lessons that year!" the one in front of me exclaims. Her obvious happiness starts to buoy me once more.

"I started listening more in middle school. I've never had an artist before or since be able to encompass what it's like to be a girl so thoroughly. I never stopped listening."

"That's so great!" I say, adding a twang to my voice. "We should get a drink together! One Jade Stone to another," I offer, wanting to treat them for all the years of support they've given me.

"Yes! That'd be amazing!"

We chat for ten more minutes, the line slowly inching forward until we are finally inside and belly up to the bar, country music pumping through the air. Once I have the attention of the bartender, I quickly order four shots, four drinks, and a Shirley Temple for Brad so he has something to hold. Brad slips his card to me and I start a tab.

Passing out the shots, our new friends raise their glasses.

"To Ryan Jade and the music of our lives!" the redhead says. It feels a little weird toasting to myself. We all clink our glasses, down the shots, and I give them the tightest hugs I can, sending all my love into them despite the fact they don't know I'm me.

Dom and I stay at the bar nursing our drinks while the girls go off and start dancing wildly. I smile at their obvious enjoyment of the night.

"Do you think we need to ride the mechanical bull?" Dom asks leaning into me, his breath caressing the shell of my ear.

"It's a requirement. Not yet, though."

We listen to the band, enjoying the music and being together. There's no awkwardness in the silence, just relaxed company. Until my favorite song, the song that led to me becoming the star I am today, is played.

I down the rest of my drink before setting the glass on the bar and grabbing Dom's arm.

"Brad, get us more drinks?" I say, pulling Dom onto the dance floor. He sets his empty glass on a table right before we step onto the floor, the colored lights dancing around us and all the other gyrating bodies.

Dom grabs my hand and spins me. My mouth drops open in shock. The moment his hand settles on my lower back, he leads me into a two-step. A delighted laugh escapes me, the happiest, most carefree sound I've probably made since becoming famous.

We twirl around the dance floor, both of us becoming more elaborate with our moves as we get comfortable. Dom is an amazing lead. Strong and sure. The dim lights do nothing to hide how good looking he is, many of the other women in the room taking notice. I don't care, this time.

Because he doesn't look anywhere but me.

The song ends and we are both breathing pretty heavy. "Want to get our drinks? Brad got us some more." He shakes his head.

"It's time for the mechanical bull."

"Should we make a bet on who will stay on longer?" I tease.

He taps his finger against his lips until his eyes light up. "Okay, if I win, you have to come to one of my games during your down time."

Not exactly a hardship to agree to see him again. So far my time with Dominic has been great. Perfect, really.

"Fine. And if I win, you have to kiss me."

I don't know why I say it. It's not like I don't want him to kiss me, but I definitely don't want it to be because of a stupid bet.

"I'm not so sure I'm going to be trying too hard to win, now," he says, his eyes heating as he pulls me a little closer to his body. My blush heats my whole body.

"If you don't give it your all, I'll make you do it again with the added stipulation you'll have to do it without your shirt."

Maybe I want to see him without his shirt on. Who knows? Not me.

"Fine. Deal."

He leads me through the crowd and pulls money from his wallet, paying for both of us. I don't remember the last time I carried my own credit card, let alone cash. Normally, someone on my team puts whatever I need on their business card.

"Ladies first," the bull operator says. I take off my shoes and knot my dress up around mid-thigh so I can use my thighs to grip.

I get settled and give the thumbs up. The bull goes round and round, up and down, twisting and shaking me. It almost feels like I'm in a blender until I'm flung off, my legs flipping over my head.

Five seconds. That's all I lasted.

The crowd cheers and I quickly right myself, sure they got to see my underwear as I flew. Dom helps me off the inflatable pad before climbing into the ring himself.

His muscles flex as he gets situated and gives the operator a thumbs up, looking much more comfortable than I felt. He moves with the bull, never surprised where it goes next. I can see his abs flex through his t-shirt on a particularly brutal bucking move. The speed increases until finally the bell rings.

Eight seconds.

He lasted the full eight seconds.

I lost and I'm much more disappointed than I thought I'd be.

He climbs down and makes his way over to me, putting his shoes back on before standing. Grabbing my hips, he pulls me close.

"Looks like you'll have to come see what I can do under the bright lights and cheers from the crowd."

"Looks like," I agree, and take him back to the bar and our drinks. "You could still kiss me," I tell him shyly, watching people dance, glass in hand.

His fingers gently tug on my chin, forcing me to look at him. "I'm not going to kiss you in a crowded bar. And I want to take this slow."

His eyes bore into mine and I can almost feel the war happening inside him. It's nice, though, this slow dance between us. Pressing a chaste kiss to his cheek, I enjoy the rest of the night, savoring the tension building between us.

# CHAPTER EIGHT

## DOMINIC

A NASTASIA WALKS THROUGH THE rental I'm considering signing a lease on, the thought of being traded stopping me from being able to purchase a house outright. We were able to fit in a quick viewing before I head out on my yearly off-season vacation with some of the guys. When she saw the kitchen, she all but cried in jealousy and made me promise to let her use it whenever she wanted. Apparently, the fact she has a professional kitchen and doesn't need mine isn't relevant.

"What do you think?" I ask her while we look out over the backyard with the jewel-like pool.

"It has everything you need and plenty of things you don't. It doesn't feel like you, though."

She's not wrong. The house is missing any sort of personality. It's gorgeous, don't get me wrong, but it feels cold, like a museum.

And no matter where I move in the house, I can't seem to get comfortable.

"I watched Ryan Jade ride a mechanical bull."

"All hail the king of segues. When did this happen?"

"When you invited me over for dinner on Saturday? I was in Texas."

"Well, well, well. My brother meets one world renowned pop star and he becomes a jet setter. How was your date?"

"It was good. Amazing. The concert was as good as the first time I saw it. This time I had a new appreciation for everything that went into it. She met with some of her fans after and, A, she was amazing. They *loved* her and it was so obvious how much she loves them."

"That's awesome. I know how much you love kids. How did a mechanical bull play into this though?"

"We went to a bar after and they had one. We made a bet, which I won, thank you very much."

"What was the bet?"

"She has to come see me play."

"Trying to win her over with the big, bad football player thing? I see right through you. How was the bar, though? Was it crazy?"

I hesitate to tell her about the disguise for fear she wouldn't be able to use it again, but it's Anya. There's no way the information would leave here.

"She wore a brunette wig. No one recognized her. In fact, we were behind some girls in line that'd come from the concert and we talked to them. They didn't realize they were talking to the person they were just watching on stage. It was crazy."

"Parker and I are nowhere near Ryan Jade level of fame, with us though, the show involved being out in the world and in normal clothes. We look pretty much the same in real life. I wonder if it's the opposite issue with her fans. She's rarely photographed when she's relaxing or not dressed perfectly. I bet it didn't compute. Plus, people aren't expecting to see her with brown hair when she was in front of them with blonde not even a few hours before."

"Yeah, I'm sure you're right. It was nice to be able to go out in public and enjoy hanging out together."

"Don't get too used to it. I doubt it'll be possible very often." We walk around the house and we get in the car. "Are you going to put an offer in?"

"No, I don't think so. There was something making me hesitate, and I think it should be an obvious 'yes' when I buy a house."

"You could always have Parker build you something. You know he'd be happy to do so."

"Maybe I should rent a house instead of buying. We'll see."

We talk about small things. Her bakery and how Parker's business is doing. I'm listening and answering when I need to, but my mind is elsewhere thinking about a certain pop star. When we pull up to Anya's house, I look over at her.

"Have you called her since?" she asks.

"We've texted a bit."

"Not good enough. You should call her. You know you want to. You have that dopey 'I have a crush' look on your face," she teases.

"I don't have that kind of look," I tell her, only slightly offended.

"Tell it to your face. Have fun on vacation. I'll see you when you get back." She gets out of my car and slams the door, and I wait until she opens the front door, and turns to wave at me before going in.

When I get home to my postage stamp size apartment, I pull out my phone to do exactly what she told me I should, but found I'm already late. Ryan texted me first. I try not to smile like an idiot at my phone. Luckily, there's no one here to see me fail so spectacularly at the attempt.

**Ryan: What are you up to?**

**Dom: Getting ready to pack my bags. I'm going on a trip with some teammates**

**Ryan: Do you need to borrow my plane? I'm happy to send it**

**Ryan: I can't wait to go on a vacation during my break. Where are y'all going to?**

**Dom: We all chipped in and chartered a plane. Thanks, though. Vegas, of course**

**Ryan: Maybe when you get back, you could come to another show. I liked having you around. And maybe I could redeem myself with the mechanical bull**

**Dom: You're on**

A hour later, I have a whiskey in my hand on the airplane. Scott, Chase, and Dwayne are dancing in the aisle, music blaring, as we wait for Tim.

"Are you ready for Vegas, motherfucker?" Dwayne asks pointing to me. He's wearing three chains I'm sure cost more than I've spent on myself in my lifetime. Then again, I was looking at a multi-million dollar house this morning, so I may not be able to say that soon. Anya convinced me if I bought a house, then the universe wouldn't let me get traded.

Not sure I believe her, but it's worth a shot.

I've never been much of a party person, but I'm trying to get out of my comfort box and try new things. This is one of them.

Plus, I've never been to Vegas other than for a game and you're not exactly exploring a city when you play in it.

"Hell, yeah!" I say, but I can't stop thinking about Ryan. I want to text her, but right now this thing between us feels private and like it's just for us. I'm not ready to break that open by telling my teammates about it. We all get there's a certain level of expectation to not talk about each other's lives outside of the team, but it happens. And it'd only take one mention in passing to the wrong person for things to blow up.

The airplane shakes as Tim jogs up the stairs, a bottle of champagne in his hands. Beneath his leather jacket, he's shirtless with sunglasses and leather pants.

"Who's ready to get laid tonight?" he asks, and the other guys all bounce around in excitement. I sit, laughing at their antics knowing, if nothing else, I'm going to enjoy watching all of them have a great time.

A limo is waiting for us on the tarmac when we touch down. The driver is well into his seventies and a hundred pounds soaking wet. His suit is pressed and his hat is slightly off kilter. There's something about him that reminds me of Dad. Not wanting him to strain himself, I help with getting all of our bags, small as they are, into the car. Once we are all loaded up, he pulls away from the plane and takes us to a steakhouse on the strip.

Dinner is amazing. Easily one of the best steaks I've ever had in my life. The guys are loud and boisterous, drawing looks from those around us, but they don't care. We're here for a good time. When the meal is done, the real party begins.

Our driver takes us to one of the most prestigious clubs you can find in Vegas. Often star-studded, it's known to have incredibly beautiful women there. We are able to skip the line, thanks to Scott sweet talking the club manager who was handing the VIP list to the bouncers when we walk up. If he plays his cards right, I think he could take her home at the end of the night.

The manager leads us back to a roped off section. One of the servers walks up and puts a chilling bottle of champagne on the table shooting Tim a wink before walking away. Dark-colored couches line the space, and I vaguely wonder how many times people have had sex on them over the years.

Tim pours the champagne out into the awaiting flutes, not caring about splashing it everywhere. He hands out the glasses before lifting his.

"Lads. I'd rather be with you than the best people in the world. Cheers!"

We all clink our glasses and down the drinks. The bubbles fizz in my throat and, having watched Anya get wasted at many a brunch, I know I'll be feeling it soon.

The music booms through the speakers. It doesn't seem to matter it's only nine at night, the club is packed. Lights flash around, illuminating and coloring the bare skin they touch. I take a better look around and see the iron cages and barely dressed people dancing in them. One hangs near the bar and the red-headed woman locks eyes with me, gyrating in a tantalizing way.

I watch, appreciating the way her body flows from one dance move to another. It would be enticing if this was a few months ago, but now? I don't care at all. She gives me a wink and moves on to others in the crowd, making them feel like the only people in the place. Two women in slinky silver dresses barely covering their nipples walk up to the rope and get Tim's attention. He leans down, one of them saying something in his ear.

With a hungry look, he undoes the rope and moves to the dance floor with them. In what feels like a blink, he's taking turns kissing them both. I almost laugh. The willingness of people to leave all of their inhibitions at home is astounding. The other guys all move off to the dance floor and I sit watching everyone, enjoying the show. A waitress drops off a smoky margarita that makes me pull up the menu on their website and take a screenshot of the ingredients, determined to make it for Ryan sometime.

"You look a little lonely," a woman's voice says. I look up and into a pair of dark eyes.

"Just enjoying some people watching," I tell her, scanning down her body. Her dress is cut down to her navel. The air of command around her is enticing and if I had met her before Ryan, I would definitely be interested.

The place where there would normally be some stirring during this interaction, sits dormant.

"Maybe we can people watch together." She waves a multi-ringed hand around, the bangles clinking together. "Buy me a drink and we can chat."

I flag down a waitress and she walks over. The woman requests a glass of champagne and I order a second drink for myself.

"Join me," I say, indicating the couch next to me.

"I thought you'd never ask." She saunters up the two steps, the swish of her hips making me think of Ryan's during one of her more vigorous numbers. "I'm Shonte. What's your name?" she asks, sitting next to me, holding her hand out, palm down.

I take her fingers and press a kiss to her soft skin, but I don't linger. "Dominic."

"Dominic. What has brought you to my fine city?"

"Spending some time with my friends."

She looks around us. "Are they ghosts?"

"They are dancing," I tell her, pointing out all the guys. It's easy to find them as they are taller than most of the crowd. "But I don't dance much."

"No? Do you not know how? I could teach you." She runs a sharp, black nail down my bicep.

"I know how to dance. I just don't like it much."

"Fair enough. Let's count how many bachelor and bachelorette parties we can find."

We spend hours together talking and laughing, alternating between making up stories about the strangers around us and talking about ourselves. The guys come and go from our VIP area, seemingly with different women every time.

"Our wedding was in Paris. It was the most romantic day of my life. When we got home, though, it was like everything changed. All of a sudden he wasn't helping me around the house. He didn't want to go out with friends. He started pinching every penny. I thought he was cheating on me and buying his mistress expensive gifts or something. When the feds came to the front door talking about embezzlement, I realized I never really knew my husband. How can you live with someone for ten years and not know them?"

I gape at her a little. "That's a crazy story. How did you survive?"

"Luckily, he was never allowed to touch my businesses, so they were able to determine what I had built wasn't made with illegal funds. It took about five years to get back on my feet. And my best friend helped me."

"And you don't love him?" I ask her with a doubtful look.

"He might have professed his love to me recently."

"And you're sitting here with me? What's keeping you from being with him?"

"He's not the person I ever pictured myself with, honestly. I was never attracted to him. It was always *just* friendship. After my divorce... I don't want to ruin our friendship." She says the last bit quietly and I know she's a goner.

"He's put himself out there and you're worried about that? It sounds like he's a great guy. If it matters what a virtual stranger thinks, I think the worst thing you can do is wonder what could have happened forever."

She hiccups, covering her mouth, her eyes surprised and I laugh.

"Sounds like maybe we both need to see what happens," she says once she's recovered.

"I plan to," I tell her, having vaguely explained the situation with Ryan, leaving out any identifying information. Tim comes up, one woman under each arm.

"You ready to go?" Tim asks and I look at Shonte not wanting to abandon her.

"Go. I'm going to go and see about a man," she says, a twinkle in her eye.

I give her a kiss on the cheek. "Thanks for hanging out with me tonight. It'll all work out. I'm sure of it."

"I hope you're right."

We walk out of the club to the limo. Shonte gets in first, our driver promising he's happy to drop her off wherever she needs to go before the end of his shift. He takes us a mile down the strip, dropping us off at a sparkling hotel.

"Good luck," I tell Shonte once I'm out of the car. She blows me a kiss and I shut the door, happy to have had such a fun night.

The guys all go to their rooms with their various guests. Not wanting to hear anything, I go to my room. Pulling up my text thread with Ryan, I drop down on the bed, snapping a picture of myself.

I send it to her with a simple good night message.

When my phone vibrates my heart skips a beat when I see she sent me a picture, too.

Her blonde hair is a wild mane. Laying on her stomach, half her sleepy face is hidden by the pillow. It's obvious she's not wearing a shirt and I feel my dick stirring.

**Ryan: Wish you were here.**

I don't remember falling asleep, but when I wake up in the morning and unlock my phone, her picture is still staring back at me.

# CHAPTER NINE

## RYAN

"**T**HANK YOU, TORONTO, AND good night!" I say into my microphone. A colorful deluge of confetti falls around me and my dancers and I wave goodbye to the screaming fans.

It takes a little over an hour and a half from the time I step off the stage to when I step foot on the plane. Despite not needing to rush, the flight to L.A. is only a little under six hours after all, I feel antsy to get up into the air. By the time we started heading to the airport, I thought Zoe was going to wring my neck in annoyance.

"Good evening, Miss Jade. The bedroom is all set up for your comfort. Would you like some dinner after we take off?" my private flight attendant, Colm asks.

"That'd be great, thank you." He hands me my usual cup of honeyed tea and I take my seat. I turn on my phone and see the normal texts from family and friends pop up. Only one makes me smile.

Dominic.

We've texted almost every day since he came to the show with me a few months ago, and sometimes we even video chat. He's been to a few more concerts. Once his picture showed up on social media about him being in the VIP tent, I had to put a stop to that.

I love my fans, but they can be rabid about anyone in my life.

And there's the stalker who thinks I'm his girlfriend. *Definitely* don't need him getting wind of Dominic.

Taking things slow has been so different for me, but it has let me see how he'd handle me prioritizing my career. My touring has scared away at least two boyfriends willing to admit it, and one that wasn't.

Cash was always so preoccupied with attending every award show, gala, and function we could, I felt like he hated when I was away on tour and unable to attend those things. And it kept me from jetting off to meet him on set, when he was starting to break into acting once his music career took off. He was great, and I loved him very much. Still, I always felt more like everything about my life was supposed to revolve around him and his career.

I tap open Dom's message.

**Dom: That blue dress makes my mouth water. So sexy.**

**Dom: Can't wait to see you tomorrow**

He's the reason I was so antsy to get on the plane. Him and his Fourth of July/Housewarming party. I'm pretty sure I single handedly stocked his kitchen, bar, and movie room from the registry. He told me I didn't need to do it, but I didn't mind.

All of his family will be at the party. I'm a little nervous, concerned my attendance will get leaked to the press, but he promised everyone there would never do such a thing. I have my doubts, though. I'll be in the background of a picture or someone will tell a friend who will tell a friend. I find I *want* to meet Dom's friends and family.

His sister I've met before, of course, which will give me one other person I know there. Plus Lorelei if she comes with Tank. He said I could bring Zoe and Paige so I'd have some friends with me. Paige jumped at the chance to meet some of Dom's teammates. The single ones, primarily.

Once dinner is done, I make my way to the bedroom and turn on a movie to fall asleep to. It might be better to wait until we get to L.A. Short of pacing the plane, I don't think I'll be able to keep myself from going crazy.

The movie and thoughts of Dom's scruffy, happy face follow me into sleep.

"Are you sure this is it?" I ask Justin, my driver and security for the night, Bradford taking the night off and letting his second-in-command call the shots.

The house feels too modern for Dom, then again, it's just a rental. It's a beautiful house, it just doesn't feel like *him*. He also just moved in and hasn't had a chance to put his stamp on it yet. It's only been a week.

I fiddle with the straps of my blue sundress that are tied in bows at my shoulders. Stars litter the skirt in red, white, and a darker blue so as to stand out. It reminds me of a dress I wore when I sang the national anthem at a baseball game for the first time. The nostalgia forced me to pick it the second I saw it on the rack.

"I'm sure. We'll be out here, waiting. If you need anything, press the button on your bracelet."

Ah, yes. The bracelet. I almost never wear it, but they were worried with the house not being in a gated community. It has a tracker and panic button in it, a compromise to Justin actually coming into the party with me. I want to make a good impression on his parents, and it's hard to do when I have security tied to my hip all night long. Instead, they'll be stationed outside.

"I got it. Thanks, Dad." I grab the card I brought off the seat and climb from the car.

"Curfew is at ten," he jokes before I shut the door behind me and Paige.

Breathing deeply, I look up at the house. The party is in full swing since I'm an hour late. Dom wanted to make sure there were plenty of people here before I showed up so I could hide in the crowd as much as possible. He's considerate like that.

My heels clack against the driveway. I could never live in a house like this. It's in a nice neighborhood but anyone can come into it. There's no gate. No guards. And the house is right on the street. All of my houses are set back on the property to allow for as much privacy as possible. Granted, with drones and long lenses, if they can find a good vantage point, they can see me.

It's creepy, but I've grown to accept it.

The front door opens without a sound.

Sparse is the word that comes to mind. Nothing in this house screams warmth or welcome. There's one small couch in the grand living room, a TV sitting on top of a plain table.

"He should have put furniture on his housewarming gift registry," Paige jokes.

"Shh," I tell her, moving to the back where the party is. "And, yeah."

We step through the back doors, my hands shaking slightly.

"Ry!" Dom says, the moment he sees me and my jaw drops.

Dom doesn't have a shirt on.

This buff, six-packed man, golden tan from the sun, doesn't have a shirt on.

And he's in the pool.

I'm drooling, there's no way I'm not. But I can do nothing but stare.

He hoists himself out, and Paige breathes out a curse. I want to gouge her eyes out.

"Get your own," I tell her, only partially joking, as he starts to walk over to me.

Water is running down his perfect body. I thought he looked good in jeans and a white t-shirt, but I'm an idiot. He should always be wet. But then I'd always be *wet* and that'd be a whole different kind of problem. His swim shorts are indecently short and they make me want to bite his muscular thighs.

If this isn't what greets me when I make it to heaven, then I'm not sure I want to go.

I hardly notice the water splashing off of him onto my feet.

"See something you like?" he asks with a cocky grin and I finally snap my mouth shut, my cheeks heating in embarrassment.

"Yes, I saw the plate of grilled hot dogs over there and my mouth started watering. I love a hot dog fresh off the grill."

Shoot me dead and bury me. I'm a fucking moron.

He laughs and runs his fingers through his hair, pushing it off his face. Muscles flex. I almost groan.

"Let's go get you one then. Hi, Paige, good to see you again," he says, holding a hand out to Paige.

"Thanks for letting me come."

"Any friend of Ryan's is welcome." He puts his wet arm around my shoulders and pulls me to the table off to the side, everyone giving us a wide berth. I can see when it registers.

The whispers start and I want to run away. Afraid I'm going to take all the attention off of Dom, I cower into his side.

"It's okay," he says, into my ear, grabbing up a plate. "Ignore them. It'll be fine, I promise." He points at various bowls and platters. "Do you want some fruit?"

Everything I point to, he puts on my plate until it's heaping full with two hot dogs, various fruits, and grilled veggies. A small plate with a singular piece of cake is all he would let me carry and only because it wouldn't fit on my other plate, his other hand filled with cutlery and my drink.

Paige follows behind us, a plate of food in her hands.

"Are you not eating?" I ask Dom, as we get situated at the outdoor dining table.

"I ate earlier. Sorry, I didn't wait. I'm on a schedule to bulk up for the season," he says, a little sheepish. I wave him away and pick up the first hot dog.

"I'm glad you did. I'd hate for you to be hungry."

"Dom, who are these ladies?" another shirtless guy asks, giving me a wink. He's attractive, in an almost fake kind of way. Like he's too perfect.

"Paige and Ryan. This is Tim, our team's kicker." I wave.

"It's nice to meet you both. Paige, you don't have a drink. Let me get you one?"

"That'd be great," she says, shy. "Let me come with you."

As she leaves, I take a bite of my hot dog and have to work not to moan. It's perfect. I don't remember the last time I had a hot dog. I could ask my chef to make me one, of course, but grilled food tastes better when you eat it outside at a party.

Opening my mouth for another bite, I notice Anastasia walk up behind her brother with a tall, blond man who looks like he should be at a biker bar rather than a backyard BBQ. I quickly set my food back down, not wanting to be rude.

"Ryan, it's really nice to see you again," Anastasia says, sitting down next to me, bumping me with her shoulder. The man takes an open seat next to Dom.

"I'm happy to be here!" I tell her, with a bit too much enthusiasm to come off naturally. I am excited to be here, and also nervous. All it takes is one picture to leak of me here with Dom and everything is ruined for him.

"I'm Parker, Anastasia's boyfriend," he says, extending his large hand. His voice is deep and rough. The musical part of my brain wonders if he can sing as I take his hand.

"Ryan. It's a pleasure to meet you." The woman next to me beams at his claiming of her, and I almost suffocate under the hearts floating around the two of them.

"Dom said you both rode a mechanical bull, Ryan. Did he tell you in college his favorite place in college was this little country bar with one? It was broken down and he fixed it in exchange for free rides," Anastasia says.

"He did not," I say looking at Dom who gives me a large, unrepentant smirk. At least it means he wants me at a game and I'll get to see him again.

"If I told you, you might not have taken the bet."

"He always cheated as a kid, too," Anya laughs.

He turns toward his sister while I continue eating the delicious food. "Please. The only way to have an even playing field with you was to cheat. You were the queen of cheating."

She sniffs, folding her arms over her chest. "I didn't cheat!"

"That's right. She just tends to change the rules as the game goes on when she's losing. That's all," Dom says to me, laughing.

Anya opens her mouth to retort, but Parker places his hand over hers, stopping her.

"Do you have any siblings, Ryan?" he asks politely. "Less feral ones, perhaps?"

Dom and Anya both make noises of protest, but I can tell it's all for show. The closeness between them is evident and jealousy inducing. Mom never wanted kids. Not that it mattered when I needed a place to go. She was ready to fight anyone to the death who came between her and me.

I always tried to be perfect for her, to limit the disruption to her life. She didn't care.

She happily took me to every guitar lesson, singing lesson, gig, meeting. All of it. When I started to take off, she even quit her lucrative job to take me around. I took care of us. It was the least I could do after she had to give up her life for me, never letting me spend a penny more on her than was absolutely necessary.

While I know not everyone stays up to date on celebrity news, or follows me, it's nice of them to pretend like they don't know a lot of personal information about me.

"I don't. More kids weren't in the cards for them," I say, not wanting to get into all the gritty details of my unconventional family.

"I'm sorry to hear that. Siblings are the worst, anyway, so you didn't miss out. I tried to mail Dom back to the stork when he was two and broke my doll," Anya says with a sympathetic smile.

I look over at the man in question with his beautiful hazel eyes. "I'm glad your plan didn't work out or I wouldn't have met him."

# CHAPTER TEN

## DOMINIC

Watching Ryan get to know my friends and family all afternoon has been amazing. She's so interested in everything anyone has to say. Anytime she's in a conversation with someone, her full attention is on them. It's one of my favorite traits. The ability to be fully present and engaged seems like a lost art in this day and age. For someone so busy and with so many people wanting things from her, I'm surprised she can stay so grounded.

Once Lorelei showed up with Tank, she loosened up a bit, able to stick to her friend's side and talk to other wives and girlfriends of my teammates.

I can't be traded away from this family.

My parents walk through the sliding glass door, Mom carrying a dish of some kind. Dad is dressed in his best khakis and a nice blue polo. I didn't tell them they had to dress up. There must've been something in my voice when I mentioned them meeting Ryan.

"Sorry to interrupt," I say, butting into Ryan's conversation with a woman I met today. She's the plus one of one of my teammates, but her name didn't stick. I turn to Ryan. "My parents just arrived. I'd love to introduce you."

"Oh! Yes, of course. Would you excuse me? It was great talking to you," Ryan tells the nameless woman who politely bows out of the conversation and goes to find her date. "Do I look okay?"

Her hands nervously run down her dress. I almost tell her she's crazy. She's stunning. The look on her face makes me pause, putting my hand lightly on her arm.

"Hey, you look great. You don't need to be nervous. They are going to love you."

"Parents don't like me much since I have a tendency to bring chaos into their son's life. Between all the fans and stalkers and paparazzi, it can be a lot."

"Stalkers? Hold on. You have stalkers?"

"Well, stalk*er*," she says, emphasizing the singular. "I shouldn't have said anything. Come on. They are looking at us and I don't want to keep them waiting."

She links her arm through mine and all but drags me to my parents, distracting me.

"Dominic, the house is beautiful," Mom says, giving me a hug. "I brought my famous fruit salad."

"Thanks, Mom," I say, taking the dish from her. "This is Ryan. Ryan, this is my mom, Gwen, and my dad, Carl."

"It's a pleasure to meet you, Mrs. and Mr. Reynier," Ryan says, holding her hand out for my mother to shake.

"Oh, sweetie, call me Gwen. And families hug," Mom says, wrapping her in a tight hug. Ryan seems taken off-guard, but quickly recovers and pats my mother's back. "I hope you didn't feel like you needed to dress up on our account."

Ryan pulls back and looks down at her dress. "Oh, um, no. I'm sorry. This was in my closet and I hadn't worn it before."

"Gwen, don't fuss. The girl wanted to look nice for our Dom, didn't you?" Dad says with a wink before hugging her as well.

I want lightning to streak from the sky and strike me dead where I stand.

"Can you both not embarrass me, please?" I say, my face pink, as Ryan gives a nervous chuckle.

"Dominic James, I gave birth to you. I'm allowed to embarrass you from now through eternity."

"Something to look forward to," I murmur.

"Are you finally ready to admit how much you're paying Ryan Jade to be here as your pretend girlfriend?" Scott jokes, before taking a drink of his beer. The guys standing with us around the fire chuckle.

"My whole bonus. Worth every penny," I joke. "She'd probably require double to agree to go to a party with your ugly mug."

The guys all laugh while I watch Ryan talking to one of our other teammates. It's taken pure force of will not to hover around her all night, but I didn't want to be clingy. The urge was there, though. In fact, all I wanted to do was sit and talk to her all night long. I should have kept this whole get together smaller. Family and my closest teammates. And her.

She and Mom spent an hour talking and laughing. Meanwhile, Dad inspected the landscaping, telling me how often I'd need to water the lawn.

Breaking away, Ryan walks up to our group.

"Hey, Dominic?" Her voice is low and slightly nervous.

"What's wrong?" I ask, making my way around the fire, looking around the party for something that might have upset her. "Is someone bothering you? I can kick them out."

"What?" Genuine confusion colors her firelight soaked face. "Oh, no. Everyone's been great. I'm hoping you have some place I could go for five minutes to sit? I just need a few minutes."

I focus on her a little more instead of looking for a perceived threat and I see what, apparently, I was missing. She looks beautiful, but everything about her has drawn in some. Maybe the world's biggest pop star, surrounded constantly by fans, staff, and everyone else, is a little introverted.

"Follow me." I grab her hand and weave us through the party, ignoring anyone calling out to us. My parents sit side by side on some pool loungers looking up at the sky and the bursts of fireworks from houses surrounding us, waiting for the big show.

We go straight through the living room to the stairs, heading up toward the bedrooms. At the top, we move to the right, toward the guest room, the only one currently with a bed, but when I reach for the handle, it turns without me.

"The fuck?" I say, when I come face to face with an *incredibly* disheveled Tim.

"Paige?" Ryan says, as she becomes visible behind Tim, equally disheveled.

"Reynier! Hey, man, you need a more comfortable bed," Tim says, buttoning the last button on his shirt. Paige's face is pink and she refuses to meet her boss's eye.

Not wanting to embarrass Paige further, I let the fact they had sex in my bed go.

"I'll get right on that," I tell him. They go down the stairs while Ryan and I go into the room. The bed is made up, but the blankets are still rumpled. "Guess I'll be sleeping on the floor tonight."

"Why not sleep in your bed?" Ryan says, moving to the chair in the corner.

"This is my bed. My old apartment could only fit a queen and I want a bigger bed in my room. It hasn't been delivered yet. Back ordered. Since I'm tall, I went with a custom bed so I'll finally fit in it." She nods, not saying anything. "Hey, I hope you don't fire Paige or anything. Tim can be incredibly charming when he wants to be. It can be hard to resist."

She gives a laugh, waving away my concern.

"No, she's fine. She's off the clock right now. I'll talk to her about decorum. I'd hate for her to embarrass you."

I give a light laugh at her smile. Then I just stand there, not sure what to do. I want to stay, but she was looking for a place to decompress, which tends to be a solitary activity.

"Welp, I'm going to get out of your hair," I say awkwardly, turning toward the door.

"Wait!" She's partially out of the chair, looking ready to lunge at me. "Stay? Please?"

*Thank God.* "Sure." I look around for somewhere to sit, but can't sit on the bed, knowing what it just saw, so I take the floor almost at Ryan's feet.

This is what I wanted the second I met her at the planetarium all those months ago. To worship this woman.

"This is a great party," she says, almost like she's not sure what to talk about.

"Thanks. They're all pretty great people. I'm glad you came." I run my finger on her calf, the skin softer than anything I've ever touched.

Her lips part, tongue wetting her bottom lip so it glistens in the low light of the bedside lamps Paige and Tim left burning. Emboldened, I let my entire hand caress her calf. Her chest starts falling more rapidly as I move north on the outside of her thigh.

"Is this okay?" I ask her, dragging my fingers back down, adding pressure to the tips, digging into her skin. She nods and spreads her legs a little. "I can't tell you how many times I've thought about touching you like this."

"I've thought about it a lot, too," she admits.

I'm drunk on her. On her heaving chest.

On her supple skin.

On the way she's looking at me.

I get on my knees, the carpeting cushioning me, and kneel before her, sitting on my heels.

"Do you like me kneeling at your feet?" I ask her, my voice low.

"Yes," she breathes.

I press a kiss against the inside of her knee and the smallest moan makes my dick harder than it's ever been. Putting my mouth on her thigh again, this time a little higher, I give her a gentle bite.

There's nothing small about this moan. Her hand reaches down, tangling in my hair. She pulls my face up higher, spreading her legs indecently wide so I can settle myself between them. So I can devour her.

I bunch her skirt up in my hands ready to shove it to her waist to bare her to me when a heavy rap of a knuckle echoes like a gunshot through the room.

"Dom?" my sister's voice says, making me want to commit fratricide at her interruption of me giving Ryan an orgasm, her hand still tangled in my hair. "Two of the guys from the team have started shooting fireworks at each other. They are pretty drunk. I think you should get out here."

"Be there in a minute," I tell her, turning back to Ryan fully prepared to let the guys blow each other up in order to get a taste of her.

"Dom, come on. You need to get out here."

I groan, dropping my head into Ryan's lap.

"Go," she whispers, letting go of my hair. I immediately miss the tension on the strands. "We were supposed to be taking things slow anyway."

"I was stupid for ever suggesting we should do that," I say and she laughs as I pull her to the edge of her chair and place a deep, rough kiss between her legs and over her skirt. I can feel the heat of her on my face and I sigh before getting to my knees.

My hand reaches down in my pants, adjusting my boner so I don't embarrass myself in front of everyone.

"I'll see you out there," I tell her and head toward the door, ripping it open. "I hate you," I tell my sister who laughs, and make my way from the room, intending to throw my teammates in a cab and send them home immediately.

I don't think Ryan has been avoiding me. Or at least, I don't want her to be avoiding me. I'm choosing to believe she's been so busy the past few weeks she hasn't been able to answer my calls.

Or texts.

For three whole weeks.

Or maybe she's avoiding me.

The rest of the party went well, or so I thought, but her silence says otherwise. Trying to keep from spiraling, I pushed all my focus into running drills with my personal trainer and lifting weights, getting my body ready for pre-season. Some nights I could barely drag myself into bed I was so tired.

I check my phone again as I unpack my bag for training camp. For the next two weeks, my priority is building deeper bonds with my brothers, and learning any new plays we've added to the playbook. Getting ready for the season. But my mind keeps returning to Ryan.

And that little moan.

This is why I didn't call Ryan. I might get traded, yet here I am, worried about Ryan, instead of focusing on football.

"Hey, Reynier," my roommate for the camp, and one of our star running backs, says.

"Good to see you," I say, reaching out to give him a high-five in welcome. While we aren't close outside of the team since he's busy with Daddy & Me classes in his off time, he's a great teammate.

"How was your off time?" he asks, dumping his bag on his bed, beginning to unpack as well.

"It was good. Went on a trip with Tim and a few of the other guys. Hung out with the family. How are the kids? Junior just turned six, right?"

His smile is beautiful at the mention of his oldest son. "He did. It was space and dinosaur themed. My wife used your sister for the cake, actually. It was one of the best cakes we've ever had."

I make a mental note to tell Anya about his praise.

"That's awesome! Thanks for supporting Anya."

"Anything for family," he says simply, and I'm touched by the sentiment. I know my connection to her was all they considered when picking Anya. She could make ugly cakes and they still would have gone with her to support her.

Once we get settled, we kill some time watching TV until it's time for team dinner. The training camp is held at a small college a few hours away from L.A. It allows us to get out of the city and away from normal life while we get back into football shape.

Excited shouts and greetings echo in the hallway as the team makes its way down to the dining hall. The first night's meal will be the traditional taco bar from a local spot run by the same couple for the past fifty years.

I load up my plate, talking and joking with some of the defensive players as we make it through the line. Tim is sitting at a table with a few of the guys we went on vacation with and I head toward them.

"What's going on?" I ask in greeting, setting my plate and drink down, taking my seat.

"Reynier, perfect. When's the next time Ryan is gonna be in town?"

"Why?" I ask, raising an eyebrow. He and Ryan talked a bit at the party after she came down from the bedroom, but it didn't seem like a friendship bloomed or anything.

"Paige was *very* flexible and I want more," Tim says, with a smirk.

My hands reaching for a taco pause in shock. I should have known that's what he was after.

"Ryan? As in Ryan Jade? You're still talking to her? I'd have thought she'd moved on by now." Scott asks.

I give Tim a look, but he's busy pushing some of his food around his plate.

"We're just friends," I say, taking a bite of one of my tacos.

"If you're just friends, hook me up!" Dwayne says with a laugh.

"We'll see," I tell him, jealousy lighting in my stomach at the thought of him, or anyone, dating Ryan.

I finish dinner quickly and make my way back to the room the moment the speeches from the coaching staff are done. My roommate is already lying on his bed video chatting with one of his kids when I get back. I move around quietly, getting ready to relax in bed when my phone rings.

With Ryan's name and face on the screen.

My heart speeds up so suddenly black dots dance in my vision. Thankfully my thumb swipes, accepting the video call, all on its own.

"Ry?" I say.

"Hi, Dom." She smiles at me, shy and unsure, and my nerves relax. Her hair is braided and resting over her shoulder. I want to give it a tug. "I'm sorry I haven't called."

I sit down on the bed, pulling my earbuds out of their case so we can have a semblance of privacy. "That's okay. You had a lot of shows and stuff."

She doesn't respond, shifting, and my stomach drops. Holy fuck.

"Was..." I clear my throat, trying again. "Was it what happened in the bedroom?" I check on my roommate out of the corner of my eye, glad to see he's busy reading now. With giant noise canceling headphones on.

Because he's the best teammate ever.

"What? No! Well, not completely."

I'm trying to not freak out, but it's becoming increasingly difficult. "Ryan, I am so sorry. I know we are getting to know each other, but it's weird because we've been talking for months yet we haven't even kissed and then the first chance I had, I jumped—"

"Dom, stop," she says, interrupting me. "It wasn't about what we were *doing*, and I'm upset we couldn't continue, more what it could mean. For you.

"That's kind of why I called. I guess Paige did an internet search for Tim after the party and a picture of you and some woman popped up from the trip you took. She sent it to me. It was just a small mention, but it would've been national news if we were to...date. It would've been all over with cheating headlines, and I don't want you subjected to that. Not that I think we're dating. Or that you want to date me. I mean, we just started talking. But we've gone on a few dates, so does that mean, *technically*, we are dating? What is the difference between talking and dating, anyway? I never understood that. I'm going to stop talking now."

Panic worms its way into my stomach at the mention of the pictures. Shonte and I weren't even doing anything, but I don't want Ryan to even *think* she'd have to worry about other women.

"She and I spent the entire night talking about the man she was in love with and people watching. The guys had all gone to dance and she came up to me. I promise you, there was nothing happening."

Watching her face, my nerves stay on high alert for any sign she's about to end this before we can even get started.

"I trust you," she says, and I relax a bit. "But I get worried sometimes that you haven't really seen what it's like to be with me. When I say that would have been national news, I'm not kidding. I'd hate for you to feel like you can't sit and talk to some woman, hell even someone like Lorelei, because it'll be on all the news channels the next day. Everything you do will be recorded. Everyone you ever talk to will be followed. Your family. All of them. And I don't want them for them because they're so great."

All of my worries about being distracted and getting traded disappear at the vulnerability shining in her eyes. There's nothing else for me to do but be transparent with what I want from her.

"Ry?"

"Hmm?" she hums, looking at something off camera.

"Will you be my girlfriend?" I ask, smiling, ignoring her warnings. "Officially?"

Her blue eyes search me through the screen. "Yes, I will." My heart soars and I want to scream.

"We can handle it. I want to date you, and if that's what comes along with it, then that's what comes along with it." My fingertips are tingling with all the excitement in my body.

This beautiful, successful, amazing woman wants to date me.

"Okay," she says, giving me a small smile. "I hope you're right."

# CHAPTER ELEVEN

## RYAN

**D**om: **Have a great** show, babe! Call me later :)

I stare down at my phone like a heartsick teenager, dopey grin firmly in place. While I haven't gotten to see Dominic in person since his party, we talk on the phone every day. I've offered to fly him out to me, but his practice and pre-season schedule didn't allow it.

Probably for the best.

I'm not sure I wouldn't have jumped him the second I saw him. And the longer we go without anyone else knowing we are dating, the better. The less pressure. Fewer eyes.

Less *everything* that comes with being Ryan Jade.

"Who has you smiling like that?" Cash says, sitting on my couch.

I clench my teeth before turning to look at him. There was a day I would have killed to have him in this room again. Now that I've met Dom? All I want to do is spend time with him.

"It was my mom," I lie.

Regret.

That's all I feel looking at my ex-boyfriend in his black jeans and band t-shirt. I never should've asked him to be a special guest for tonight's show back when we were setting up the tour. We were making the list of people to reach out to and I was missing him. Missing him made me do a lot of stupid shit.

Like wanting him to see me succeed without him and inviting him to perform with me.

Now I don't care what he thinks and wish he wasn't here.

"I remember when you used to smile like that when I'd call you." He has a joking tone, but he's not wrong. I was infatuated with him. "I could make you smile like that again, if you'd give me another chance."

Any time we've talked since the A-list movie star he left me for broke it off with him, he's been trying to get back into my good graces. There were so many times I wanted to hear those words from him, a part of me flutters slightly.

I open my mouth to respond, a knock at my door stopping me from the inevitable downward spiral of thinking about our relationship.

"Come in," I call out, patting a piece of hair back into place.

"Well, well, well. If it isn't my best daughter."

I freeze at the voice, caught by a memory of crying in a cold shower trying to wake my dad up.

"Holy shit, you're Sebastian Slate," Cash breathes, oblivious to my pain. "Sir, I am a huge fan. You're one of the reasons I picked up a guitar."

"Thank you, son. That's awfully nice to hear."

"What are you doing here?" I interrupt without turning around, numbness trying to take over my body. It's been almost seven years since the last time I saw him as Margo loaded him up into the car to drive him to rehab. Based on the headlines, he's been in and out of facilities over the years.

"Aren't you going to say hi to your old man?" His twang has come out. When his band went big, that was the first thing the record label told them to lose. No one wants to hear a punk rock band that sounds like they belong on country radio.

I turn to look at him. His blond hair is a shade darker than mine, but well kept. It's been cut and styled so unlike the shaggy, greasy mess I'm used to, I almost don't recognize him. Color tints his full face and his eyes twinkle.

This man in pressed khakis and a polo shirt is not one I've ever seen before. Then again, I've never really known Sebastian to be sober. The longest stint was when I was six and he first started to teach me to play guitar despite my hands being too small.

That time ended with his worst downward spiral and me calling the cops, because he was yelling and smashing things. The fear I felt coats the back of my tongue as the memory washes through me.

"Why are you here?" I ask again, folding my arms over my chest.

The band he helped found kicked him out after almost a decade of his antics, finally sick of his shit. They were able to find another guitarist who was able to take them to the next level since he wasn't too drunk to help write songs and better their craft.

His money started running out when I first started making it. It didn't take long before he came crawling to his daughter begging for help, selling me lies about getting clean.

"Why, I wanted to see my daughter, of course. Come over here and give me a hug." He takes a step toward me, arms wide, but I step back, bumping into my vanity. "I thought we could grab some dinner after the concert. Your friend here could come with us."

"Yes, I'd love to," Cash says, flashing a bright white smile, turning his eyes to me silently begging.

I glare at him and remember all the times in our relationship he put making connections above what I needed, and any hint of a flutter dies.

"We aren't going to dinner with Cash. We aren't going to dinner at all." I want to say yes. The seven-year-old inside me wants her dad, wants his attention, but there's too much buzzing in my brain.

Too much of the past bearing down on me.

Zoe walks in, nose buried in her phone, unaware of my fight between staying present and drifting into the past.

"Ryan, you have about ten minutes—" She stops abruptly when she looks up and takes in the scene. "Sir, you can't be back here." She presses the button on her earpiece and calls for security.

"There's no need for that, I'm Ryan's father." His smile is beautiful. It's the one that made all the women, including my mother, fall in love with him. They kept her, and then me, hidden not wanting to ruin his playboy rep.

It's the smile that lights my face and part of me hates him for the similarity.

"Dad, I have to get out there. I'll call you next week." I don't know if it's a lie or not. A part of me will always be his little girl, but Margo and Matthew are the only parents I need or want.

Hurt lives in his eyes, but the well of empathy within me is bone dry. Especially now, when I have to go out and perform for sixty-three thousand fans.

Zoe and security usher him out of my dressing room without any issues. I slump down in my chair, breathing deeply, head in my hands. Cash bounces around talking at me, but I don't listen. I can't listen. When Zoe returns, I've collected myself. I'm ready. Because I'm a professional.

"Find out who let him in, and fire them," I tell her, brushing past her to the golf cart waiting to whisk me away from all the memories and broken promises lying at my feet.

Stagehands move me this way and that. Arm up. Foot in a shoe. Hair over the shoulder so my dress can be zipped. Shoulders pulled back to remind me to stand tall. Guitar strap dropped over my head. Neck of the instrument placed in my hand. Hands pushing me to my next entrance spot. A poseable doll.

I'm silently told to smile.

And I do.

Because I'm a professional.

The lift rises and I stand up into the lights, expression perfect. Hair perfect. Clothes perfect. This is everything I've ever wanted in life and right now I hate it.

I hate the fans.

I hate the lights.

I hate the words coming out of my mouth as I sing and perform.

I hate this world that took my father from me.

But I'm a professional and the show must go on. So I sing. And I dance. And I pretend to be happy. I make everyone in the stadium feel like I'm singing to them personally. That this show is just for them. And on a regular night, I'd be happy to give that to them. To be perfect for them.

But not tonight.

"Mid-set speech. Forty-five seconds," the robotic voice in my ears says.

"How's everyone doing out there?" I ask and they scream. It tries to warm me, but I'm too cold, too numb so that I can make it through this. "I want you all to know how excited I am that you're here with us tonight. These next songs helped me through a hard time and I know, from all the messages you've sent, they've helped you, too. How about we do a little healing together? Right here, right now."

My fingers strum the next notes, and I see their faces change when they realize what song I'm about to play.

"Intro in 5, 4, 3," the voice fades out and I sing the first word.

Because I'm a professional.

On and on and on we go until it's time for Cash to come out.

"You know, you have been an amazing audience tonight," I tell them, trying not to sound as robotic as the voice in my ear. "In fact, you've been so amazing, I think you deserve a little surprise. Do you think you deserve a little surprise?"

They meltdown.

But it's not like how I melted down when Sebastian forgot it was my birthday and passed out drunk, falling into the pool, taking my cake with him. It's not how I melted down when he fell off the wagon the first time.

No, their screaming comes from their excitement as Cash walks up behind me, microphone in hand, waving to the crowd.

It's not at all like my screaming as I watched my world burn down around me.

I hug Cash with a smile on my face.

I open my mouth and sing.

Because I'm a professional.

The hot chocolate in my mug warms my hands, but does nothing to warm my heart. I consider not calling Dom, breaking our nightly phone call ritual. But that's never been me.

I'm always there for the people I care about. Reliable and trust-worthy.

I'm not my father.

But with Dom, I don't have to be fake. I'm not Ryan Jade right now. I'm Ry. The phone rings until he finally picks up, sweat trickling down his face.

"How was the concert?" he asks, smiling at me, trying to catch his breath.

"It was good," I say. Not technically a lie. It was good. Just not for me. "Are you busy? I can call you back."

"Absolutely not. You're saving me from the killer workout my trainer gave me. He's lucky I didn't die doing all of those sprints.

I meant to be done before you called, but Anya called me in the middle and talked for thirty minutes."

"How's she doing?" I ask with genuine care. Dom's sister is incredibly sweet and I like her a lot. I want to get to know her away from Dom. Maybe become friends, even.

"She's great," he says, smiling. "Her business is booming all thanks to you and I don't think she could be happier. Or more stressed."

"She would have blown up all on her own. I only gave her a little push."

He nods and finally looks at me. "Are you okay?" The concern in his voice warms me in the way nothing else has.

I take a deep breath and let it go.

"My dad showed up at the concert today," I tell him.

"That's great! How was that?"

"I haven't seen him in almost a decade, so it kind of threw me off balance a bit."

"Wait." His brow crinkles, thinking, realizing the lie I told him. "I thought you just threw a party for him and your mom."

I didn't tell my last two boyfriends about my biological parents. Deep down, I think I knew they weren't there for me. Or maybe I just know that Dom's different. He's not going to judge. Or get excited about who my dad is. The only boyfriend I'd told about my dad was so excited I was related to *the* Sebastian Slate he didn't even listen to anything else I said.

"My aunt and uncle raised me. They are my parents. But not the ones that created me. My mom left when I was little. I don't even remember her. She stayed with my dad just long enough to leave me with him. He was in the middle of touring, though, so he sent me off to my aunt's. I was with him when he wasn't touring and out of rehab. My dad is Sebastian Slate."

I watch him digest this, sadness filling his features.

"I'm sure seeing him tonight was hard. I'm sorry you had to go through that alone. I wish I could've been there for you."

"Yeah," I say, a small smile on the edge of my mouth. "I wish you could've been, too."

And I mean it. He opens his mouth to say something, but I cut him off.

"I was thinking, I have a bet to fulfill. When can I come watch you play?" I ask and his whoop of excitement pulls a real smile from me for the first time since Dad walked into my dressing room.

# CHAPTER TWELVE

## DOMINIC

I T WAS EASY TO pick the season opener for Ryan to attend. She started her break six days ago and it will go through November, when she picks back up and finishes the tour the first weekend of February. Sure it was a distraction to avoid talking further about her biological parents, but I wasn't going to push her. It took everything in me not to fly to her and hold her in my arms.

To try and erase the sadness and disappointment tinging her features.

Once she told me Sebastian Slate was her father, I felt stupid for not catching it sooner. She could be his twin, her features slightly softer. But that doesn't change anything for me. I'm not interested in Ryan for the people she's related to or the lifestyle that she has.

I'm interested in Ryan for the person she is.

**Ryan: I'm in**

**Ryan: Good luck!**

**Ryan: If you score a touchdown, I'll kiss you after the game ;)**

I have never wanted to score a touchdown more in my life. And that includes playing in the Super Bowl.

**Dom: Consider it done**

The second Ryan confirmed we were still on for the game, I let Coach Williamson know about the situation. I knew that people in the front office would have to get involved.

Geoff Haley is the head of media relations for the Thunderhawks and there's no one greater in the business. Within a few hours of letting Coach know Ryan would be attending the game as my guest, I was in Geoff's office with Coach, her, and her immediate team on speakerphone.

We ironed out any details that needed Ryan's input.

Did she want to use the player's entrance? No. She'd be walking in the front door this one and only time since no one would be expecting her there.

Would anyone be joining her in the suite? Yes. My family, Zoe, and a few others.

Did she have any plans to come to any other games in the near future? Yes. Every game when she's not on tour.

After that, we quickly wrapped up, Geoff giving Zoe her phone number so all the logistical and security details could be ironed out before the game. Once they were both off the phone, Geoff looked at me seriously.

"I know I don't have to tell you this, but you need to be prepared for what is going to come next. These are the last few days as a semi-private person. From the moment a camera catches her in the box, that's it. There's no going back. If you go to the store, you'll be photographed. If you go out drinking and hug a friend's wife hello, rumors will start. Everything you do and say will be splashed on magazines worldwide.

"You've always had your head on straight. Make sure it stays that way. You will have a press conference Monday morning. It's going to be the biggest one you've ever had. I promise every outlet will be there."

"I'm ready for it," I told him.

"Okay. Here's my number." He slides me his business card, much less intimidating than Ryan's, with a handwritten number on the back. "Keep it in your phone. Text me, day or night. If plans change, if she's joining you at an event, if you're traveling to see her. No matter how small and inconsequential you think it is, I want to hear about it." He stood, holding his hand out to me.

"Got it," I said, standing, gripping his hand.

"I hope you do," he says, as Coach and I left.

Coach Williamson grabbed my arm, stopping me.

"This is going to be a big year for us," he says, rubbing his fingers over his mustache. "I'm not one to say who my men can and can't date, or even if they should be dating, but you're an important member to this team. I want to make sure your focus is on this season."

"Yes, sir. My devotion to this organization has never wavered. There's nowhere else I'd rather be," I told him, hoping to keep my name out of any trade talks.

"Alright, then. That's all I'm going to say about the matter."

We turned and walked down the hallway, side by side, and I wondered if I had just lied to my coach.

No matter how ready I was in Geoff's office, I'm nervous now. But I know my family will take care of Ryan. I'm sure Dad will love being in a suite. Normally I buy their tickets down in the regular seats.

*"How can I get the full experience if I'm not with the fans?"* Dad always said whenever I'd offer to put them in a suite with other players' families.

"Alright, men! It's time," Coach says clapping. We circle up, ready and warm. "This year is about redemption and tonight is the first step on our path there. Take care of the man beside you. Do your job. Never quit. And never surrender! Hands in. Team on three." We all put our hands in the middle. "One. Two. Three."

"Team!"

We hustle out of the locker room and into the tunnel waiting. I put my helmet on and wait to hear my name. For the first time, I'm part of the starting line up. And they are going to call my name.

"At wide receiver is number eighty-two, DOMINIC REYNIER!"

And the crowd goes wild.

I jog out, hyping up the crowd in the way I watched hundreds of players before me growing up. Calling for more chants and more noise. Beating my chest.

My blood is pumping with impatience for the game.

And then I look up and I see her blonde hair gleam. I point to her, running to the sideline to join my teammates, and I feel like I can fly.

"Second down, gentlemen. Let's end it here," Logan Samuels, our quarterback, says before calling the play. We line up and the ball is snapped.

I try to break free of the defense, but they are with me step for step. The defensive linemen swipe ours to the side. Shrill whistles cut through the crowd cheering, calling the play dead, our quarterback beneath a stack of defensive players seven yards behind the line of scrimmage.

"Fuck!" Tank yells, climbing to his feet, pulling people off the top of Samuels. I try to quickly catch my breath and avoid looking up at the suite.

It has been a struggle to stay focused this entire game, wanting to check out Ryan as often as possible, but I've managed. I look up at the game clock.

Four seconds.

That's all the time we have left, but it's enough to get off one more play. Six points down, we need a touchdown and the extra point to win.

Tank is pressed against my left side in the huddle. Scott is pressed against my right. Logan stands in the middle, a general ready to lead his troops.

"Trips right bunch f shuttle, Tom and Jerry right yellow," he says before bringing his hands together in a sharp clap and we all break.

The play is one of the more straightforward in our playbook. I line up on the right side, prepared to get the ball in case the other two options are covered. My blood surges as Logan goes through the silent count.

With the snap, I run. Not a single guy is covering me as I sprint to the far right side of the end zone. Turning, I look back and the ball is already in the air toward me.

The throw is perfect. I reach up and cradle the ball to my chest as it comes down in my arms. Referees raise their arms in the air, indicating a touchdown. Cheering drowns out all thoughts in my head. My teammates slam into me, slapping any part of me they can reach.

Shoulder.

Back.

Head.

I take my helmet off the second I hit the sidelines and look up at the suite, grinning at Ryan who's jumping around cheering. Tim jogs onto the field and puts it through the uprights without any effort and that's all it takes to win our home opener.

We all make our way out onto the field, shaking the hands of the other team, talking to players we've gotten to know over the years. Before long, I'm jogging back into the locker room.

Geoff is waiting in the tunnel, and the second I'm beside him, he falls in step with me.

"Everything went great," he says before I can even ask. "Everyone is clamoring to get a picture of the two of you, so be prepared for every phone and camera to be in your face."

I nod. It's everything we anticipated. But I didn't realize how *bright* all the flashes would be. We walk through the area where certain fans and season ticket holders get to stand and cheer for us as we come back into the locker room. Normally, the area is filled with about fifty people; today it's closer to a hundred.

And all of them are screaming my name. This is a first. Some of the fans would call out to me after games, wanting pictures and autographs, but this is the first time *everyone* seems to be interested in me. It's almost overwhelming.

I wave but nothing more. The locker room doors shut behind me and I take a breath.

"What the hell is going on?" one of the guys calls out as Geoff and I enter the room. It's not a requirement for me to tell the guys about my relationship, but I feel like I'm hiding it from them if I don't.

Geoff gets everyone to quiet down, but before he can say anything, I cut in.

"I'm dating Ryan Jade," I tell them and a locker slams. The silence is almost oppressive with the undercurrent of shock. I walk to the locker and begin getting undressed.

"She lose a bet?" one of the guys calls out playfully getting a round of laughter. Friendly ribbing is a part of being on this team and spending so much time together, but when it comes to Ryan, annoyance flames bright in my chest.

I walk away and get into the shower, Tank the only other one inside. He nods at me before dutifully turning his gaze.

"Lorelei says she's one of the best people she's ever met. She was great at the party, too. I hope it works out for you both," he says. "I'm happy for you."

"Thanks, man," I say, soaping up my chest, my annoyance lessening.

# CHAPTER THIRTEEN

## RYAN

The family room is beautiful. I try to stand in the back so Dom can hug his parents and sister first, but his mom grabs my hand and yanks me to the front.

"Dom is going to want to see you. This is the first time he's ever brought a girl to a game before," she says.

That's the third time she's told me that today. It's almost like she never thought Dom would find someone. Which is crazy because he's kind, smart, and funny.

And hot as fuck.

If he wasn't a professional football player, he could have been a cover model. The kind that all the teens girls hang up on their walls and their mothers secretly love.

And I owe him a kiss. A kiss I really want to give him.

His hair is wet when he walks in, and it makes me think of him lifting out of the pool at his party.

And the water running down his body.

A body that I want to lick.

I shift, trying to shake off the heat pooling between my thighs as he smiles at us. Gwen shoves me forward, causing me to stumble and smack into her son's chest. It's a good chest. Dom's arms come around me and settle at my low back.

"My number is on your chest," he whispers. "It's the sexiest thing you could wear."

After Dom won our bet at the bar, I had Zoe find me a few options where I could get some team merchandise. When I saw the shop she found that would create a custom corset top from any jersey that you want, I knew I had to have one. My only stipulation to her was that I wanted Dom's name on the back and she knocked it out of the park.

The top is figure hugging but comfortable and easy to move in with the added bonus of making my boobs look fantastic. Not a requirement, but always appreciated.

"You haven't seen my lingerie drawer yet," I whisper, no filter between my mouth and hormones. His eyes heat. "Then again, I do have your last name on my back. Maybe that's even better than lingerie?" I ask, egging him on.

"You need to stop. I can't say hi to my mom with a hard on."

I giggle at his predicament. "You played great. Congratulations on the win." Up on my tiptoes, I press a kiss to his cheek.

"Thanks for coming. I'm glad you're here."

I step back and his arms drop, leaving me cold where his warmth seeped into my bones.

"You played great, sweetie," Gwen says, wrapping him in a quick hug.

"Thanks, Mom." He presses a kiss to her cheek before turning to Carl.

"You helped my fantasy team," his dad says and I laugh.

"Dad watched his team more than the game," Anya jokes and I don't think she is wrong. He was checking the app constantly throughout the game, watching his points go up every time Dom touched the ball.

Dom throws his head back laughing before hugging his dad. "Glad you're not going to have to bench me."

He steps back and addresses all four of us. "Let's get out of here."

We all fall in step around him heading out the double doors. The hallway is void of anyone that isn't a part of the team or family and I'm incredibly thankful for the consideration. Dom and I have chosen to date. That doesn't mean his family should have cameras shoved in their faces.

I have no doubt our pictures were taken in the suite, and I warned them every interaction and facial expression would be analyzed. They didn't care, though. They were there to support their son and brother, and by extension, me.

My aunt and uncle always support me, but it's impossible to keep a pang of pain from flashing at the thought of how parents *should* be.

Dom pulls the car into the garage, quickly pressing the button to shut the door and close out the world. After the game, we went our separate ways from his family and my security team, wanting to make it home before photographers started following us.

His hand hasn't left my thigh the entire drive. Cash never used to touch me in such a casual, intimate way. It's nice.

"I think this was the first time I've sat in the front seat of a car in ten years," I tell him, still feeling a little awkward. Even though we talk on the phone almost every day, there are nerves jittering inside me now, anticipating what I hope will come.

"I'm glad we could manage it this once. Let me get your door."

He gets out of the car and jogs around the front. His garage is huge, and basically empty, so there's plenty of space. A smile lights my face as he opens my door and holds out his hand. I take it and step down. His eyes draw me in. The door blows my hair across my face as he pushes it shut, but I'm so lost in him I don't even hear it close.

"Are you hungry?" he asks, voice husky. *Not for food*, I think. But I can't say that.

"You know what I'd love? A drink."

"Let's get you one then." Dom doesn't drop my hand as he moves to the back of the car, opening the door, pulling out his bag, and closing it before I can take a step. "Come on."

The garage connects to a laundry room with three different pairs of jeans hanging from a drying rack. Moving through a door into the kitchen, I realize the door to the laundry room is hidden behind faux cabinet doors so you'd never expect for a room to be back there. One of my houses has a similar design, but instead of a laundry, it's the pantry.

We walk into his house and I marvel at it now filled with furniture. Without people milling about, and trying to impress his parents, I have a second to take in the space. It's modern, but with the new furniture and art, it no longer feels cold and stiff.

"What would you like?" he asks, dropping my hand and moving over to the built-in bar.

"I'm not picky."

Nodding, he pulls out his phone, swiping before moving around to grab ingredients.

"In Vegas, I had an *amazing* margarita, and I thought you'd like it. I took a picture of the description, but I haven't made it before. Don't judge me too harshly. Deal?"

"Deal," I say, trying not to show how much the gesture means to me. Not only did he think of me, he took the picture and bought everything to make me a drink he thought I'd like?

Cash never would have done that.

Shaking the thoughts of my ex from my mind, I sit on a stool at the island and watch him move about his kitchen. When I was here during his party, it almost seemed like the house didn't fit him.

Like it was too much.

Too grand.

But I remember feeling like that too when I bought my first house. It was a three thousand square foot penthouse and was nicer than anything I'd ever stepped foot in up to that point. Now I feel at home anywhere, no matter the grandeur.

It calms something inside me I didn't know was agitated to see Dominic acclimated. Like he can fit in my world and not be spooked.

Maybe.

Hopefully.

He turns toward me, his ever-present smile on his face. "Want to go sit outside?"

"Absolutely."

I follow him through the dining room with a table set for twelve, opening the large glass door for us, and we step out. The evening is perfect. Getting to spend it with Dom? Even better.

The pool lights are on, lighting the undulating water, giving the perfect ambiance. We leave off the other lights, choosing to enjoy the city lights instead. Dom leads me to a new, comfortable looking outdoor sofa and motions for me to sit.

Once I'm firmly planted, he hands me my drink and joins me.

"Looks like you decorated," I say, taking a sip and humming in pleasure at the perfection. I look at him when he doesn't respond and he's just staring at me.

"You can't moan like that, or we aren't going to have time to finish these drinks," he says, staring at my mouth. He shakes his head and takes a drink of his, giving a sharp nod of approval. "Yes, I decorated. Or really, Parker's friend, Charlie, and Lorelei decorated. I only had to give them my credit card."

"Well, they did a phenomenal job. It's very you."

"Even though I'm just renting the place, I like things to be comfortable, and they are great at making spaces feel welcoming and homey. What's the point of having a chair no one wants to sit in? They should open a business."

"I like to furniture shop myself. The hunt for the perfect piece lights my fire." All of my houses have been meticulously filled with furniture I *love*. Hiring designers is great, but picking pieces out on your own is even better.

"You're way better at it than me, I'm sure. Anya used to say I must be color blind because of my inability to pick colors that look good together. I try to tell her I just don't care and pick what works. I guess that's not a good enough answer," he laughs.

"Definitely not."

Dom takes another drink and looks out at the view. The only thing I can look at is him.

His full lips.

His straight nose.

His soft, wavy hair.

My fingers move to the nape of his neck and I begin playing with the strands there, letting my nails gently scrape his skin.

"Hey, Dom?"

"Hmm?" he hums, not looking at me.

"I owe you a kiss." That got his attention and arresting eyes to look at me. "Can I kiss you now?"

He takes the glass from my hand and sets both of our drinks on the side table beside the arm of the couch.

"Fuck, yes," he says, leaning toward me, but I stop him with a hand to his chest.

Long lenses.

It's only a matter of time before people uncover where Dom lives, if they haven't already, and we would have no idea if they were out in the darkness snapping pictures of us from a mile away. The views are nice up here, but it's easier to get a good angle and snap a picture.

I grab his hand and pull him off the couch, taking him inside. I don't want our first kiss to be splashed on the front page of the internet tomorrow. He follows me without a word, leaving our drinks where they sit.

# CHAPTER FOURTEEN

I TAKE HIM TO the door I know holds a bed behind it, unsure where his room is. The knob is cold in my hand as I turn it and pull us into the darkness within. At our movement, ambient lighting turns on, casting us in a warm, candle-like glow.

We both kick off our shoes, Dom shutting the door behind him. He lets me pull him, following all the unspoken directions I give. Moving to the bed.

Sitting on the edge.

Leaning back on his hands and watching me, curious, but oh so turned on.

I prowl toward him, moving my body in the sexy way my dance teacher taught me. Slow and sensual.

"Lay against the headboard," I tell him, and he does.

My legs straddle him as I climb onto the bed, my hand pushing on his firm chest until he lies down beneath me.

His cock is thick and hard when I sit on his lap, but I ignore it. For now.

I start at his neck, letting my lips glide over his pulse point before pressing a kiss below his ear.

"I hope you know, that doesn't count for our bet," he jokes. I can feel the words vibrate in his chest.

"Shh," I say, laughing, but it relaxes me. Exactly what I needed. I settle my weight down, lying fully on top of him.

His large hands come to my hips, gripping them, and moving me against his erection as I kiss along his stubble covered jaw.

"Ry," he whispers, a hint of begging in the nickname I love hearing on his lips.

I brush my lips over his, and they are as soft as they look. They part for me, immediately, and he leans up, trying to press a kiss to my mouth, but I move back and look down at him.

"Patience," I chide, grinding down on his lap at the same time, letting him know I'm just as turned on.

Leaning back down, I press my lips to his, running my tongue along the full bottom one. He parts his immediately and I consume him.

Our tongues move over each other. He tastes of tequila and the kiss is perfect. Exploring. Patient. Gentle.

We pull apart and I look down at him.

"My turn," he says and flips me onto my back, pinning me to the foot of the bed. He grinds into my center and I arch, moaning at the friction. He takes my mouth and this kiss is anything but patient.

Or gentle.

It's passionate. And smoldering.

Marking.

He claims every part of me, his hand running down my thigh and hooking my leg over his back before doing the same with the other.

"You taste amazing," he says, panting, pressing hot kisses down my neck to the swell of my breasts, pulling my top down. I can't do anything, don't want to do anything, except take everything he's giving me. He palms my breasts, pushing them together. He bites one nipple. I hiss, but as his tongue soothes the sting, I moan. Moving to the other, he repeats his actions.

And I'm dripping wet.

Needy.

Desperate for more.

"I can't wait any longer to have you inside me," I tell him, my hands reaching for his shirt.

"Thank fuck." He sits up, reaches over his head, grabs the shirt at the nape of his neck, and pulls it off in one swift motion.

Whoever planted that move in the collective male consciousness deserves a fruit basket.

His arms, abs, and chest all flex.

They deserve a fruit basket every day for their entire lives.

"How do you like it?" he asks, eyes roaming my body.

"Rough."

Desire lights his face. "Perfect."

A hand reaches down and settles on my throat. With a strong grip, cutting off my air, he pulls me up to him.

"Your turn," he growls and I almost come on the spot as he climbs off me, and flips me over like I'm a doll, here for his pleasure. I'm okay with that. "Fuck, that's sexy," he says, running a hand where his last name is.

He gives me a sharp slap on my ass, causing me to yelp, before he grabs the zipper and frees me.

"Don't move," he commands as he climbs off the bed for a moment. I turn to look at him and thank whatever god made him as he unbuttons his pants and drops them, his dick standing thick and proud at attention.

My mouth waters. There's time for me to taste him later. Right now, I need him between my thighs and nowhere else. He gets back on the bed and I move to undo my skirt. His hands stop mine.

"Leave it."

"Dom, I need you. Please," I beg.

"I believe I remember someone telling me to be patient," he says. He grabs a handful of my hair and pulls me into a sharp arch, a moan falling from my mouth at the manhandling, his stubble scraping against my cheek. "Don't worry, I'm going to give it to you."

He rips my hanging top off me with his other hand before pushing my skirt up around my waist.

"Look at how wet you are," he says, pushing my thong to the side and running his fingers through me, shoving two in roughly. "I need to see you."

Letting go of my hair, he flips me over again, settling between my legs.

"Condom?" he mutters, pressed against my entrance.

"Birth control. Fuck me. Now."

I can't wait another second, wrapping myself around him as he shoves into me and we both groan at the feeling. My walls pulse as they acclimate to the intrusion. He pulls out slowly.

So slowly before pushing back in. The move is almost gentle and at odds with everything else so far. Dom does this twice more and stills.

"God, these tits." He grabs them both, squeezing and twisting my nipples. I arch at the pain. Reveling in its bite. "They are perfect. And this pussy? I've dreamed about this pussy."

"Dom," I say, my tone only a little whiny for him to move, my walls pulsing around him.

"Did you dream of my cock, Ryan?"

"Fuck yes," I say, trying to move and fuck him if he won't do it, but he holds me still.

"Did you touch yourself to the thought of me taking you?"

He pulls out, inch by inch, and I almost cry at the emptiness.

"Yes, I thought of you. I came faster than ever before."

He slides in just as slowly and I want to cry with need.

"When all those people were chanting your name, did you think about how I'd make you chant mine?"

"Yes," I moan as he pulls out again.

This time, he slams home and I cry out in pain and pleasure.

"You're such a good girl, Ryan," he grunts, pounding into me with such force we shift until my head is hanging off the end. I don't even care.

His strokes are slow, the force punishing. It's exactly what I need. Like he knows my body better than I do.

"Faster," I beg, needing everything he can give me. "You feel so good. Give it to me, please. Please, baby."

He picks up speed and I know I'm not going to last long. He's already my addiction.

"That's right. No one has fucked you this good have they?"

"No," I cry.

"Only me?" he asks, and it's right there. I know I'm only a few seconds from coming.

"Only you. Dom! Only you!"

I chant his name as I come, dark spots dancing in my vision, and I hear his grunt, his cock pulsing deep inside me as he finds his pleasure in my body.

Dom is passed out, naked, and gently snoring. Granted, it's three in the morning and he not only fucked me into oblivion, he also played a football game.

My core is so sore and tired I almost can't close my legs. We rested up and then took each other again. It was easily the best sex I've ever had in my entire life.

Like a glacier moving through the water, I slip from under Dom's arm and out of the bed.

"Fuck. Me," I mouth silently at the pain throbbing from my vagina. Between Dom's size and the...vigorous pace, every single muscle on my body is sore.

Moving into the bathroom, I curse. I look as thoroughly used as I was. My hair is a tangled mess and bite marks cover my tits.

Making my way out of the bathroom, I grab the robe he gave me to wear between sessions. Dom shifts, and I pause mid-step, making sure he stays asleep before heading out of the room.

The house is lit just enough I can move through it. I make a mental note to have one of my homes updated with similar lighting so I can move through the space without turning on overhead lights.

One thing about me is I am a night person. All of my most creative inspirations have come in the middle of the night. But without a piano here, I'm not sure what to do with the melody currently playing in my mind.

I begin opening doors, going on a self-guided tour, knowing Dom would want me to treat his home as my own. It's easy to figure out which bedroom is the one he uses, the bed being giant compared to the cramped queen we're currently in. I close the door on this room quickly, not wanting to invade his personal space.

Going downstairs, I move through those rooms as well, making a quick pit stop for water and my phone. Each room is ordinary and expected, if not perfectly furnished.

That is, until I come to what seems to be the media room.

There's a giant screen taking up one wall with so much seating in front of it, you could fit almost twenty people. That's not what I care about.

Over in one corner is a keyboard.

I move toward it and notice it's a digital piano. Not only that, it's also the brand I favor. I run my fingers over the ivory keys wondering if Dom is musically inclined.

Typically, if someone plays the piano or is a songwriter, or anything musical, they make sure to tell me about it when I meet them. Not Dom.

Granted, Dom isn't a boaster, either.

I pull the little stool out and begin playing the melody in my head. As I hear it out loud, I tweak it where it's not quite correct. Grabbing my phone out of the pocket of my robe, I set it to record and begin playing, humming the words that aren't written. I get to the chorus and realize it's fully formed as I sing.

*I was drifting like a feather in the wind,*
*Chasing broken stars where dreams couldn't begin,*
*But you're my lighthouse, pulling me close,*
*In your arms, I found what I needed most.*
*After storm after storm, I'm steady and free,*
*In the calm of your touch, it's all new to me.*

I finish out the song, singing the few verses that come to me as I play. The last note rings out and I hit stop on the recording, saving it until I can get in the studio to fully flesh out what's taking shape.

Clapping from the doorway startles me, my racing heart starting to settle as Dom makes his way to me. My heart squeezes at the soft look in his eyes. He kisses my shoulder before pulling an ottoman over to sit next to me.

"That sounds pretty," he says, tucking my hair behind my ear. His fingers trail down the side of my neck in a delicate touch so at odds with his demanding ones from earlier.

"Thank you. Did I wake you?" I ask, worried.

"I woke up and you were gone. This room has a lot of sound-proofing. If the door hadn't been open, I wouldn't have heard anything even when I came downstairs." He takes my hand, linking our fingers. "Could you not sleep?"

"I had an idea in my head. Had to get it out. I was prepared to hum it into my phone until I found the keyboard. Do you play?"

His cheeks pink and it's the cutest thing I've ever seen.

"Uh, no." He clears his throat and his blush deepens. "I called Zoe and asked if you needed anything while you were staying with me. She mentioned you write a lot of songs in the middle of the night and suggested a few things. There's a guitar in that closet." He points to a door I didn't even notice when I came into the room. "I put it away so no one would mess with it. Do you want it?"

I melt at his thoughtfulness. This man I've known for less than six months, went to great lengths to take care of me. Something no one but my parents have done, unless I was paying them to do so.

"Not right now. Right now, I want you to take me back to bed."

He stands up, picking me up in his arms as he does, throwing me over his shoulder. A squeal escapes me. "That I can do," he says, giving me a light smack on the ass, helping to write another verse in my head.

# CHAPTER FIFTEEN

## DOMINIC

SWEAT COLLECTS AT MY hairline and my lower back. I've needed to pee for fifteen minutes. But Ryan is currently draped over me, passed out, and I'd rather die in a sweaty puddle than wake her.

However, if I wet the bed, I don't think I'll ever be able to get her into a bed with me again. And now that I've had her under me, I know I can't go back.

I try sliding out from under her, but her arms tighten around me, throwing a leg over my own for good measure.

I'm trapped and I have no other choice.

"Psst. Ryan." I jostle her a little, but she doesn't wake.

"Ryan," I say louder.

Nothing.

I bring my hand up and begin running my fingers up and along her perfect breast, all the way down to her hip. Up and down.

Over and over, making my touch heavier with each pass. She begins shifting and I hear her breath catch.

"If you try to fuck me one more time, I think my vagina is going to go on strike," she says. Or at least, that's what I think she says, the mumbled words almost indistinguishable.

"I'm pretty sure I couldn't get hard right now, even if I wanted to. I need you to move so I can go to the bathroom. Otherwise, I'm going to wet the bed like a toddler."

She shifts off me, eyes firmly closed, grumbling angrily something about cutting off my dick before killing me. I'm not too worried about the particulars as I sprint to the bathroom, leaning over the toilet just in time.

Washing my hands after I'm finished, I move back out to the room. Since I've been gone, Ryan has covered her head with a pillow and somehow dislodged the fitted sheet, the mattress standing out against the linens. I chuckle at the sight; glad I closed the blackout shades so she can hide from the light.

Leaving her to rest, I make my way to my bedroom to take a shower. She looked so sexy leading me last night, I didn't want to stop and make her change course to this room. So long as there was a bed, I didn't care.

The curtains to the floor to ceiling windows are pushed back against the wall. Since I didn't sleep in the room last night, I never closed them. Daylight creeps in, the lights in the pool clicking off as I look down over the backyard. Our glasses from last night sit on the table and I smile at the thought of the kiss that started everything.

The best night.

I press the button on the wall and the mechanism in the tracks starts whirring and the curtains move. Turning, I walk into the bathroom, the warmed ceramic tile my favorite feature. My clothes hit the floor and I step into the shower enclosure.

With my eyes closed, I let the steamy water rush over my face and wake up my body. Cold air sweeps over my bare ass and back but is quickly replaced with a warm body. My dick stirs when arms encircle my waist, a kiss is pressed against my spine.

"Good morning, sleepyhead," I say stroking the hands on my stomach.

"It'd be better at ten," she says against my skin and I laugh.

"You didn't have to get up." I turn in her arms.

With a finger under her chin, I lift her face and drop my lips to hers. She shifts, a hand reaching down between us, grabbing my rapidly hardening dick.

"Ry," I whisper, breaking the kiss. "I thought you couldn't take any more?"

She strokes me and I moan, pleasure radiating through my body.

"I'll always be able to take more of you."

That's all she needs to say. I grab the backs of her thighs, forcing her to jump up and wrap her mile long legs around my waist. I press her against the wall and push into her. She hisses through her teeth and I pause, letting her decide if she wants this, raining kisses against her neck.

"Make me come, Dom," she commands and I'm happy to oblige.

"It'll be my pleasure."

Twenty minutes later, I leave a satiated Ryan falling back asleep in my bed. I give her a kiss goodbye and gently twist her nipple, pulling one of my favorite sounds from her mouth.

Despite the house being quiet as I step into the garage, it doesn't feel empty like it does when it's only me. Ryan's presence adds weight to the air around me, making this house feel more like a home.

The garage door ascends as I move to the driver's side door.

My name rings out, my mouth dropping as I see the number of people in front of my driveway. I knew there would be interest in my relationship with Ryan, but a small, naïve piece of me never thought people would be at my house. Especially when I'm heading to a press conference to give them exactly what they want.

A statement on the woman in my bed.

High-pitched squeals and some signs catch my attention off to one side, and that's when I realize some of Ryan's fans are here, too. It's not just the press hunting us and by extension, me. It's the very people claiming they love her. I head toward them and the sound of camera shutters irritate me, but I keep Geoff's warning in mind about not letting them see any emotion.

"Hi, y'all!" I call out of the crowd. "I have to head to the facility. If you could please create some space, that'd be great. I don't want anyone to get hurt."

They yell out questions at me, but I ignore them and make my way back to my car. The attention makes my skin itch. I'll get used to it. I have to, if I want Ryan in my life.

Pulling my car from the garage, I back up through the space the crowd made for me, blinded by the flash of the cameras in my face, and make my way to the Thunderhawk facility.

Geoff comes into the locker room, fingers flying across his phone screen. "Are you ready?" he asks, finally looking up.

I look around me and wish my teammates were here to support me. "Yes."

He turns and heads out and I walk behind him, feeling like I'm heading to stand in front of a firing squad. Ryan is worth all of this, but it's intimidating. I've never had people interested in me outside of football before, other than one interviewer that asked me about Anya being on *House of Desire*. If this is how Ryan feels every time she leaves the house, I'm impressed she hasn't become a hermit.

Geoff pulls open the door to the media room and when I step over the threshold, the low hum of conversation turns to a tidal wave of yelled questions. There are news reporters filling every square inch of the floor available. There's no way we aren't breaking fire codes with the number of people in this room. Geoff steps up to the podium.

"Thank you all for being here today. Dominic will take questions for ten minutes, and then Coach Williamson will take over to talk about the game on Sunday."

He steps away from the microphone and motions for me. My heart races as I take the stage, flashes blinding me as everyone raises their hands waiting for me to call on them. I point to the woman in front, standing calmly.

"Mr. Reynier, how did you meet Ms. Jade?" she asks.

"You can call me Dominic and I met her helping my sister deliver the cake she ordered for her parents' wedding anniversary," I answer.

I point to a man in a shirt that reminds me of Ryan's eyes.

"How long have you two been going out?"

"I'm going to keep that between the two of us," I tell them and immediately point to a woman in a polka dot dress.

"How do you feel about the majority of Ryan Jade's songs being about ex-boyfriends or men she's had crushes on?"

I knew I was going to get this question, and I spent the weeks leading up this moment coming up with the perfect answer. The true answer.

"It doesn't bother me at all. Ryan Jade is an incredibly talented artist who draws from personal experience. There's a cliche of 'write what you know' for a reason. By sharing her life in her songs, she's given people, including myself, the knowledge they aren't alone. I'm awestruck at how vulnerable she's been in her career."

I point to a guy with fluffy white hair. "Do you love her?"

A chuckle escapes me. "Next question."

They all laugh and I point to a random person. "Do you hope she writes a song about you?"

The song she was writing in my own media room flits through my mind. "I'll be honored if she writes a song about me."

"What if it's a breakup song?" someone calls out and they laugh again.

"Then I hope it's the best breakup song ever heard," I joke, knowing if we ever broke up, I'd never be able to listen to her music again, so it wouldn't matter.

I'd be too crushed. The reality of how quickly I've fallen for her floors me like a solid hit from a defense. Thankfully, Geoff steps up and lays his hand on my back.

"Alright, everyone, that's time. Thank you, Dominic."

I walk off the stage to more camera flashes and yelled last-minute questions. The noise is blocked when the door shuts behind me and I almost run into Coach.

"Well done, kid. She's a lucky girl." He claps me on the shoulder and walks into the media room.

Taking a deep breath and releasing it, my nerves calm now it's all over.

The world knows.

Now we can go about living our lives.

# CHAPTER SIXTEEN

# RYAN

"Can you see anything?" the voice says on the other side of the glass.

I'm currently trapped in the corner of the entryway, hoping no one saw me come down in one of Dom's shirts I found in the dresser and no pants. The front door has a wavy glass in it, but it doesn't keep prying eyes from being able to see shapes and movement through it. And considering his press conference just ended, if there's any movement, they will know it's me.

**Ryan: Dom's house isn't safe anymore. He needs a new one. Today. Send me listings.**

I hit send on my text to Zoe and get a reply back almost immediately.

**Zoe: He's not going to let you buy him a house, Ryan.**

**Ryan: Don't care. I'll tell him it's a friend's or something. I have to protect him.**

**Zoe: Okay. Give me thirty minutes.**

The faces pressed against the glass are gone when I look up. Sighing with relief, I run on tiptoes to the kitchen. Movement by the pool catches my eye and I drop down behind the kitchen island.

My heart is racing.

Deciding I'm going to have to be hungry for right now, I lay down on my stomach and army crawl to the hidden laundry room door. From my vantage point, I can easily make out the indention where the door handle is. My hand slips in easily, and I twist the knob. The door bangs shut as I kick it closed and finally relax. Too bad this room isn't a walk-in pantry so I can snack while I wait for Dom.

He mentioned going to the press conference, but I don't know if there are other team things he has to do on Mondays. Would he have to practice today? That seems like it'd be overkill, considering he played a game yesterday. What do I know, though?

He is a professional after all, and professionals require a higher level of dedication.

I chew on my thumbnail wondering if I should text and ask him when he's coming home when my phone begins vibrating with the listings Zoe is sending me.

Swiping through the thirty or so options, there are only three I can actually see Dom living in. I click the link on the last one, the mid-century modern architecture of the outside catching my eye. And then I see the note on the listing.

"One of a kind, Parker Hightower original."

Anastasia's boyfriend talked about his construction business and the custom homes they make. I asked around in my circles if anyone had heard of Parker. One of my producers recently moved into one of his builds and I know he *loves* it.

The seventeen million dollar price tag seems reasonable when I swipe through the pictures and see all the little touches even million dollar mansions don't always take into consideration. I back out of the listing and heart the link so Zoe knows which one I mean when I text her.

**Ryan: Buy it. Cash. 24 hr close.**

Seven minutes later, my phone is ringing and I answer it.

"I called the realtor. Apparently, the house is already empty. I guess the owner had to move to New York last minute. The lawyers are working on the contracts now and everything should be done by the end of business," she says, no greeting. Whenever Zoe is *on*, all the niceties go out the window in favor of brevity and getting the job done.

"Perfect. Put it in a trust only Dom is the beneficiary of."

"You know he'll have to sign paperwork. Are you sure you don't want to buy it and let him live in it? That way, if something happens, you can sell it?"

"No. It's his house."

"Ryan—"

I cut her off. "Just do it, Zoe."

"Consider it done."

I hang up the phone and sigh.

It's not very often I have to pull out my boss voice, but sometimes it's a requirement. Zoe is basically an appendage. She's not only my employee but also one of my best friends. Those blurred lines can cause me headaches when, on the rare occasion, she's trying to advise me as a friend.

I hate when I have to do it, at the end of the day though, Zoe *is* my employee. No matter how much I love her. No matter how many drunken late nights we've spent up talking about dating and pedicures and childhood trauma.

The garage door starts whirring and I get up off the floor almost shaking with excitement to see Dom. If I were a little less excited, I might take notice of the similarities between me and a golden retriever awaiting its owner's arrival.

In the name of self-preservation, I ignore the comparison.

The garage door is closing as he walks into the laundry room, jolting with shock at my presence.

"Is something wrong?" he asks, not closing the door. Maybe he doesn't want to shut off his means of escape should I be here waiting to drop a verbal bomb on him.

"No," I tell him truthfully because when he's standing in front of me, I can't seem to think of anything that could be wrong. Then I hear people screaming Dom's name and I remember. "Actually, yes. The curtains on the back windows are open. And people have their noses pressed against the glass in the entryway."

His face drops.

"Fuck. I forgot to close those." He gently pushes me aside and moves into the house. I hear the fabric moving. "Okay, it's clear."

My eyes prick with tears at how it's not even been twenty-four hours since the game and he's already being forced to hide.

"I'm sorry," I say, moving into the kitchen, stopping at the island. Running my finger along the veining, I refuse to look at him. Until his fingers gently grip my chin, lifting it.

His brow creased in confusion. "Sorry? About what?"

I wave my hands around me. "All of this."

Dropping the hold on my face, he sweeps me into his arms. "You don't have anything to be sorry about. I should've closed the curtains. And I'll get some for the front glass, too. I think so long as we're back here, no one can see us."

"Is it bad?" My question is muffled by his shirt, but I don't move my face.

He pauses and I know, I *know*, he's going to lie to me. To spare me.

Because he's a good guy who doesn't deserve any of this.

"There's just a lot of excited people. I'm one of them."

I pull back and look up into his hazel eyes.

"How many are out there?"

Reading my face, he blows a breath out through his nose. "Two to three hundred."

My eyes almost bug out of my head at the insanity of the number.

"Dom," I say gently, "we can't stay here."

We stare at each other for a moment, and when his shoulders slump slightly I know I've won.

"Yeah, I realized that. Tank warned me about getting into a gated community. I didn't think he was being serious. I should've known better."

"There's a house that I think you'll like. Parker built it. A friend owns it and is willing to let us stay there," I lie. But it's a lie for the greater good. His safety is all that matters to me.

"I can't stay at your friend's house." He pushes off the counter and out of my arms, pulling open the freezer. My favorite brand of frozen pizza makes an appearance and I salivate.

"This is how it's done in my world," I tell him. "Normal friends might loan you a shirt or drive you to the airport. Rich people loan you houses or planes. It's no big deal."

That's not a lie. This is absolutely something that happens in my circles. In fact, my team of house managers know they could have guests arrive at any of my houses any time, day or night. One of my friends from high school, really my only friend from high school, moved to Nashville ten years ago with her producer husband. When he got drunk and backhanded her, she and their kids were stashed away at my house with security within the hour of the phone call.

I see in his eyes he wants to reject the offer, so I change course.

"If you want to stay here, I can't stay with you. I'm sorry. It's not safe now." All of my houses have been broken into at one point or another. Luckily, I've never been home. I don't tell him this, not wanting to scare him away.

It's a low blow. I know pulling at Dom's need to take care of people in his life will get him to agree. I'd feel bad about it, if there wasn't a legitimate security risk.

"Okay," he says, moving to the oven and setting the temperature, leaving it to preheat.

"Okay," I say with relief. "Wanna watch a movie? They said it won't be ready for a while."

"Sure, sounds good." The slight dejection in his voice worries me. It reminds me of how Cash sounded when I wouldn't want to go to his favorite dive bar for a drink or let him drive me around in his new convertible.

Worry if my life is going to ruin this before it even has a chance to start takes hold, and a small seed of panic is planted.

Seven hours later, Bradford and Justin pull identical black SUVs into Dom's garage.

"Which one do you want to ride in?" Brad asks, following me into the dining room where Dom and Zoe are.

"Is this necessary?" Dom asks, looking between me and my head of security before turning back to signing the supposed rental agreement in front of him. Zoe flips through the pages so fast, I know he's not getting a chance to read them, as she notarizes the pages, making the house his.

"If you want privacy, yes," Brad states in his no-nonsense tone.

"I know it's crazy. We want everyone off our tail for as long as possible and this will help," I tell him.

He nods and gives a smile and signs the last page. I feel like I haven't seen his smile in days, despite it just being since this morning. Before he left for the press conference.

Before he knew what came in the Ryan Jade package.

"I'm sorry, Ry. It's a little overwhelming. I'm sure your friend's house is great." He moves toward me and I reach up and pull his face down to mine, giving him a searing kiss. He opens his mouth to me enthusiastically and we ignore the other people in the room.

"I'll make it up to you," I tell him, innuendo in my voice.

"I'm heading out," Zoe says, pushing all the paperwork into her bag. I wave to her and then focus on the task at hand. Getting us to the new house. Grabbing Dom's hand, I pull him behind me to the garage and toward the car furthest from us.

Opening the back hatch, we both climb in, lying on our sides. Brad comes over and looks at me, waiting for me to give him permission. I nod. He reaches out and grabs a handle, pulling the black shade over us. Light tries to squeeze in around the edges, but the cover is custom and the gap is almost imperceptible. The car shakes as the hatch is closed and the driver climbs into the front seat. Brad always makes sure to use different members of the security team for this detail and to not always be the one driving the car I'm in so the paps don't ignore the decoy car.

The engines rev and the garage doors are lifted. Dom and I are silent as we back out of the garage. His fingers unexpectedly brush my hand. I grab them and bring his large hand to my cheek, holding it there.

"You're worth it," he whispers, and I almost can't hear him. Or maybe I don't trust the words. Words plenty have said but have never been true.

"I hope so."

His fingers trace my face, feeling, as if he wants to memorize me.

"I know so."

He kisses the tip of my nose, my giggle the last sound we make for the hour drive.

Dom's new house is only fifteen minutes from his old one, but before we can go there, we have to lose any tails we picked up. Right as I'm contemplating throwing back the cover, opening the hatch, and climbing out at the next stop just to get feeling back in my leg, the engine shuts off.

"We're here," Bradford calls from outside the car.

"Thank fuck. I felt like I was being driven out to a pasture to be shot like in a mafia movie or something," Dom says, getting out and almost falling to the ground on dead asleep legs. Brad and I chuckle as he fights to stay standing, shaking out his legs. I move to the edge of the car, letting mine dangle over the edge.

Blood rushes back into my extremities and with it, pins and needles.

Dom comes to stand in front of me, his control over his body returned.

"I will say, your friend has great taste in houses. This one is beautiful. It's *exactly* the type of house I love. You said Parker built it?"

My heart squeezes at his enjoyment of his unknown gift. "That's what I was told," I fib.

"Guess I should have taken Anya up on having him build me something." He holds his hand out to me, which I take, letting him pull me to my feet.

"Guess you should've."

# CHAPTER SEVENTEEN

## DOMINIC

TANK PULLS ON HIS cleats, tying the laces, readying for practice. My jaw cracks with a yawn as I wrap tape around my ankle.

"It's just weird, not sleeping in my own bed. I'm sure I'll get used to it," I say, finishing my story about the new house. Putting my foot back on the ground, I test my taping job.

Perfect.

"At least now you won't have to deal with door-to-door marketers," Tank says with a smile over his shoulder at me.

"Shit, my tape just ran out. Hey, Reynier! Throw me yours," one of the guys calls out, across the locker room. I lob the roll towards him and he catches it one handed.

Turning back towards my locker, I grab my mesh jersey, throwing it on over my moisture wicking undershirt.

"That's definitely a bonus," I say, addressing Tank once more. "Maybe I should do something nice for her. Make her dinner or something. Show her everything is going to be okay."

"What if you took her out? When's the last time you've been on a date?"

"It's been a while. Where should I take her?"

"There's this awesome place called The Giving Tree. Lore and I went there for our anniversary. Go there. It's amazing." Tank pulls on his jersey.

Running out of time before practice starts, I snatch up my phone and send a quick text to Zoe, asking her to get us a reservation for tonight. When a thumbs up comes back, I toss the device back into my bag and jog out to the field.

Practice takes hours but feels even longer with the anticipation of surprising Ryan tonight. The second our team meeting is done, I dash out of the facility and race home, calling Zoe on my drive to get everything organized.

"Ry?" I call out, accidentally slamming the door behind me in my excitement. "Ryan? Where are you?"

The door to her makeshift music room opens at the end of the hall and she sticks her head out, hair slightly disheveled like she'd been running her fingers through it in frustration.

"Did you call for me? Sorry, I was listening to something I recorded while you were out."

"Do you want to go out on a date tonight?"

Her smile is my favorite slightly crooked one. "Hell yes."

"Then we should probably go get ready."

She comes bounding out of the room and leaps into my arms, pressing a kiss against my lips.

"How much time do we have?"

I put her down and check my phone. "About an hour."

"First one upstairs gets the big shower!" she says, running from me, my name written across her back. She must have stolen one of my team t-shirts while I was at practice. So long as she's wearing it, I'd give her anything she wanted.

There's something about my name on her that makes my inner caveman *very* happy. I'm sure the fact she wasn't wearing a bra under the shirt played into a bit as well.

Exactly one hour and twenty minutes later, we arrived to The Giving Tree. One of the security team moves the black SUV right in front of the restaurant we are going to and I quickly parallel park in the space.

My only stipulation when I called Zoe was I wanted to drive us. She conferenced in Bradford and we discussed the logistics of making it happen. It was agreed the security team would save us a parking spot so we could be right in front of the door. Without valet, they didn't want us to have to walk very far.

"One time, at the beginning of my career, I had to do a shopping trip to this store that paid me to be there. And there were photographers, of course. The only spot available required me to parallel park. Something about having all those people watching me gave me performance anxiety and I bumped into the car behind me. I ended up having to leave my insurance information under their windshield wiper," Ryan says as I put the car in park.

She looks beautiful.

Favoring corset tops lately, she is in a dark maroon one that shoves her boobs up with a sheer, sparkly long-sleeve shirt over it that's tucked into a leather skirt.

The thigh-high boots almost had me on my knees back at the house, and every time I look at her, my mouth waters.

I've dated beautiful women before, but there's something about Ryan that sets my blood ablaze and I can't get over it.

"Dad wouldn't let Anya or me take a learner's permit without knowing how to park in every type of situation. He would set up cones in the street and make us park over and over until we could almost do it with our eyes closed. At the time it was so annoying. All of my friends were getting their licenses and there I was, parking five thousand times.

"I never realized how useful of a skill it was until I was walking down the street and a woman rolled down her window, crying, asking if I could park her car for her because she didn't know how. I called my dad and thanked him that day."

"I bet she was very thankful for the help," Ryan says, touching my arm. My car quiets as I turn the key.

"So thankful she went to dinner with me," I tell her with a grin and she laughs.

"I bet you a thousand dollars they were fake tears!"

"They worked, if they were! Stay there, I'll get your door."

A car passes and then I open the door and exit, moving quickly to get to the angel in my front seat. I open her door, holding a hand out to help her. She swings her long legs out first before pulling herself out with my help. A gasp echoes in the air and Ryan looks over my shoulder, smiling and giving a small wave to the early twenty-something year old now stopped on the sidewalk. Without letting her go, I close her door before taking her hand.

"Ready?" I ask and she looks up at me smiling.

"Always."

I've driven by this restaurant many times in my life. In childhood, we never could have afforded a place like this, but once I could, I realized I didn't really have any interest in it. For the most part, I keep my day-to-day life pretty much the same as I did growing up. No fancy meals or clothes. My biggest concession was getting two cars. One daily driver for practice and this 1970 Chevy Chevelle I could drive around in for special occasions like tonight.

The security team moves in around us, their eyes never stopping from surveying every possible angle.

"Good evening, Ms. Jade, Mr. Reynier. We have your table ready, if you'd like to follow me," the hostess says.

I follow Ryan down the hallway and when we turn the corner, my jaw drops.

The entire place feels like I'm walking into a fairy garden. Flowers are everywhere. Every square inch of the ceiling is covered in them, and bare light bulbs hanging down. Garlands drape along surfaces. The chairs are in light pinks, purples, and greens with gold accents everywhere. But the real beauty is the tree.

In the center of the room is a stained-glass sculpture in the shape of a tree trunk. I look closer and see the branches crawling through the flowers on the ceiling, little lights twinkling.

"Wow," I say, my eyes flitting around the room, not able to stop taking it all in.

Ryan giggles and pulls on my hand. "Come on."

We follow the hostess to our table in the back, and as we move through the space, I notice the phones. Almost every table has a phone pointed at us, but Ryan seems oblivious. Or, most likely, immune.

But I'm not immune.

I want to ask them to please let us eat in peace, then remember I'm no longer afforded that privacy. If we are in public, we are on. It doesn't matter that we are on a date. Us being here is going to be reported on.

Pushing the thoughts from my mind, I pull out Ryan's chair. She smiles up at me as I take my own seat, Bradford and the two others setting up at the table flanking us. The hostess hands us our menus, tells us our waiter's name that my brain doesn't hold on to, and then excuses herself.

"This place is beautiful. I can see why you love it," I tell Ryan, the low lighting making her skin and eyes glow.

"I signed my first recording contract at this restaurant. It was the fanciest place I had ever been in at the time."

"Didn't you start your career in Nashville?"

"I did, but they wanted me to meet some executives out here."

We pause our conversation when the waiter arrives. Ryan makes a few suggestions for drinks and food, which I take, and then we are alone together once more.

"What was it like growing up doing this?" I ask, taking a sip of my drink as delicious as Ryan told me it would be.

"Honestly, it was lonely a lot of the time." Her face goes pensive and a little sad. "There were a lot of things I missed out on because I was busy trying to get my music seen by as many people as possible. I never went to a school dance. I had a few friends growing up, but no one stuck around. My mom was my best friend. She or my dad were at every show, but in the beginning, it was mainly her. Sebastian never gave her money to raise me despite basically leaving me on her doorstep.

"My dad had a better paying job, so he kept working while she and I traveled around. Fairs. Bars. Pretty much any place that let me perform, we were there. And then one day, some guys from a label were in the crowd. I became an 'overnight sensation.' Everyone at my school was making plans to go off to college and stuff and there I was, signing my first record deal hoping for everything I have now."

Her teal eyes are unfocused, lost in her thoughts and memories.

"Do you ever regret it?" I ask when she comes back to the present. "Choosing this as your career?"

She looks around, takes in the people watching us. Recording us.

"Music is my life. I was born to be Ryan Jade. I couldn't be anything else."

Surprisingly, I understand that.

When I stepped out onto the football field, everything clicked. I went to school and got a degree to appease my parents, and to have a fallback in case I got hurt, but I always knew professional football was for me. It was my path. What I was called to do.

I couldn't be anything else.

Well, that's not entirely true. I could be other things. Just like I'm sure Ryan could be other things. But those other things would never be enough. They'd never fill the cavernous emptiness not having music or football would leave in us.

A cute girl with a braces filled smile, seemingly a tween, tries to step up to our table. Bradford intercepts her before she can get more than half a dozen feet from us.

"I'm sorry, miss. I'm going to have to ask you to back up," he tells the girl. Every single phone in the place is now obviously on us filming this interaction as her face falls, but she doesn't put up a fight. Shoulders slumped, she turns to go.

"Wait, it's okay," Ryan calls out. She stands and moves to the girl. "Hi, there. I'm Ryan. What's your name?"

"Scarlett," the girl says, shy.

"Scarlett, huh? Our names kind of match! We both have color names. Scarlett and Jade."

The girl lights up at this. "Yeah, we do! The popular girls at my school call me Scarbutt, though, and tell me it's a grandma name."

"I think it's a beautiful name. Kids used to make fun of me for being named a boy's name, but you know what? I wouldn't want to be named anything else."

"Me neither," the girl says, bolstered. "Would you sign this?" She holds out a napkin and pen.

"I'd love to!" She takes the items and scribbles her name before handing them back. "Hey, Scarlett, would you mind taking a picture with me?"

Bouncing in excitement, Scarlett nods. Ryan turns toward me. "Dominic, could you take our picture?"

I push up from the table immediately, pulling my phone from my pocket. "I'd love to."

Ryan crouches down getting eye level. "Say cheese," I instruct and they both do. I take a few pictures, making sure to get a few options for Ryan before letting them drop their smiles. As Ryan finishes the interaction, I take a few candid shots.

"Is that your boyfriend?" Scarlett whispers, pointing at me.

"Yeah, it is," Ryan says, claiming me. It makes me want to puff up my chest. Even though we just said we'd date and see where this thing goes, I've considered myself to be her boyfriend. I wouldn't be seeing anyone else so long as Ryan was there, official title or not.

The girls giggle and I take a picture, smiling at the joy in their faces.

I take Scarlett's phone and snap a few pictures for her as well, and then the encounter comes to an end.

"Thank you so much for coming to say hi to me," Ryan says holding out her arms. Scarlett immediately goes to her, hugging her tightly.

"Bye, Ryan!"

"Bye, Scarlett," she waves and once the girl's back is turned, she goes over to Bradford.

"Go have her parents sign the release," she tells him, and he moves into immediate action as we both sit back down at the table. "Can you send me that picture?"

I take my phone back out and send her all the shots I took. "What release?" I ask as she begins typing on her phone.

"So I can post these," she says, not looking up at me.

"Ry, are you sure you want to do that?" All the publicity centered on Scarlett makes me nervous for her.

"Yes. Those kids won't dare call her Scarbutt anymore."

Of course. She's protecting her. Fighting for her.

I never should have doubted.

Bradford comes over to our table, giving Ryan a nod. She types for a few seconds longer before tucking her phone away once more. My phone vibrates and when I look at it, I see it's a social media notification.

Ryan Jade posted a picture of her and Scarlett giggling together and the world goes wild.

Dinner was phenomenal. No one else interrupted our meal. The food was amazing, almost making me cry it was so good, and the company was perfect. Ryan and I joked and talked, not a single minute of the date with an awkward pause. Our waiter comes out one last time and when I ask for the check, he tells us our meal was comped. Easily a three thousand dollar dinner, and we didn't have to spend a dime. I tipped him the amount we would have spent, figuring the money would be more useful to him than the restaurant anyway, and we make our way outside.

Flashes blind me as we step outside, paparazzi yelling at us to look this and that way. Brad and the team flank us, keeping everyone back as we make our way to my car.

My car that is completely destroyed.

"She's mine" is spray painted over the custom paint job. The front windshield is smashed in, a rock sitting in the middle of the glass.

The destruction must register to Brad at the same time because we're football tackled into the back seat of the black SUV in front of my car. Once our door closes, the driver whose name I still haven't memorized, zips out of the spot and speeds toward the house.

"Dom, I am *so sorry*," Ryan says, tears in her voice.

"Why are you sorry? You didn't destroy my car." I say, taking her into my arms and kissing the top of her blonde head. But she pulls back, her bottom lip between her teeth.

"No, but it's my fault."

"How is it your fault?"

She looks at me, her eyes shining with unshed tears, silently begging me. For what, I don't know.

"I have a few stalkers, but there's one that we don't know who it is. The letters come from all sorts of places and we can't link them to anyone. And he always talks about how I'm his and he'll come for me one day so we can finally be together."

My heart sinks at the fear in her voice. It must be terrifying to have people think they know you, that they *own* you, when you don't even know they exist. It's not like there's a lot they can do if he only sends physical letters. No IP address to trace. No social media to find.

I think about how she hid in my laundry room.

How she insisted Bradford and his team cover the house 24/7.

Why riding in my car can't happen anymore. Not when she can be seen through the untinted glass. Not to mention I know I don't have the driving skills needed if someone were to follow us.

"Too bad, you're mine now. I'm not giving you up."

A tear rolls down her cheek and her bottom lip quivers.

"Baby—" I start, but she cuts me off.

"If you want to end this now, I understand. It's a lot. With the fans and the stalkers and the *cameras*. It's too much." She scoots away from me and looks out the window, tears silently streaming down her face.

In one of her songs, she begs the person to stay. To believe she's worth the chaos of her life. The chaos of her stardom. It's one that I always thought was beautiful, but I never understood.

I do now.

The pressure that sits on her shoulders. She is Atlas trying to hold up the crushing weight of the world's expectations, and I see how her muscles strain. I reach out and grab her arm, pulling her toward me.

"I'm not leaving," I tell her as she cries into my chest, quietly begging me for my words to be true.

# CHAPTER EIGHTEEN

## RYAN

Dom and I sit outside in the lush, private backyard, a favorite spot for us. My feet are tucked under his thigh, a book I'm not paying attention to in my hand. In the weeks after his car was vandalized, the cops couldn't find anything. The guy was in all black and hid his face.

While they were searching for a suspect, I was expecting our relationship to disintegrate like a mirage. But there he is, watching tape and taking notes for his game on Sunday. I walked on eggshells around him for about a week before he finally snapped and told me he wasn't going anywhere and he needed me to relax a little. It's not that I didn't hear the words, or even trust he meant them.

It could change.

And I don't want it to change.

"You're staring," he says using his fingers to zoom in, brow scrunched as he picks something apart. His tongue peeks out as he makes a note in his notebook. Apparently, he picks a different color notebook every year. This year's is a teal green like my eyes. It made my heart squeeze when he picked it. A silly thing, but touching all the same.

"You're pretty. I can't help it." It's not a lie. He's freaking gorgeous and sometimes I get sucked into watching his expressive face.

He puts his pen behind his ear and flips the tablet cover over the screen and gives me his full attention. His large hand wraps around my ankle, the calloused palm rough against my skin as he gives me a yank. That's all it takes for me to be ready for him.

My phone vibrates across the coffee table, distracting me.

"Hold that thought," I say, unable to ignore the call. Without taking my eyes off him, I answer it. "Hello?"

"Ryan! It's your dad." My stomach drops.

I changed my phone number three years ago when it was leaked to the public, and I know I never gave the new one to him. My stomach tightens with dread.

"How did you get this number?" Dom's eyes snap to me. I pull my leg out of his grip and set my feet on the concrete, like I'm getting ready to run.

"From Margo, of course. She was my sister before she was your aunt." That can't be right. Mom would never give him my phone number without asking me first. In fact, she most likely wouldn't even ask me, always wanting to shield me from whatever scrape he's gotten himself into. "Sweetie, I wanted to call and tell you congratulations on your new relationship! Donald seems like a great young man. Shame about his car though. You know, I had a fan break into my car once and lay in the back seat naked." He laughs, but I don't feel any humor at that situation or Dom's.

"His name is *Dominic*." I sigh, pinching the bridge of my nose in annoyance. "What do you want, Sebastian?" I push up and begin pacing around the pool, counting my footsteps on each lap. Dom's arms are on his knees and his eyes are watching me like I was him. His are filled with worry, whereas mine were filled with wonder.

The tone of his voice tells me he's about to ask me for money. Again.

"Well, sweetie," he starts, sugary sweet, "the money you gave me ran out. I have a lot of debts to pay before I can start with a clean slate, and I was wondering if you'd be able to help your old man out. I want to do everything I can to stay clean this time."

It's an old, effective threat. And he knows it.

No matter what I do, give him money, don't give him money, it doesn't make him more or less likely to stay clean. I've tried tough love at Margo's urging. I've tried getting him into the nicest facilities money could buy.

I've given him incentives for every week he stayed clean.

None of it mattered.

He always relapsed. No matter how much I distance myself, no matter how much I consider Matthew to be my dad, Sebastian will always be my biological father and the little kid inside me will always want him to be sober. I'll always wish I was enough to be sober for.

Tears sting my eyes, but I refuse to let them fall.

"Fine," I breathe. "I'll tell Zoe to wire you some money."

I can hear the smile in his voice. The smile I always wanted to have directed at me. "You're the best, kiddo!"

"I have to go now," I tell him on my third lap around the pool, sadness and disappointment slithering around in my gut.

"Sure, sure. I miss you, kiddo. You, me, and this Diego should get together soon."

I don't even bother to correct him this time, the misnaming of Dominic making it obvious he didn't care about anything other than getting money.

"Yeah, we'll see."

I end the call and keep my back toward Dom and try to collect myself. My eyes don't stray from my feet as I complete two more laps. Three steps from finishing another, I stop. Dom is blocking my path.

"Want to talk about it?" he asks.

"No," I say, shaking my head so my hair blocks my face.

"Okay. If that changes, I'm here."

I nod. When the first tear falls, he moves to me, wrapping me in his strong arms. The place I feel safe. And wanted. Enough.

I'm not sure I could survive if Dom decided my life was too much for him, and I swear to myself, I'll do everything I can to keep him from feeling the weight of it all.

Thirty minutes before kickoff, I've pushed open all the windows to the suite, wanting to give my brilliant best friend Taylor the full game day experience. She's the only one I've talked to even a little about Dom with because I know it won't end up on the front page.

I just wish she'd be able to meet him today.

"How was your dinner?" I ask. She happened to be in town for a meeting with a potential donor and decided to join me for the first half of the game.

"It was amazing. I think we'll be getting a seven figure check to push us over the edge to make some prototypes of the new design."

"That's awesome!" I feel my phone vibrating in my back pocket, interrupting our conversation. Pulling it out, I see Mom's face and smile. It took a few days for me to get over Sebastian's phone call. Being around Dom definitely helped.

"Hello, Mother," I say in a fake British accent, a joke between us after we spent a day watching movies between my shows. Somehow, every single movie we picked had a British actor. By the end, we were trying to imitate their accents.

Needless to say, it left us in a fit of giggles on the couch and it's been a bit with us ever since.

"Hello, daughter! Where are you?" she asks, a look of confusion on her face.

"I'm at Dom's game," I say, flipping around the camera and showing her the field.

After visiting Dom in July, I told Mom about him, too excited to keep it to myself any longer but not wanting the press to hear about it. Since I've been staying with him during this break, they have talked a few times when she has called me. After the first time, she texted me later, simply saying *"That one's a keeper."*

Something she's never said about any of my other boyfriends. She knew they weren't for me long term. After a huge blowup when she tried to tell me to be careful with Cash, she started keeping her thoughts to herself unless I asked.

And even then, I didn't always want to hear the truth she gave me.

With Dominic, I was desperate to know she liked him.

"That looks very nice. I can call you later, sweet pea," she says, giving me an out I don't want.

"Hi, Mrs. Sampson," Taylor says, poking her face into the call. Mom waves, calling out a hello.

"No, no. It's fine. Do you wanna see the suite?"

"Yes! Take me on a little tour."

I bounce a little in my boots. "Okay." I scramble back to the door and start.

"You walk in, and there's these pretty pictures." I show her the shots of the stadium and team through the years done in an editorial style.

"Those are nice," she says. I know she doesn't care, really, but I love that she indulges me.

"Aren't they? Then you come in and it's a little dining area. And there's a bar back here. Kevin the bartender." Kevin waves at my phone with a smile before I move on. "There's a little kitchenette here where Lucia, our server, normally is, but she's down getting the food ready. And then all the seats!"

"That's a very nice setup you've got there. Dom's taking good care of my girl."

I flip the camera back around, focusing it on my face once more. You'd have to be blind to miss the happiness that seems to be radiating out of me.

"He does at that," I say, no hint of innuendo despite how well he takes care of me in *that* area, too. This is my mother, after all. I keep all of that talk for my girlfriends. "Hey, can I ask you something real quick?"

"Of course!"

I move to the back of the suite, as far away from anyone I can and whisper.

"Dad called me. He said you gave him my number?"

Her face turns thunderous, but she keeps her voice low enough, I have to hold the speaker to my ear to hear her. "That son-of-a-bitch. He stopped by the house asking for money. Your dad was coming in from the grocery store and called out for help with something heavy, and I rushed to help him, leaving Sebastian, *and my phone,* in the living room. He must have guessed my password."

"Is it still your house number from childhood?"

She nods, a sheepish look on her face. "I'll change it today. I'm so sorry, baby."

"It's okay, I know you didn't plan on seeing him or anything." I move back toward the front of the suite so I can watch what's happening on the field.

"I'm sorry all the same. Anyway, I was just calling to chat. I'm going to let you go, baby. Call me later. And tell Dom I want to meet him in person soon."

"I will. Love you." I blow her an air kiss, which she returns, and turn to see Anya, Parker, Lorelei, and an unknown family behind me.

"Good day for football!" Anya says, giving me a hug in greeting.

"It's a great day for football," I say, returning the embrace. I have fallen in love with Dom's sister over the weeks, glad I can call her a friend. "Hey, Parker."

"Hello," he says giving me a hug, but it's not as engulfing as Anya's. He pulls me into his side with one arm and I squeeze around his middle.

I imagine it's how a big brother would hug his little sister and it sets my heart a flutter. Lore wraps me up in a hug, but I don't say anything, not wanting to interrupt the phone call she's finishing.

My friends and family are great. I love them all. There's something about these people that makes me feel whole.

Loved.

Wanted.

Just for being me.

"Will you get us some drinks, babe?" Anya asks Parker. His eyes are so filled with love when he nods, I almost have to look away.

"Ryan? Do you want one?" he asks.

"Please."

He turns to go talk to Kevin who has a list of our favorite drinks at the ready. Anya turns to the family standing, looking out on the field.

"Ryan, I want to introduce you to Liam. He's my shop assistant. These are his parents, Bridget and Nathan."

Liam comes bouncing over, just waiting for his chance, a bright smile. His excitement is infectious and I find myself bouncing with him.

"My girlfriend is a huge fan! She didn't believe me when I told her you'd be here, but you're here and that's amazing and I was wondering if you'd take a picture with me so I could send it to her?" All the words come out in a rush, pulling a laugh from me.

"We should do one better and send her a video!" I suggest.

We record the short video, and I share a few words with his parents who seem as kind and lovely as Liam. Anya and I make our way to our seats, sitting next to Taylor. Introductions are made quickly.

"When do you go back on tour?" Anya asks, clapping at some announcement that was made and I didn't hear. Hopefully, it wasn't something important that will lead to headlines like "Ryan Jade Hates Animals: Pop Star Didn't Clap for Thunderhawk Animal Shelter Program."

"Next week," I say, and she must hear the sadness in my voice because she turns her honey-brown eyes on me.

"Going to miss my brother?"

"Yeah. Especially sleeping with him." I say and she slaps her hands over her ears.

"La la la la la I don't need to hear this," she sings and I laugh.

"No!" I say, pulling one hand away so she can hear me. "I *actually* mean sleeping. He's a good snuggler. Makes me sleep better."

She gets a dreamy look on her face and turns back to glance at Parker. "I know what you mean."

Feeling our eyes on him, he looks over at us and gives Anya a wink. I think I swoon with her at the gesture. He strolls toward us, cups in hand. I take mine first, and then he hands Anya her rum and coke before taking his seat next to her. His free hand immediately settles on her thigh while he looks out at the field.

I wish that Dom could be up here with me, watching the game and be coupley like Anya and Parker. But watching him play sets me on fire.

It's all I can do to wait until we get home to tackle him myself.

"Okay, sorry about that. One of my clients is being a shit," Lorelei says, flipping her hair over her shoulder. "Hi, Ryan. I've missed you!"

"Hi, Lore. I've missed you, too! I've been meaning to text you about finding some art for Dom's new house."

I freeze, hoping that Anya doesn't think anything of my slip-up.

Lorelei begins typing in her phone, nodding. "I'll put a reminder in my calendar to call you tomorrow. I can either come over and you can show me the space or video call. Whichever works for your schedule. Anya mentioned it was a friend of yours's house. My team can make sure the hangings are temporary, and we can talk about renting the pieces."

Lorelei is the best art broker I've ever found. She has a keen eye for emerging artists and can elevate any space with her finds. I've had her do four of my houses.

"Perfect."

"Ugh, shit. I need a drink. One sec," she says, quickly making her way to the bar.

I turn toward the field now that the players are being announced. I clap for all of them, but as Dom's name is called, I stand, cheering loudly.

"Get the fuck out of here, you stupid bitch!" a man in the opposing team's jersey yells in the section in front of me and I ignore him. The few games I've come to, Thunderhawk fans have been incredibly welcoming and kind to me. There have been a few hecklers before today, always in opposing team colors, yelling at me how Dom sucks.

A loud bang startles me and suddenly I'm being knocked off my feet. I look up and Parker is laying on top of me.

"Are you okay?" he asks, frantic. I can feel his heart sprinting.

Or that might be mine. I don't think I've taken a breath in the last ten seconds.

"I'm good. I'm surprised you didn't tackle Anya," I joke, trying to defuse the fight-or-flight response my body is currently going through.

He gives me a sheepish grin. "She threw herself down before I could, so I came for you."

"I appreciate that," I tell him with a pat. Bradford is on the stairs, looking out at the crowd, gun in his holster. Which means the threat is not lethal. "Do you think you could get off me now? I'm having a hard time getting air."

"Oh, God," he says pushing up. Parker stands, then reaches down and picks me up like a doll, setting me on my feet. "Sorry."

"No problem." I turn to look at Brad. "We good?" I ask.

"Some guy threw a full beer can at you. Hit the glass instead of your face. Security got him. Should we go?" He looks at me and must see the answer on my face because he moves to take a seat directly behind me.

"I'm good," I say, embarrassed. Liam's mom squeezes my arm and I almost crack. Luckily, the incident doesn't seem to have dulled Liam's enthusiasm.

Subdued, I sit back down in my seat. Lore grabs my hand, linking our fingers together.

"Are you okay?" Anya asks, a concerned look on her face. All I do is nod.

"I've had a full beer dumped on me when I was on the field standing by the wall," Lore tells me. "People have also yelled heinous things about Tank to me, when we were beating their team. I'm not excusing it, or saying that behavior should is normal, but I want you to know you're not alone. Every wife and girlfriend has a similar story. Sometimes they hate us for no reason."

For the rest of the game, I don't leave my seat. I clap. That's the extent of my cheering, not wanting to draw attention to myself any more than I'm sure has been given to me. There's no way the whole incident wasn't recorded and splashed across social media and the news almost instantly. Tears prick my eyes as the game pauses for the two-minute warning.

All of my willpower has gone into staying in this seat and not letting them see they can get to me. I hate that I won't be able to come to next week's game because of the tour. I don't want to give them the satisfaction of knowing they succeeded in their goal.

Because they did.

I'm rattled.

We knew that my attending these games would be a bit of a security risk. The team has done everything they can, with my security, to mitigate every risk they could. But if I'm in public, there will always be a level of danger, no matter how small.

"I know it's easier said than done, but don't let that guy get to you. He's an asshole who's upset he's not a professional athlete and decided to take it out on you," Anya says. She doesn't look at me, but I can feel her watching me out of the corner of her eye.

"I know," I say, pushing back the tears.

"Every game you're at, I can tell the difference in how well Dominic plays. He loves having you here. Thunderhawk fans love you. My family loves you. And we're glad you're here."

A single tear escapes.

"I'm not sure I'm worth everything he has to go through because of me. He's not going to be asked about that amazing touchdown he scored by the reporters. He's going to be asked about how his girlfriend had a beer thrown at her. I don't want to take anything away from him because I'm causing problems by being here."

This time she looks at me, holding my gaze and not letting me go.

"I promise you, he doesn't care. All he cares about is you. And he's too hardheaded to ever let something he wants be taken away from him by some drunk idiot that can't keep his damn mouth shut. He wants you, Ryan. No matter the baggage you bring. He wants you. Don't take yourself away from him because you think it'll be better for him. It won't be." Not trusting my voice, I look out toward the field. She bumps her shoulder into mine. "Plus, have you ever seen Dom mope? It'll make you want to drown him to get it to stop. Don't make me have to drown my brother, Ryan."

I laugh, the words not enough to convince me he wouldn't be better off without me. Everyone's better off without me, it seems.

But I'm too selfish to let him go.

# CHAPTER NINETEEN

## DOMINIC

A WEIGHT HAS BEEN lifted off my shoulders with the trade deadline coming and going without my departure from the Thunderhawks. It doesn't mean I'm safe forever, just until March. There's a lot of time left to prove myself. The next forty-eight hours will be the last hours before I really need to lock in and focus for the remainder of the season.

Luckily, we didn't pull a Thanksgiving game. This season, we'll be playing Sunday like normal. Which is perfect, as it allows me to finally meet Ryan's parents.

"I can buy a plane ticket, babe. You don't have to rent me a whole ass jet. It's only me," I tell Ryan, packing the shirt Anya helped me pick up for tomorrow night. Nerves make my hand shake a little.

I feel dumb being so nervous to meet my girlfriend's parents, but here I am. Like I'm sixteen again. Maybe it's because this is a relationship I could see myself being in long term and I want to make a good impression on them.

"Would you rather spend every minute together we can or get mobbed in the airport?"

I hem and haw, making noises like I'm trying to make a choice when it's really no choice at all. She laughs and continues without it. "The last time I was in an airport, sitting at the gate, it became a security nightmare. It's not worth disrupting the entire place."

I pick up the phone and look at her perfectly made-up face.

"I didn't think about it," I tell her honestly. The level of fame I've gained over the last few months has made many things harder than they used to be. The locals try to leave me alone and let me have a normal life. It's all the tourists who make going out hard.

And most of my personal life has evaporated, just like Geoff warned me it would. Not that I mind.

For the most part.

Sometimes I miss being able to do things in relative anonymity. I wouldn't trade my relationship with Ryan to go back to that life, though. Reminding myself the interest in my life is because so many people care about her keeps me from going out of my mind when I feel like I'm living in a fishbowl now.

A photo was snapped of me talking to a hostess at a dinner with a few of the guys and the next day the headlines talked about us breaking up already. I might have to take a page out of Ryan's book and buy a wig.

"I know. And I'm sorry to make it a necessity. I promise it's worth it. Plus, flying private is better."

She's not wrong. We drive right up to the plane and get on. Within twenty minutes, we are normally taking off. The rules that apply to the everyday person when it comes to, well, basically anything, don't apply to someone of Ryan's stature.

"Dominic, it's time to go," Justin, my lone security guy, calls out to me from the living room. After the car incident, Ryan tried to give me half of her security when she left to go back on tour, but I refused, compromising at Justin.

"Babe, I have to go. Have a great show. I'll see you in a couple hours."

"Text me when you land."

I blow her a kiss and hang up the call, pocketing my phone. Grabbing up my duffel, I sling it over my shoulder and then pick up my hanging bag, careful not to wrinkle the shirt inside. Ryan promised me her parents would long be in bed by the time we got to the house and I could meet them first thing in the morning. I was thankful for the time to sleep before meeting them after the four hour flight.

And so I could kiss my girlfriend hello without feeling like they are watching me. After three weeks without seeing her in person, I'm almost desperate to get my hands on her. Which will also have to wait until tomorrow so her body has a chance to rest after the show. A grin splits my face as I walk down the stairs at the surprise I have for Ryan waiting in my bag.

An unfamiliar ceiling is the first thing I see upon waking. I fell asleep with Ryan in my arms, but sometime throughout the night rolled onto my back. Even when I'm not holding her, she's always touching me in sleep. Looking down, I see her butt is pressed against the outside of my thigh. My dick starts thinking about how nice of a butt it is, too.

I turn on my side, spooning her from behind. My hand runs down her body, following the various dips and valleys of her figure, before palming her ass and giving it a squeeze. I repeat my path and she begins shifting in her sleep, pressing herself against my hardening crotch.

She reaches backward, grabbing a handful of the hair at the back of my head. Twisting her face to the side, I claim her mouth in a searing kiss. We both break away panting.

"Good morning," I say, staring into her beautiful eyes.

"Good will be once you've made me come," she says, pushing her ass against my hard dick.

I groan, thrusting into her, my dick settling between her cheeks. We dry hump each other for a moment like randy teenagers until I still her with my hand.

"No orgasms this morning. I have plans for you tonight."

"Sexy plans?" she asks, her voice deeper than usual after her concert.

"*Very* sexy plans," I promise. If her parents' house had a different layout, I wouldn't be doing what I have planned. But over the years, Ryan had an additional primary suite added on the opposite side of the house for whenever she stays over. "I'm going to go take a shower."

I kiss her shoulder and climb from the bed. Stretching, I take in the view of the property they own through the window. I can picture a young, pigtailed Ryan running around the yard screaming and playing games. With a smile, I move into the shower.

Once I'm done, I wipe the steam from the mirror and shave my face. Pale arms circle my waist and a kiss is pressed against my back.

This has been a great morning.

"You smell good," Ryan says, taking a deep whiff.

"It's your soap," I tell her, washing the remnants of shaving cream from my face.

"Well, it smells better on you."

"You better get in the shower if you want to have time for phase one of my sexy plans."

"There are phases?" she asks, moving around to look me in the eyes.

I give her my most lust filled look. "A few of them."

She purrs at the promise and I slap her ass as she walks into the shower.

Once I have my pants on, I open the side pocket of my duffel and look down at the supplies. My heart races a bit, worried about Ryan's reaction. I'm pretty sure she's going to be into it, but you never know on things like this.

When she walks back into the bedroom, I want to hit the floor at her feet and spend my life there worshiping her for the goddess she is.

The towels drop and she strikes a sexy pose. Her skin is pink from the water I know was molten lava level hot.

"I'm ready for phase one," she says, all thoughts but being inside her eddying from my brain.

"Get on the bed on your hands and knees." I barely get the words out.

If she's naked much longer, my plans are going to go out the window and I'm going to fuck her right now. She crawls onto the bed, following my instructions and my mouth waters.

I grab the lube from the pocket of my bag and squirt some on her ass. She squeaks at the cold but holds still. I begin rubbing the lube all over her tight hole. Her body tenses as I begin working a finger inside her.

"Relax, baby," I coo and almost come when she does, trusting me. "Tell me to stop and I'll stop."

She doesn't and I melt.

"Has anyone taken you here before?" I ask. She moans as I slowly work a finger in and out, adding another gradually.

"No."

"Good. This is mine. *You're* mine."

"Yes, I'm yours," she moans.

By the time I have her ready, I'm rock hard, precum leaking from the tip of my dick. Her thighs are slick with her arousal and I can tell she's on the edge of coming. I grab the brand-new butt plug from the pocket and squirt lube on the tip.

"You're doing so good, baby. Almost done."

"Dom," she moans.

"I'll give you what you need in a minute. Trust me."

"I do."

Those two little words make me pause at how good they sound from her mouth. I kneel back on the bed behind her once more and begin working the plug into her ass. Her moans become desperate and she starts pushing back against the silicone toy, taking more and more into her body until it's fully seated. I kiss her lower back, gently thrusting the plug in and out of her.

"I need to come, Dom. Please, please, please," she begs and I give in.

Grabbing her, I flip her onto her back and her eyes are wild looking back at me. A pink flush colors her skin and I know it's no longer from the water. I grab her legs and throw them over my shoulders and immediately dive face first into her pussy, fucking her with my tongue. Her hands go to my hair and she begins grinding me. I lick and suck and kiss her dripping pussy, shoving two fingers in with zero resistance. Legs squeezing my face, she comes with a shout, going boneless as I lick her through the last of her release.

"That was a great phase one," she says, her head lolling on the side as I wipe my mouth with her discarded towel. "Do I need to get on my hands and knees again to remove it?"

A grin slowly spreads on my face. "You're wearing it all day."

"What? It's Thanksgiving." Her eyes bug out of her flushed face and I want to laugh. I've never seen her so discombobulated.

"Yup."

"My parents are going to be there."

"Uh huh."

"Dominic. I can't wear *a butt plug to Thanksgiving with my parents*," she hisses. I grab the remote from my bag and turn it on. She jolts in surprise, mouth agape. "Oh, fuck."

Her muscles clench and she groans, her hand reaching down to her clit. I move quickly, slapping it away.

"No touching." Affront flashes in her eyes and I have to bite back a laugh. I turn off the vibrator and her body relaxes.

"You need to take this out of me," she commands, but I ignore her. I move to the closet and take out my button-down shirt. She gets off the bed, and grabs her clothes for the day from her suitcase.

The door to the bathroom slams and the laugh I've been repressing sneaks out. As I tuck my shirt into my pants and slip my belt through the loops, she opens the door, all but ripping it from its hinges.

Her hair is fluffy with untamed curls from the humidity last night and the orgasm this morning.

She looks breathtaking in her neediness and I wonder if I have made a deeply grave mistake. How am I not going to have a raging hard on the entire day, knowing she's wearing my plug?

"You okay, babe?" I ask her and her nostrils flare.

"I'm going to use you like a sex doll later and I don't care if you come or not." She jabs a sharp nail into my chest. I don't mind her ire. It's definitely turning me on.

"That's not the threat you think it is, gorgeous."

I move to the bathroom and quickly brush my teeth and wash her dried arousal from my mouth. I come out of the bathroom, and the crazed look has calmed in her eyes and I think she's gotten a little more control of herself.

"Ry," I say grabbing her shoulders, "I can take it out, just say the word."

She softens. "No, I want it. I just go a little crazy with wanting you. It's like I'm on fire whenever you're near and to have a constant reminder of what's coming? It's going to be painful to wait. I want this, though. You. Sexy surprises. All of it."

Kissing her, I squeeze her ass, unable to keep my hands from her. "I don't want to wait either. The pain of waiting will make the pleasure even better."

When we are ready, she grabs the door handle but pauses, looking back over her shoulder.

"Sure hope it's not awkward meeting my dad knowing I have a butt plug in," she says with a wide grin and opens the door stomping out.

I can feel the blood drain from my face and now know for a fact I made a mistake.

# CHAPTER TWENTY

## RYAN

I'M SO KEYED UP, I'm ready to explode. The plug in my ass shifts with every step and by the time I'm entering the main house, I'm on the brink of orgasm.

Now, I *really* don't mind the plug. In fact, it's something I've been wanting to try for a while.

What I mind is how *goddamn* horny I am going to be.

All.

Fucking.

Day.

When the vibration started moving through my body, I thought I was going to cry out in ecstasy. And then he cut it off before I could find my release. I'm ready to edge him until he begs me to end his suffering. And then I'll edge him some more.

Turnabout is fair play, after all.

Mom is in her favorite Thanksgiving apron with my fourth-grade handprints painted to look like turkeys on the front with the words "You're the Gravy to my Mashed Potatoes." She's worn it every year since I made it and the fact she's kept it all this time makes my heart squeeze.

"Mom," I call, and she looks up at me, her face breaking into a smile full of love. She drops the potato and peeler onto the counter and wipes her hands, making her way around the island I had custom made to her specifications after years of complaints there wasn't enough counter space.

"My baby is finally home," she coos, pulling me into her arms and giving me a strong hug. I hold onto her, breathing in her faint vanilla scent.

"I missed you."

"I've been counting the days." She pulls away and wipes the tear from her eye.

Mom has always been incredibly supportive of my life and everything that comes with it. I know she wishes, some days, my dreams had kept me a little more local and with more free time. Dom clears his throat behind me and I smile, something I can't seem to stop, despite his being in the doghouse.

"Mom, this is Dominic, my boyfriend."

"Hi, Mrs. Sampson, it's a true pleasure to meet you. Thank you for inviting me into your home for the holidays," he says, so formal I melt a little. He sticks his hand out for her to shake, but she bats it away and envelopes him in the same hug as me.

"Go ahead and call me Momma Margo. Thank you for taking such good care of my little girl," she says and I catch his eye giving him a heated look and a wink. Pink stains his cheeks at the silent innuendo.

"It's been my pleasure, Momma Margo," he says, his eyes going wide at the implication as he pulls back from the hug. "I mean, she's easy to take care of." I slap my hand over my mouth trying to stifle my giggle. "I mean, happy Thanksgiving."

His face is so red, I'm pretty sure if I put my hand on his cheek, I'd get burned from the heat of his embarrassment.

"Is there anything we can help you with, Mom?"

She turns to look at me. "I have it all under control. Why don't you go introduce Dominic to your father?"

I grab Dom and pull him from the room. He calls out a goodbye to my mom. Once we are in the dark hallway, I push him against the wall, plastering my entire body against him before pulling his face down to mine. He tries to keep the kiss PG, but the plug shifts and makes me pant into his mouth.

"Let's go back to my room real quick. I'll suck every last drop of cum from your dick and you can use those talented hands to get me off." I rub myself against his leg like an animal in heat as I speak. It does nothing to give me relief.

"As amazing as that sounds, seeing you desperate like this is turning me on even more than I thought it would." Dom grabs the back of my neck and gives me a kiss that's almost all tongue and heat. "Now come on. It's time I meet your dad."

This time, he's the one dragging me down the hallway until he notices every yearbook picture is hung on the wall in order. Starting at senior year, he stops at each one and I almost roll my eyes at the outfit and hair choices I made. My mom tried to talk me out of the pag boy haircut in seventh grade, the shortness not a good look with my curls. Did I listen? No. Now it's forever memorialized on the wall. Dom gets down to second grade and stops.

"This is the cutest picture I've ever seen," he says with a laugh. "Do you think your mom would still have a wallet-sized version I could have?"

"You are not carrying that picture in your wallet," I say looking at my seven-year-old self.

My blonde hair is in pigtails, one slightly higher than the other, and I have a big, holey grin on my face having lost three front teeth two days before the picture. The bow and ears on my Minnie Mouse shirt are visible, the rest cut off.

"I'll ask her myself," he says, quickly looking at the last two pictures before we get to the end of the hall and I pull him into the living room.

"Dad," I call from the doorway and he startles in the dark brown leather recliner I bought him for the Christmas before last. Mom was ready to burn his old one that was riddled with rips and holes in the backyard.

"Now there's my favorite daughter," he says, slapping his hands on his thighs before standing. I laugh at his joke, the same joke I've heard every time I see him since I moved out on my own. His potbelly has gotten a little bigger since the last time I saw him, and his shirt is barely covering it.

Dad's arms wrap around me and he kisses the top of my head. The announcers from the Thanksgiving Day parade drone on in the background like every year.

"How's the shop?" I ask once he lets me go. "Dad owns an IT infrastructure company," I mention to Dom who nods.

"Good, good. Still standing. The new kid I hired is a putz but he has promise." He turns his eyes to Dom and grins behind his bushy beard. "And this must be the superstar football player. It's good to meet you, son."

Dom takes the offered hand and gives it a shake. "It's nice to meet you, too, sir. Thank you for having me in your home."

"Any boy that makes my daughter as happy as my baby girl has been since she met you is always welcome here." He claps him on the back before turning back to the TV. "Now, what do you know about Thanksgiving floats, Dominic?"

"Not a dang thing, to be honest."

"That makes two of us." He sits back in his chair and waves at us to take a seat on the couch.

We spend an hour watching the various floats and performances in the parade in New York City, Dad declaring each float his favorite. At the end, Dad stands and states he needs a beer, promising to bring back a drink for both of us as well. The moment he's out of the room, Dominic's hand goes into his pocket and my back bows as the butt plug begins vibrating.

"Are you going to come before he comes back?" Dom whispers into my ear, eyes trained on the doorway.

My nipples pebble beneath my bra, and I want to rip my clothes from my body and beg him to mount me right here. Pleasure builds, heat radiating out from my core. My pussy clenches around nothing, desperate to be filled, and my fingers dig into Dom's leg.

"He's in the hall," Dom warns. I'm so close, I almost don't hear the words. When the vibrations stop, I'm at the precipice, about to fall into blissful oblivion. My body slumps against the couch and

I look at Dom my chest heaving. "Pull yourself together, Ry. He's walking in."

I sit up, ignoring the throbbing between my thighs.

"Here you go," Dad says, holding the beers out to us by the necks of the bottles. We take them with a thanks, the cool glass nice against my heated skin.

I look up at Dom, the bottle pressed to my lips and he gives me a wink before taking a drink from his.

This is going to be torture.

It took ten years for dinnertime to arrive, I'm sure of it.

Dom turned on the vibrator two more times throughout the day. Once while I was in the restroom, my knees almost giving out when he stopped it once more with me on the edge of orgasm. The second time Dad was showing him a car he was working on while I set up the table. Mom yelled at me from the kitchen to be careful when she heard me drop one of the plates from her 'fancy china' they received as a wedding present back in the day.

Even without the vibration, the plug had me in a state of constant arousal with Dom rebuffing every attempt I made to get him to take me rough and quick.

"The food looks delicious," he says, pulling my chair out around the wood table Dad made Mom for their first anniversary. My grandma's lace table runner sits under all the dishes, making me nostalgic for the holiday dinners we had at her house when I first came to live with Margo and Matthew.

"Thank you, Dominic. It's filled with love," Mom says. She always told me love should be the special ingredient that goes into anything you do for someone you care about.

I take my seat and Dom moves to take his across from me. The second he's seated, I kick off my shoe and begin running my foot along the inside of his leg until it's rubbing against his semi-hard dick.

Dom gives me a look that tells me to knock it off, but I don't, needing him to feel the same need I feel. Mom says a quick prayer and we all begin filling food onto our plates, my foot coming back to the floor.

"So, Dominic, how did you get into football?" Dad asks, and the conversation starts.

We tell stories. Laugh. Drink. And have the best holiday dinner I think I've ever had.

Dominic is perfect. He flatters my mother every chance he gets and talks everything sports with my father. Every minute that passes, my feelings for him deepen. It's amazing how well he fits into my family. And my parents like him and approve.

Seeing how quickly they take to Dom, how his fun-loving personality draws them in, I know this is what I've been waiting for.

Mom looks at me before shifting in her seat and focusing back on Dom once more and I know it's time for 'the talk.'

"How have you been handling everything that comes with Ryan's life, Dominic? Has it been rough with her back out on the road?"

He chews the last bite of his pumpkin pie, contemplating his response. I hold my breath, nervous for his answer, wondering if this will be the time when he tells me it has been too much.

"I miss her when she's out on the road, but I know she's doing something she loves, so I'm glad she can do that."

"And everything else?"

He looks between my parents before wiping his mouth with his napkin, putting it next to his empty plate.

"It's hard. I'm not going to lie to you, it's been a big change." My heart drops. Before I can lower my gaze to the table, his eyes lock on mine. "Ryan is worth every sacrifice I have to make."

My heart starts beating again.

"We've always thought so, too," Dad says, raising his glass in a salute, Dom returning the gesture.

Once dinner is over, we clear the table, Dom and I washing the dishes that don't fit in the dishwasher by hand. The silence between us is comfortable, and I feel the first flutter of love for this man who has come into my life and added so many things I didn't realize I was missing.

The scrub brush in my hand pauses. *Love.* It's been so gradual, I almost missed it. Growing up, falling in love felt like a descent into madness, but being with Dom hasn't felt like that. It's felt calming, easy.

I'm falling in love with Dominic Reynier.

I wait for panic or surprise at the realization, but there is none. Just happiness at the possibility of my feelings growing even deeper for this man.

Finishing up the last dish, I rinse it before handing it to him to dry.

"I need you," I tell him. This time, it's not a desperate cry for pleasure, but a need to show him how I feel with my body, what I'm not yet willing to say.

"Let's go to bed."

We move to the living room, my parents cuddled on the couch as in love as the day they first met, and call out our goodnights before making our way back to my room.

Dom shuts the door to my room behind us, and I kiss him, pouring everything I can into the kiss to thank him for today. He breaks away.

"You said you needed me," he says, kissing along my neck, nibbling the skin there.

"I do."

"What will you do to have me?" he asks. My answer spills from my lips without a moment's hesitation.

"Anything."

"Anything?"

"Anything," I confirm.

He moves to the chair in the corner of the room that I sit in when I want to write a poem that inevitably turns into song lyrics and sits. His legs are spread and he looks like a casual king surveying his kingdom.

"Take off your clothes." I follow the instructions, my mouth watering at this dominant version of him. "Now get down on your hands and knees."

I drop to my knees and his eyes heat with lust. The wood floor is hard beneath my palms, but I don't feel it.

"Crawl to me." My hips sway as I slink across the floor to him, my arousal pouring from me at my submission.

No one else ever made me feel safe enough for such a display of trust.

"That's the most beautiful sight I've seen," he says as I sit back on my heels at his feet. "Take out my cock."

I do, giving him a few pumps before taking it between my lips. My desperation for release is still there, but my need to taste him is stronger.

"Holy fuck," he moans, jolting back, and I swirl my tongue around his tip before taking him to the back of my throat. Hollowing out my cheeks, I suck him off as I pull back, diving back down the second my lips get to the tip.

Bobbing my mouth up and down, his thigh muscles tighten, until he grabs a handful of my hair and pulls me off him.

Panting, he looks down at me. "That's enough of that. Get on my lap and show me how much you need me," he commands.

I pull myself off the floor and straddle him, thankful my chair is bigger than normal and easily fits us both. I grip his dick at the base and line it up with my opening. I fuck the tip, enjoying the way his mouth opens and tongue wets his bottom lip.

"I thought you said you needed me." His voice is rough and I can feel it between my thighs.

"I do."

"Then take me, Ryan, and stop fucking around."

I feel myself slicken more at his words and begin impaling myself. His thick shaft feels even bigger with the plug in my ass. I go slow, taking him in inch by inch.

"I said take. My. Cock," Dom says impatiently. He grabs my hips, pulling me down hard as he thrusts up into me. The pain of being so full is beautiful, delicious. "You're so tight, baby. You take me so well."

His hands run over my body as he praises me and I breathe through the intrusion. I pull myself up inch by inch, and we groan together as I sit back down taking him once more.

"Ride me, Ryan. Take what you want from me. I'm yours. Make yourself come."

# CHAPTER TWENTY-ONE

## DOMINIC

S HE THROWS HER HEAD back, body quaking. It takes everything in me not to follow her, but I have plans for tonight and
they don't include my premature ejaculation. Boneless, she leans
against me, the last few tremors of pleasure passing through her
body. I settle my hands on her ass and stand and make my way over
to the bed. Dropping her down on top of the comforter, I begin
rubbing her clit.

"Too much," she says, her head lolling.

"You can take it. I know you can." I grab the plug and pull it from
her and toss it on the towel I left on the bedside table this morning.
One hand continues to rub her slickness around, the other grabs the
bottle of lube, popping open the lid.

I let the liquid drizzle out, landing on her abused core and begin
working it toward her ass before lubing up my dick as well.

"Look at me, Ryan," I command, putting the bottle down and spreading her legs wide. Her eyes are unfocused but quickly filling with heat once more. "Say stop and I will."

She nods and I press the tip of my dick against her lubed ass and begin working myself in, one excruciating inch at a time.

"You're too big, Dom," she whines, meeting me gentle thrust for gentle thrust.

"You can take it. Don't you want to be full of me? Don't you want me to claim this ass as mine?"

"Yes."

My dick is only half way inside her and I'm already sweating, my orgasm building at the base of my spine. But I need her. I need to claim her.

Mark her.

Own her.

Ryan Jade is mine and I want her to feel me imprinted on every inch of her skin.

After minutes of working myself inside her tight, hot ass, she's taken me to the root. My dick twitches once I'm fully seated and I can't move. My mind thinks of every non-sexy thing it can to keep from exploding right here and now. Once I'm back under control, I begin pumping.

Her tits bounce and shake as my thrusts get harder and harder.

"Don't hold back," she moans, her head tipped back. "Give it to me as hard as you can, baby. Make me feel you for days."

"I'll give it to you," I grunt, picking up the pace and intensity. The sound of our skin slapping together echoes through the room. "This ass is mine."

I drop down on top of her, settling my weight onto one forearm next to her face and hooking her leg over the other, adjusting her position so I can better fuck her.

Sweat runs down my back as her nails scratch her ownership into my skin. I've never been one for scratching, but these marks are Ryan's and I want everyone to see them. See what I do to her. See how I drive her wild. How the pleasure I give her, shatters her.

I rut into her like a beast, groaning as I feel her body tighten.

"Don't come yet, baby. Wait for me," I say, knowing it won't be long.

"Dom, please. Please, I need to come. Make me come, baby. Make me come."

"Shh, baby. You don't want your parents to hear how much you love me using you like this, do you?" She shakes her head and I keep going, my heart racing as I try to keep my pace steady and unrelenting.

Her mouth opens, eyes screwed closed, and I know she's going to come. There's no stopping the train she's on. Her back bows off the bed and she comes with a scream. I slap my hand over her mouth, muffling her cries, tears leaking from her teal eyes. Once she's come down, I remove my hand. She reaches up and grabs the back of my head, pulling me mouth down into a searing kiss of panting and tongues.

"Fill me up," she begs as I continue to fuck into her.

"I'll fill you up. I'm going to come in this tight ass." My strokes become undisciplined as I let my orgasm start to take control. My grunts are wild, driven by my need to get as close to her as possible. I'm probably squishing her with my weight, but I don't care as I feel my dick swell.

Every muscle in my body tightens and then my vision whites out as I come. My cock jerks with spurt after spurt of cum until I collapse, spent.

Ryan's nails that were scoring my back now gently scrape my scalp, moving down my back. I purr like a contented cat into her neck as I catch my breath.

"That was the best sex I've ever had," she says and I laugh.

"Every time I have sex with you is the best time," I tell her, truthfully, and I wonder if it's because of the feelings I'm developing for her, or the fact we're very compatible. It seems like, any time we're together, we are able to anticipate each other's wants and needs. It has led to some amazing sex that leaves me feeling more and more connected with Ryan.

The few girlfriends I've had before this never felt permanent. Football always came first and they never changed how I felt about that. Ever since our first phone call, it's felt different with Ryan. There's been a connection that wasn't there before. One that made me think about what I want from life, not only want I want from football.

I'm still dedicated, still focused, but Ryan is as important to me. Something I never thought possible. Maybe Anya was right after all. Maybe I *could* have both.

"Stay here," I tell her, giving her a kiss and hoisting myself off her, pulling my spent dick from her body, cum leaking out of her. Caveman like pride lights in my stomach at the mess I've made of her.

"I think someone could chase me with a knife right now and I wouldn't be able to go anywhere."

A chuckle escapes me. The floor creaks beneath my feet on the way to the bathroom. Snagging the washcloth off the hook, I wet it with warm water and take it back to her. She hisses in pain as I begin cleaning her up, careful to be as gentle as possible.

"Flip on your stomach. I'll give you a massage," I tell her as I take the cloth back to the bathroom.

"This won't be one of those massages that ends in sex is it? Because I need at least an hour before I'm going to be ready to go again." She's on her stomach, her hands a pillow under her face.

I grab a real pillow from the top of the bed and drop it by her. She grabs it, resting her head on top with her arms underneath.

"Do you have any lotion in this room?" I ask, and she points to the bedside table on the left.

I recognize the bottle as the one that appeared in my bathroom after one of her visits. When I spied it on my vanity in the morning, I smiled. Seeing the tangible sign she viewed my space as her space made me so happy I could have broken out into song. But I didn't. Because that would be a crime against the art.

"Oh my God, that feels amazing," she says on a moan, melting into the bed as I begin rubbing between her shoulder blades.

"The trainers taught me a trick or two over the seasons. Now hush."

She mimes zipping her lips and throwing away the key and we settle into silence. I work the lotion into her skin, peppering her back with kisses as I go, taking liberties with her where I can. Ryan falls asleep after twenty minutes, her breathing evening out, but I keep going, wanting to take care of her.

"I think I might be falling in love with you," I mumble against the skin of her lower back as I kiss her there. She might not have heard me, too lost to relaxation, but I don't mind.

What matters is I heard the words, and in saying them out loud, a piece of me settles into place I didn't know I was missing.

# CHAPTER TWENTY-TWO

"Who are you texting?" I ask Ryan, making conversation. My fingers put the finishing touches on my bow tie. It only took three different training videos to finally get it right.

"Karter and Sky," she says with an eye roll. "They want me to meet them in Singapore to go to some party or something? I don't know."

"Don't they know you're on tour?" I don't mean for the question to come out the way it does, but it seems like every time Ryan hears from these friends, they want something.

She puts her phone down and looks up at me. "They don't really pay attention to my schedule. It's kind of a lot to keep track of."

I nod, not responding. Being in the middle of a world tour, it's pretty easy to find out the dates of the stops, but they are her friends to manage and if it doesn't bother her they don't put in that little bit of effort, who am I to tell her otherwise?

"What do you think?" I ask, turning around in front of the camera.

The tux is the first custom piece of clothing I've ever owned. I wanted to make sure I look nice for this year's team charity auction, where I'm one of the items up for bid. Paige found the best local spot, and when I walked in, I knew she was right. The owner was a fifth-generation tailor, learning the trade from his father as he did before him. Pictures lined the walls of the family in the store over the years, and it reminded me so much of my parents' house that I instantly felt at home. When the owner saw it was me, he told me anything I wanted would be on the house.

While a perk of dating Ryan, it's one I refused to accept. I paid for the materials and agreed to make three posts on social media wearing the tux with credit going to the store instead of paying for the labor he put into the clothes. It was something I had planned to do anyway, so it made me feel bad. Then Paige showed me the effect I've had on local businesses as I've been photographed wearing things I buy around town.

Every single one of the stores has posted how much their lives have changed and their dreams are coming true, all because I decided to buy something I liked.

So, I know the shop owner sees the loss of money for this tux as an investment in his business.

The work he has done was perfect, and the fact he was willing to come to the house for one fitting in particular due to my game schedule was a huge help. I plan to get any suits I need from him going forward.

"Hmm, I don't know. Maybe you should take it off and put it back on," Ryan jokes through the phone. While it's an off day for the tour, we decided she wouldn't attend tonight's gala with me, instead wanting the attention to go to the organization we are raising money for. Wanting to be a part of it all, she graciously donated a VIP experience for four to her tour for the auction.

With the few days off, she went to see her parents for an early Christmas, not wanting to completely miss the holiday due to touring.

"Um, hello? I am in the room!" Anya says hip checking me out of the way, twirling around in the pale blue dress Lorelei helped her find. "What about me? What do you think?"

"You look amazing!" Ryan squeals. She made sure to give me the number of her makeup artist for Anya once she agreed to be my date, like last year. "Wait, do I see something sparkling on a very specific finger?"

"You just might," Anya says coyly, shoving her left hand as close to the camera as possible. "Parker proposed last week!"

They both squeal as Anya recounts the proposal in her new bakery and I watch them, happiness burning brightly.

"Wait, last week? Dom, did you know she was engaged?" Ryan asks, turning her attention back on me.

"I mean, yeah."

"And you didn't tell me?"

I rub the back of my neck feeling sheepish. "Obviously, they were going to get engaged! Plus, I kind of...forgot."

She rolls her eyes at me. "Men," she says in a teasing tone. "Well, I'm excited. Congratulations."

"Thank you," Anya says, with that dreamy look she's had on her face all week.

"Hey, you still haven't told me I look amazing," I say, pulling Ryan's attention back to myself.

"Sorry, babe. You look amazing, too."

"Thank you." I feign annoyance, pulling down on the bottom of my jacket, snapping it into place. "How was your day?"

I give Anya a shooing motion to get out of the room so I can talk to my girlfriend for the last few minutes before we have to leave. As the door clicks shut behind my sister, I watch anxiety light Ryan's expression.

"Don't freak out, but my ex-boyfriend, Cash, called. He wants me to have a writing session with him at a recording studio in L.A."

I scoop the phone up off the dresser it was resting on, the happiness I was feeling moments ago ebbing away with a tinge of jealousy. "Writing session for what?"

"A song." Rolling my eyes, I wait. She sighs. "Okay, so it *might* be a love song."

"Your ex-boyfriend wants you to write a love song with him?" I ask, my voice full of disbelief. "Why can't someone else do it?"

"Because he thinks I can help him with the writer's block he's having about it."

I hear Zoe scoff off screen and I call out to her. "What is she not telling me, Z?"

"He's been hitting her up since before you two started dating about meeting up. My guess? It's a ploy to get back with her."

Ryan gives her employee a hard look before standing and going into the bedroom so we can have some privacy. It's not that I mind her writing with this guy, but a part of me wonders if she does this, will she remember what it's like to be with someone who understands her life.

I try. I appreciate her music. I'm happy to let her write whenever she wants or to run off to the recording studio real quick to record something.

There will always be a part of her life I'll never fully understand and Cash could give her that.

Plus, she doesn't know I'm falling in love with her.

Over the past three weeks, there have been multiple times those words have almost slipped from my lips, but we've only been dating a few months, officially, and I don't want to scare her off.

"I know it sounds bad, but this is a normal thing. Sure, he might have ulterior motives, but it doesn't matter. I'm with you. There have been plenty of times I've needed someone to brainstorm with me and unlock new ideas.

"When I have writer's block, I'd do anything to break it. Including asking my ex to have a writing session. This is a normal thing. I promise."

"Okay."

"Okay?" she repeats, skeptically.

"It's not my favorite, but this is your job. I would never want to stand in the way of that."

Her face softens and she gives my favorite lopsided grin. "Tell you what. You've never been to a studio. Why don't you come with me? We can schedule it for after one of your practices. I think you'd have a lot of fun. And once we're done, we can go on a date or something. What do you say?"

Smiling, I give her the answer I know she wants. "Sounds perfect." A muffled voice reaches me and I check the time. "Babe, I have to get going okay? Have a good night. I'll call you in the morning."

"Have a great time. Tell Anya to win you! Can't have you going to dinner with anyone but me!"

I laugh and start making my way out of the room. "Will do. Good night."

"Sweet dreams."

I blow her a kiss and hang up the phone, jogging down the stairs. Everyone is waiting at the car for me. As I climb into the blacked-out SUV, jealousy comes roaring through me at Cash being a part of Ryan's professional life. At his ability to understand her, and her creativity, in a way I never will.

"Are you ready to talk about it?" Anya asks, sliding into the seat next to me. My bow tie is hanging loose around my neck and my starched white shirt is unbuttoned to my breastbone.

The auction ended an hour ago, Ryan winning a dinner with me via Anya's bidding on her behalf. The team mingles and some of the players start to get drunk.

I might be one of them.

"Talk about what?" I ask, trying to get the last dregs of my drink from my glass, ice smacking into my face.

"Whatever it is that has you drinking enough for two and put that grumpy look on your face."

"I'm not grumpy," I tell her, but it's a lie.

She knows it.

I know it.

She stares at me, unrelenting until I sigh.

"Ryan is going to help write a song with her ex-boyfriend. *Cash.*"

"Okay."

I wait for more of a reaction, but none comes. "That's it? That's all you're going to say? 'Okay'?"

"What do you want me to say? I'm sure she works with other artists all the time. It's a small industry, all things considered. I'm sure it happens all the time."

"Well, this one will be a love song."

"Now we're getting somewhere. And you're upset people will think they're back together?"

I think about it for a minute and look around, watching my teammates. Tim is hitting on the owner's daughter, the one I flirted with the year before last hoping she would bid on me, Paige at the bar getting a drink. Tank is dancing with Lorelei in a way that suggests exactly what they'll be doing tonight. Coach Williamson is sitting at his table next to his wife, trying to get some water into her. About twenty minutes ago she threw her shoes across the room, irritated she had to wear them. When I saw the size of the heel, I couldn't say I blamed her.

"Kind of? Not really, I don't think. Zoe said he's been trying to weasel his way back in. Since before we got together."

An angry storm cloud look takes over her face, protective instincts kicking in.

"And you think she's going to choose him? She'd be an idiot to think he was a better choice than you." Her voice shakes and I grab her hand.

"No? Maybe? I don't know. We haven't been together long and they have a history and he's into music and she's into music and they'd make better sense together. Plus, I constantly have pre-season and practices and games that keep me busy nine months out of the year."

"Dom, do you *want* her to choose him?"

The thought of ending my relationship with Ryan sends a panic through my blood, burning away some of the drunkenness I'm feeling.

"Fuck no, I don't," I almost yell.

She pats my shoulder in a consoling manner, looking around the party.

"Okay, okay. I shouldn't have even asked. What do you say we get out of here, huh? I think you've had enough for tonight, and all of this will look different in the morning."

"Yeah, okay." I grab my phone from my pocket and type out a message to our driver, asking them to bring the car around.

I wobble on my feet for a moment before I steady myself. Helping Anya stand, I say goodbye to the players nearby before grabbing our coats and heading for the door.

Flashes blind me as we walk through the exit. Justin gets out of the SUV and begins walking up the red carpet to meet us. My concession with him coming tonight was he'd wait in the car, knowing no one would take a shot at me in a room full of professional football players.

With Anya's hand in mine, I pull her behind me, walking through the screaming paparazzi. I don't say anything, using my body to protect her, but suddenly she's shoved into my back with an oof and stumbles. I turn and catch her before she can hit the ground and my anger, mixed with the alcohol, gets the best of me.

"Get the fuck off my sister," I yell, pushing one of the photographers near her. I don't care if it was him that bumped into her or not.

This is my sister. Not me. Not Ryan. Anastasia. The person who never signed up for this and is here only because she was doing me a favor. I shove the photographer again for good measure, even more flashes going off now I'm making a scene, but I'm so angry I don't even care. All I want to do is live my life. Not be hounded all because I like a girl.

Justin rushes in, shoving people out of the way, grabbing me and Anya. We rush to the car, Anya between us. He shoves us into the car, closes the door, and the second he's seated behind the wheel, he peels out.

"Are you okay?" I ask Anya, checking her for bruises. She slaps my hands away from her.

"Yes. Stop touching me, you nut. They just bumped into me. You didn't need to shove that guy."

"He could have hurt you! Over a picture of me walking to the fucking car!" I yell into the silence.

She puts on her customer service face, the placid mask meant to calm. "But he didn't. He bumped me. If I hadn't been in these heels, I wouldn't have even hit you, that's how gentle it was. And you lost your cool in front of all those people. You realize that's going to be front page news?"

"I don't care. I don't care what they say about me! They need to stay away from you." My chest constricts and I can feel myself getting lightheaded from the inability to pull in a deep breath. I take off my jacket, throwing it into the cargo space behind us, needing to get some air into my lungs, but it doesn't help.

"Dom?" Anya grabs my arm. It does nothing against the tornado turning inside my brain, blowing all rational thought away. "Hey, Dommy. Look at me."

She grabs my face and forces me to look at her. Our eyes lock and she takes slow, deep breaths, encouraging me to follow in the same pattern.

"There we go." Finally, I calm, tears filling my eyes. "I don't think you're so mad about me getting pushed but actually, a little bit scared Ryan is going to think you're not good enough for her. And that, despite loving her, she'll pick someone else."

"Holy fuck, I shoved that photographer. I could get charged with assault! I might get kicked off the team." Panic begins rising in me again.

If I don't get kicked off, they might trade me after the season. Away from my family, *my home*, because I can't keep my shit together. Seeing me start to spiral, Anya stops it in its tracks.

"No, you won't. You're not going anywhere. You're not going to get charged, and if you do, we'll get you a bomb ass lawyer. It's going to be okay. I promise."

I can feel my lip tremble, my emotions sitting much closer to the surface tonight. "What if I lose her because I can't deal with all this craziness?"

"You won't," she says, pulling me into her and holding me like she did during thunderstorms when we were growing up. "You can handle this, Dom. It'll die down eventually and it'll be fine."

I wrap my arms around her and close my eyes for the rest of the trip. "Thanks for being my sister."

"I didn't have much choice in the matter, but I'm glad I am either way."

# CHAPTER TWENTY-THREE

S TANDING ON THE LINE of scrimmage, I try my best to focus on the game, but my brain isn't cooperating. It's been a week since me shoving the photographer was plastered all over social media and the morning news. My mouth automatically says 'no comment' every time someone comes near me. I think Geoff might have nerves of steel because when I called and told him what happened, he barely even batted an eye, immediately jumping into problem solving mode.

I did all the things you'd expect. I apologized. I expressed remorse. I admitted I lost my cool and I'd be working on it in the future.

The league, thankfully, didn't do anything except fine me for conduct unbecoming of a player, which cost me a cool fifty thousand. At least I didn't lose my position.

And the photographer declined to press charges, stating the picture he was able to snap on his way down was worth every bump and bruise he received. He must be right, too, because it's been the picture used in every single story run since.

I called Ryan to tell her what happened and she was concerned, more for how I was handling the stress of everything than because it was going to be plastered everywhere. Zoe took care of worrying about that, reminding me how everything I do now reflects on Ryan as well. As if I needed reminding. I haven't called or texted her much since, afraid Zoe will have convinced her to drop me and save her image and it'll all end.

The referee blows his whistle indicating the end of the quarter. This has been the hardest game I've ever played in. Not only is the opposing team almost impossible to stop, it's like they have our playbook memorized. No matter what we do, they have an answer for it.

We huddle in a circle, the offensive coach talking to us about the next play we're going to run. It must be obvious I'm not entirely present if the slap to the side of my helmeted head is anything to go by.

"Get your shit together, Reynier or I'll throw your ass on the bench!"

"Yes, Coach!" I respond. At this rate, there's no way I won't get traded at the end of the year.

We all clap when the huddle breaks, and I'm a half second slower than everyone else. My feet feel heavy as I line up on the right side, Rhubarb, the strong safety across from me.

"Hey, Reynier. How does it feel to be more famous for being Ryan Jade's little bitch than your stats?" he calls out. I try to ignore him.

Normally, it's easy to ignore the trash talk. Lately, it's been turning to Ryan more and more, setting my teeth on edge.

The ball is hiked and I explode off the line straight at the safety before cutting in and running five yards. My blood sings with adrenaline.

Logan throws the ball to me, but it's a little too high. As I jump into the air to catch it, my legs are hit out from under me, sending me into a midair cartwheel.

Every molecule of oxygen in my lungs leaves in a whoosh when I slam into the ground. Bones groaning, my vision starts to tunnel before snapping back into focus. The crowd is booing, but I don't care. It's more important for me to get air back into me than it is to have the fans cheering for me.

Not that they'd ever be able to take the kind of hit I just did.

Tank's face blocks out the lights above me.

"Are you alive?" he asks with a smile on his face. I hate him. I flip him off so he knows. "Oh yeah, you're alive."

He helps me get into a seated position and the trainers come sliding in around me.

"I'm fine," I tell them before they can start asking me a dozen questions. "Got the air knocked out of me."

I reach out a hand to get some help getting to my feet, and someone gives it to me, like I knew they would. This is a team, after all.

"You need to leave for a play, son," the ref says, once I'm back on my feet. They called an injury timeout when I didn't pop back up. Even though I was fine, it's the rule.

I don't reply, jogging off to the sideline, the trainers in my wake. The guys line back up and play resumes. My backup runs down the field and catches the ball, securing us the first down. He jogs over and I slap him on the back before taking my space once more.

"Maybe Ryan Jade will let me break her back like I did yours. I bet she moans like a little whore," Rhubarb says, and this time I see red.

The ball is snapped again. I ignore the called play and run like a steam engine straight for the safety, taking him out at the knees. The hit is dirty, I can admit it. Yellow flags fly in from every direction imaginable and the play ends.

Hands rip me off the guy and set me to my feet, pushing me to walk back to our huddle.

"She might have picked you now, but you know she spreads her legs for every guy with a hard dick and a dollar! That's how she got to the top!" he yells as his teammates try to usher him back to their side. My control has reached its end.

I break free from my teammates' grasps and sprint toward him. His yellow teeth are bared in a snarl. Fingers weaving into his face mask, I throw him down to the ground. Fists land anywhere they can reach. He gets a few good swings in, but I don't care. All I want is to break him.

Another member of the opposing team tackles me down to the turf and begins beating on me. Whistles screams. Fans cheer. Words are exchanged. The bench clearing brawl only lasts for a few moments, despite feeling longer. I'm breathing like I've run a mile, pacing trying to dispel all the pent-up aggression raging within me.

When order is restored, the penalties start getting called.

"Personal foul, unsportsmanlike conduct offense number eighty-two that's a fifteen yard penalty. Number eighty-two is also disqualified for the remainder of the game," the ref calls and I deflate.

My team is screaming about the unfairness of the call, but it's more for form than because they believe it. I have never been tossed from a game before. One of the members of the sideline staff comes over, ushering me into the tunnel and back to the locker room. I rip my helmet off to jeers from the crowd. Beer rains down on me as I pass between stands and into the shadows.

The game continues without me. Metal smashes into cinder block, the door meeting the wall when I storm into the locker room. I throw my helmet.

Another first.

"FUCK!" I scream at the top of my lungs.

Dad's disappointed face comes to mind and my eyes swim. One thing he always taught me was to never let my emotions rule me on the field. You always have to be in control, calculating. But I had no control. I was a storm screaming and howling, looking for someone or something to destroy.

I hit another person.

My ass hits the bench in front of my locker hard enough to bruise. Leaning my forearms on my knees, I stay like that until the end of the game when my team comes pouring in. In another first, I don't celebrate our win.


My phone won't stop vibrating, so I put it on silent. Text messages from Ryan and my family have poured in steadily over the past hour. I ignore them all and walk into the media room. Just like after the game where Ryan and I went public, it's standing room only. Cameras record my every move so I make sure to hold myself high despite the shame I feel. This time, Geoff doesn't introduce me and I don't plan to take any questions.

I step up before the firing squad of pens waiting for a shot at me.

"First, I'd like to apologize officially to Rhubarb. I'm ashamed of my actions today and the pain I caused him. I also want to apologize to the fans, coaches, and teammates I have here with the Thunderhawks. My actions today hurt the team and that's unacceptable. To my parents, I'm sorry for not being the son you raised. Being a professional athlete is a blessing. It's something very few people ever achieve but many dream of. I get to live the dreams I've had since I was a little boy every single day I step into this facility and today, I cast a shadow on everything I hold dear.

"Being on a team is about unity and cohesion. Caring about the whole instead of the individual parts that make it up. It requires selflessness and humility. Love. Respect. Today, I cared about myself above the team and put pressure on my teammates to make up for my lack of fortitude.

"Today was a mistake that hurt another person and I'll always regret my actions. I'm prepared to shoulder the minimum one game suspension and any further consequences my brothers, coaches, and the league deem necessary. And to the kids that love football, I'm sorry for disappointing you most of all. I hope you learn from me what *not* to do and continue to be a better person than I was today. Thank you."

I begin to step away from the podium and questions ring out. They pass over me like fog.

"How does it make you feel that Ryan Jade bought the house you live in?" one reporter calls out, stopping me in my tracks.

I search the crowd of faces and land on the guy I had pushed a week prior, a smarmy grin on his face.

"What did you say?" I ask and the room goes quiet. Tension radiates as they see my fuse had been lit again and they wait for the explosion.

"I asked how it makes you feel that your girlfriend bought the house you live in? You *did* know she bought it, didn't you? Do you often accept such extravagant gifts from your paramours?"

All the noise becomes buzzing in my ears. My mouth gapes open and closed like a fish out of water.

"That's all for tonight," Geoff says, rushing in and putting his arm around me, pulling me from the platform.

Ryan said the house was owned by a friend. It's not hers, I'm just borrowing it. Granted, I've never heard of someone letting a stranger, for all intents and purposes, become a squatter without paying rent. But I also don't run in the circles Ryan runs in. All of these thoughts want to come out, to defend myself, defend Ryan, but they don't.

If she lied about this, what else did she lie about?

"Go ahead and go home for the night, Dominic. I'll come up with a plan and we'll talk in the morning," Geoff says when we get to the locker room.

All I can do is nod. Grabbing up my bag, I head for the exit where Justin is waiting for me. The drive home takes forever. My brain stutters on one word.

Home.

It's not my home. It's a place I live and I sleep, but it's not mine. It doesn't matter it's decorated to my tastes or I've spent so much time in the backyard I can name the flowers that make up the garden.

It doesn't matter it's where I started to fall in love with Ryan.

Because it's not mine.

The lights are on at the front facade and I stare at it. It's my dream house, honestly. One I could never afford. When my old house was swarmed, I was so panicked, I didn't give any thought to the strangeness of the situation.

I could go back to my old house, but I know it'd be swarmed and make Justin's life harder. Pulling out my phone, I video call Ryan the second I'm in the door, ignoring all of her texts.

"Dom! Thank goodness. What—"

"Do you own this house?"

Her eyes get big.

"What?"

"Do you own this house, Ryan?"

She watches me for a second and I see her weighing her options. She's considering lying to me and I'm watching her do it, my heart breaking.

"Yes." At least she told me the truth, I guess.

"Why?" I ask, my tone edging toward anger. "What didn't you tell me?"

"Because you never would've moved in if you knew I bought it for you," she defends.

The world stops spinning, I'm sure of it. Or at least, my world stops spinning.

"You bought it *for* me? You didn't already own it?"

I see the moment she realizes she fucked up register on her face. We're in too deep now. She's kept this from me for months, and I can see the fear of me leaving take hold. The one that comes round and round any time there's a problem.

"Dom, baby. I'm sorry, okay? I wanted you to be safe and it was the quickest way to make that happen in a long-term way. And it was all my fault you needed to move, so it made sense I'd buy the house for you. It's in your name and everything, so you own it. You can keep it, of course. It's a gift for putting up with my life. I knew you'd never accept it. I just wanted you safe."

"I don't want to keep it," I tell her. No matter how perfect it is, I can't take something like this from her.

"Okay, we can find you another one, then!" she says, trying to right the situation.

My anger shifts. She doesn't get it. It's not about the fans and the cameras and the pictures and the invasion of my privacy. It's that she thinks I'm not here for *her* but for what she can give me.

"I don't need you to buy me things, Ryan. I'm not your friends. I'm not your dad. I'm not Cash!"

She jerks back like I've slapped her. And I have. It might have been with my words instead of a hand, but the sting is no different.

"I'll reach out to my realtor and she'll call you to list it." Tears are in her eyes as she hangs up.

I stare at the black screen for a moment before hurling it across the room with a shout, my anger winning one more time.

# CHAPTER TWENTY-FOUR

## RYAN

***Is Ryan Jade headed toward violence?***

*I*N THE PAST FEW *weeks, we have seen an increasingly distressing pattern. Violence from Dominic Reynier. From pushing a photographer that accidentally bumped his sister, to getting into a fistfight on the field, earning himself a one game suspension. It makes this reporter wonder: Is Ryan Jade next?*

*With this pattern of explosive anger, you have to wonder what's been going on in the privacy of the home the singer bought the football star.*

*"Dominic is not a violent person," his sister, Anastasia says, behind her bakery counter, who met and fell in love with her fiancé on reality show* House of Desire. *"Dom is the best brother and one of the best men I've ever met in my life and you should be ashamed for suggesting otherwise."*

*We reached out to some of Dominic's ex-girlfriends who have re-fused to give us a comment. Was that from fear, I wonder? That now, paired with Ryan Jade's resources, he would retaliate? Who's to say.*

*The Jade Stones, the name fans of Ryan have given themselves, have taken up a petition on social media, begging the singer to break up with her boyfriend.*

*"She deserves so much better than him. She's smart, beautiful, rich. She could have any man she wanted and yet she's with this abuser? It's dumb. We care so much about Ryan and just want her happy. We figured if we got this petition going and it took off, she'd realize how concerned we all are for her and want to get help. We are looking out for her. No one knows her better than we do and it's time we stepped in," one user, @Cindy_Loves_Ryan, the creator of the petition, says.*

*Despite her fans begging her to leave, Ryan stays.*

*Is her team too concerned with placating their cash cow to say any-thing? What about Zoe, her longtime manager and friend? Doesn't she care how Reynier is dragging her client down?*

*Or is everyone too concerned with the record breaking Radiance tour to care?*

I slam my phone down on the makeup table, fuming. After end-less needling, Dom finally told me what was said to him on the field. We talked about it for hours. How every move he makes will be over scrutinized. How letting his temper win out would never be possible. Especially not in such a public manner. And he agreed, saying he understood and knew it had all gotten to be too much.

And then he went to bed.

I wanted to call him all night to make sure we were good and he was still in this. But I tried to give him his space after Zoe convinced me there wasn't anything more I could do.

Wanting to save Dominic's name, I almost had Zoe leak to the press what happened. Ultimately, it was decided it'd be better not to acknowledge the issue. Like always. Let them say whatever they want and know, behind closed doors, that's not who Dom is.

It can be hard, not defending yourself. A year into my career when a particularly scathing article about how I lipsync and we use someone else's voice on my records made me almost quit after finally getting my dream, I retaliated. I did an interview talking about how what they said wasn't true and gave my side of the entire thing. Apparently, I protested too much, which meant the rumors were true.

Convinced I was about to lose my career, we decided from that moment on, we'd hold a wall of silence when it came to the press. Of course, there are some rumors we respond to. Never directly. It's always "a source close to the singer denies the pregnancy claims" or "sources say the relationship is alive and well despite the distance and busy schedules." Because no matter what choice I made, it was the wrong one.

It can be even harder not defending a person you love, I've found.

The knock on my dressing room door startles me out of my angry thoughts.

"It's time," Zoe says, opening the door despite me not calling out to come in.

"Okay," I say, standing tall, taking one last look in the mirror to make sure everything is perfect.

My hair.

My clothes.

My makeup.

My smile.

Perfectly in place. Perfectly laid. Perfect, perfect, *perfect*. It's what they expect of me. What they demand. Every move I make? Perfect. Every word I say? Perfect. Everything my boyfriend does? Perfect.

The golf cart whisks me to the stage and my stomach hurts from all the anger I feel.

When I hear them screaming as the graphics on the stage indicate the show is about to start, I know I'm pissed, the fuck, off. At these people and their petition. These people think they can buy my music and concert tickets and that gives them the *right* to think they have a say in my life. That they know me.

They don't know anything about me except what I want them to know.

They don't know how broken down I feel whenever I think about my father.

They don't know how it's hard to believe I'm a person sometimes when all their phones are pointed at me.

They don't know the soul shattering pleasure I get when I'm wrapped in Dom's arms.

The person they know is fake.

I crouch onto my platform, mic in hand, and the robotic voice starts counting down in my ear. Putting on the mask, I push my anger away. My mind tinkers with a new song my anger is writing while the muscle memory of hundreds of hours of rehearsals takes over.

I put the mic to my mouth and sing.

*Pulse of the party, with a groove so sweet*

*Catching dreams like confetti, dancing on our feet*

Later, sitting down at my piano, I give my body a breather from the marathon this concert is. I haven't been able to feel my feet in over an hour. My muscles are strong, resilient, from working out with Dominic whenever I stayed with him. He spends so much time in the gym, making sure he's in peak form for the season, if I didn't go with him I would've hardly seen him.

"How are you all liking the show so far?" I ask the crowd, playing the wrong melody on my piano. It's not my next song but the one I was writing in Dominic's house.

The one about him.

I think of the article, of all the other bad things people must be writing about him and my eyes prick.

"You know, it's been a hard few weeks," I tell the crowd and they start to settle down, unsure where this is going. "Sometimes, in this life, even when we have something we want with every fiber of our being, there can be times it frustrates us or makes us mad or sad. Do you ever experience things like that?"

They cheer their agreement.

It might seem silly, feeling like I'm having a legitimate conversation with them since they can't respond, but I know I am.

"These past few weeks have been hard because I've had to watch the man I care about get dragged because he wasn't perfect. And it's interesting, don't you think, how we hold some people to a level of perfection we ourselves could never reach?" I see the ones closest to the stage start to squirm a little.

My fingers begin moving of their own accord and I know I'm going to share a piece of me with them. Because I want them to understand. I want them to see the real.

And I want them to get it.

"Would you all mind if I did something I don't normally do? We'll get back to the original set list in a moment, but would you mind if I shared with you a new song? One that's not finished yet?"

They explode.

The only time they have ever heard new music before was when I release an album. Never a minute sooner. I need them to understand what I feel for him. Despite my anger tonight, I want them to know me. I love them so much for giving me the life I always wanted.

The life that led me to him.

And I hope he's watching, too.

"You have to forgive me if I don't get every note perfect, yet. This is the first time I'm playing this in its entirety. I started writing it at three in the morning when I couldn't sleep because I realized this could be the one."

They cheer, quieting quickly, absorbing every note I play.

When I sing, I can hear the difference in my voice and I wonder if they can hear it, too. How much this means to me. The song was going to be more of a pop song, but this stripped-down version, I know it can't be anything but this.

This song doesn't need the drums and guitars, and all the other pieces. It needs me. And my heart. And my piano.

I pour everything I am into every note. I'll never give a greater performance than I'm giving right now. Then again, I'm not performing. I'm simply giving voice to my heart. It's why I started singing and songwriting to begin with.

So I could find a way to voice all the feelings I've felt. To make them real and memorialize them. Process them. Move past them.

The final notes die and a tear rolls down my cheek. I hope it's enough for Dom.

I hope *I'm* enough for him.

A beat of silence fills the stadium and then I look out at the crowd, jaw dropping.

Every single person is holding up their phone with their flashlight on, fireflies in the darkness. They don't cheer and I realize I don't want them to. Instead, they see me. RyanJade Marie Collins. Possibly for the first time.

I swipe the tear from my face and clear my throat. "Are you ready to keep going on the Radiance tour?" I ask, slipping back into the Ryan Jade they know. This time my fingers start to play the right song and I finish out the concert.

It's a little more raw, but it's the best second half of a concert I've given.

When I go back to my dressing room, my phone is sitting on my makeup table where I left it. One simple text showing.

**Dom: Come home. I miss you.**

# CHAPTER TWENTY-FIVE

"**B**RAD? WHAT ARE WE doing here?" I ask, weary. I'm tired and want to get home to Dominic. He turns around in his seat and smiles at me.

"Having fun."

"Fun? What fun is at a high school?"

He doesn't respond, instead getting out and opening my door. I look at him, staying seated. He rolls his eyes. "Don't make me forcibly remove you from this car."

"You work for me, you know," I tell him, following his instructions. It wouldn't be the first time he's thrown me over his shoulder and marched me in somewhere. Luckily, no photographers were around for the other times.

He's silent as he leads me down a sidewalk to a door on the side of the gymnasium. I'd be concerned he was taking me to murder me or something, but why would he do that in a school? He could easily do it in the woods and hide me somewhere no one would find me. I'd be dead before I even knew what was happening.

When the metal door slams shut behind us, lights turn on and my jaw drops.

Thousands of twinkle lights are draped over the basketball court. Paper flowers cascade in a river from an archway and lead all the way to where I'm standing. A glittering disco ball spins from the rafters and some slow song plays in the background, too soft for me to name it.

And there at center court is Dominic in his tuxedo he wore to his team's Christmas ball.

I walk over to him, our arms going around each other's waists automatically.

"What is all of this?" I ask, awed at all the work. Even if he hired people to do all of this, I know it took hours to set up and arrange.

"This is your Christmas present. You said you never went to a school dance before. I thought we could remedy that. School is out for winter break, so we don't have to worry about anyone stumbling in on us. The principal is a fan, and she was happy to keep it a secret if you're willing to sign a CD for her. I have it over there." He points to a bag next to the bleachers.

I go to my tiptoes and press a kiss to his soft lips. "This is amazing. If you had told me, I could have worn a dress!"

A throat clears behind me and I turn to see Elaine, my hairdresser, her baby wrapped against her front, sleeping deeply. "Madam, your fairy godmother awaits."

She motions to the locker room and I turn back to Dominic, tears in my eyes. "You did all this for me?"

"You wrote that song for me?"

"You saw it?"

"I did."

"I'm sorry I didn't sing it to you first. Make sure you were okay with me sharing it," I tell him.

"There's nothing you should be sorry for. Now go get ready." He presses a kiss to my forehead and shoos me over to the locker room.

Among the lockers is a rack with five dresses on it. The bathroom counter is covered in all the products Elaine normally brings for me as well as a few hair tools.

"I'm so glad you're here," I tell Elaine, hugging her around her sweet baby. She had sent me pictures when he arrived in the hospital parking lot, unwilling to wait for his mom to get inside the doors, three weeks early. "How are you feeling? Look at his hair!" I exclaim in a whisper, running my finger gently over the crown of his head.

"He can't sleep anywhere except for on me. Wouldn't have it any other way. We could talk about this baby all night, but I want to talk about this man. Ryan. I don't think I could have created a better one for you."

I smile at that. He truly is perfect. I'm silent for a minute.

*"I think I love him,"* I want to say, but hold myself back, the words stuck. "He's amazing. I'm incredibly lucky," I say instead.

"He's been working on putting this together for a few weeks now. You deserve someone caring about you like this."

My throat clogs with emotion. No one has ever done something like this for me. Cash celebrated holidays with me, sure, but it was always on some exotic beach at a five-star resort. My gifts were always over the top and nothing I cared about. Cars, jewelry, whatever he thought would be big and flashy and sweep me off my feet.

But this, *this*, is what I always wanted.

For something thoughtful and heartfelt. Not something big and flashy just to be big and flashy.

"Don't cry, you'll get puffy," Elaine tells me, fanning my face while I blink rapidly. Once I'm under control, she pushes me to the creaky old chair, presumably from the coach's office, and forces me down into it.

"Do you want to go natural or full glam?" she asks, turning me toward the mirror.

"Natural, please."

She nods and begins moving around, the baby not caring one bit. In twenty minutes, she has my face refreshed and my hair in professionally messy waves, the front sections twisted and pinned at the back of my head. We move over to the dresses together and look at the options. They are all beautiful, of course. There's one I think would be perfect.

The pale pink silk glides over my skin like water as Elaine helps drop it over my head. She zips me up and gives me a whistle.

"You've worn some gorgeous gowns and outfits over the years, but this is the most like you I've ever seen."

She's not wrong.

The dress is unembellished and simple. In its simplicity, the exquisite construction shines. The sheath traces my curves like Dom's hands have done many times, and I know I'm going to have to go home with this dress after tonight. It's my first high school dance dress, after all. How could I be expected to part with it?

Elaine adjusts my hair, adding pale pink flowers here and there to go with the dress.

I step into a pair of delicate shoes and make my way back out to the gym.

For a second, the scene changes in my mind. Instead of walking toward Dom in an empty high school gymnasium, he's standing at an altar, our friends and family surrounding us, and my dress isn't pink, but the lightest of creams. I shake the image from my head and walk toward him.

"You look breathtaking," he says, the lights reflecting in his eyes.

"You look incredibly handsome," I tell him, taking his offered hand. He pulls me close and we sway to the music. Spinning in slow circles, it feels like we are the only people in the world. "This is the best present I've ever gotten."

"I'm glad you like it."

Dom spins me around and I do a double take. "Is that punch and cookies?"

He grins, making my heart race. "What's a school dance without refreshments. We can try and spike the punch later. I made sure to sneak in my flask."

I laugh as he spins me under his arm before pulling me against him once more. The place I always want to be.

"Ry, I want to apologize for all the drama and scrutiny I've brought down on us the past few weeks. I know it's blown back on you and that's nothing I ever wanted to have happen."

His face is drawn with worry and I find my thumb reaching up to rub away his frown lines.

"Be careful your face might freeze like that." Something Dad always said to me. "Yes, I got some flak for everything. It doesn't matter what we do, Dom, eventually they were going to start to turn on us. This is your first time going through this cycle, but it's not mine. I don't care what they think. I don't care what they print. The people who matter know you. I know you. That's all that matters to me."

This time when he spins me, it's a bit slower.

"How do you do it? How do you deal with all of this? How is having every move you, or someone around you, makes scrutinized worth it?"

Normally, a question like this raises my hackles, but I can see he's genuinely curious how I deal with it. And maybe looking for a way to deal with it, too.

"Can I show you something? Tomorrow?"

He tilts his head. "Show me what?"

"You'll have to wait and see."

He considers, but I know he was never going to tell me no. "Okay."

I snuggle closer to him, laying my head on his chest, and there we sway. Tucked into our own little bubble, where no one and nothing can get to us.

# CHAPTER TWENTY-SIX

## DOMINIC

RYAN IS IN HER brown wig and sunglasses, a duffel bag in one hand, and a strap to a guitar case thrown over one shoulder. Ryan's security team surrounds us, Justin enjoying a day off while I'm under Bradford's watchful eye. We are met at the back of the hospital by the director.

Every line of the woman's face tells me she has a no-nonsense approach to life. It's her eyes that belay the deep-rooted compassion for others.

"Miss Jade. Thank you for joining us. If you'll follow me."

We walk to a bank of freight elevators and she presses the button to the tenth floor. When the doors open, the space could not be more different. The ward is a bright explosion of color, burning my retinas. Children's drawings line the walls. A kid in a little car propels himself forward, his little legs working hard to push himself. A nurse follows him, pushing a pole with various bags of fluid hanging down, connected to his arm.

For the brightness, the floor is eerily quiet.

"We have a room you can change in over here," the woman tells us, and leads us to what seems to be an empty office. The blinds are drawn down over the window looking out onto the floor.

"Thank you," Ryan says, and we walk in, our security and the woman standing outside.

She is a flurry of movement as she starts to strip off her wig and the clothes she threw on over her costume. She pulls the shoes out of her backpack before shoving all the clothes in.

"What are we doing here, exactly?" I ask. It took less than four hours for Zoe to have this entire visit set up once Ryan called her this morning. By the time I got home from practice and showered, we were ready to go.

"You'll see." She stands up adjusting her flowery dress and takes her guitar from its case. "How do I look?"

"You look like Ryan Jade."

She kisses me, slightly breathless. "Perfect. Let's go."

We leave the bag and case where they sit. When she pulls open the door, a nurse walking by stops, dropping her clipboard.

"I thought it was a rumor," she whispers, eyes wide beneath bangs covering her forehead.

The manager snaps her fingers at the nurse. "News of this visit is being kept under wraps. Is that clear?"

"Yes, of course. Sorry, I was surprised. Welcome."

"Maxine, here, is the lead nurse on the floor," the manager says.

Ryan hands Zoe her guitar and claps her hands. "Amazing! You can help me then, if you have time. I want to visit any kids who'd be interested in meeting me. Parents and siblings, too. Would you be able to help me with all the names and a little about them before I go into each room? Not their illness or anything, but what they like, dislike, things like that."

"I'd be happy to do that," Maxine says, grabbing up her clipboard. "Why don't we start over here?"

She leads us to the first door on the right. It's covered in paper made to look like the rainbow with puffy white clouds.

"This is one of our older kids. Her name is Katelyn. She's fourteen and this will, hopefully, be her last stay with us after this round of chemo. Her favorite subject is math. She sings in her school's choir. And she's a big fan. Her mom is Kathy. She's a single mom. No siblings."

"Got it. Thank you," Ryan says. She knocks on the door before pushing it open at Maxine's nod. "Hello!"

I hear a gasp and an ear splitting squeal before an older woman's voice telling Katelyn to get back into bed. When I poke my head around the corner, I see Ryan and Katelyn swaying in a tight hug. Ryan doesn't let go first, something she told me she does on purpose after I watched her first meet and greet. She said she never wanted the kids to feel like she didn't want to hug them. I think that might have been the first nail in the coffin of me falling in love with her.

And this one is the last.

They finally part and Katelyn moves back to her bed, rainbow socks pulled up to her knees. Ryan focuses on Kathy while Katelyn gets situated and holds out a hand.

"Hi, Kathy. I'm Ryan Jade. I was hoping, with your permission, I could spend a little time with Katelyn."

"Yes!" Katelyn answers for her mom, who smiles at her.

She takes Ryan's hand, shaking it. "It sounds like Katelyn very much wants to spend time with you. Thank you for coming."

"It's my pleasure," Ryan says earnestly. She turns back to Katelyn. "I hear you like to sing with your school's choir, and I was wondering if you wanted to sing with me?"

If I thought the squeal when Ryan walked in the room was loud, that was nothing compared to this one. I think my eardrum might have perforated with the noise. Ryan, of course, is unfazed.

"Yes, oh my God. My friends are never going to believe I'm about to sing with Ryan *freaking Jade.*"

"Language," Kathy chastises, but Katelyn is beyond hearing it.

Zoe steps up to Ryan's side and hands her the guitar. She slings the strap over her head and begins strumming a few strings.

Katelyn's voice is beautiful. She misses a note here and there, but I can tell it's more due to the lack of warm up and nerves than talent. Once they are done singing, Ryan sits and chats with Katelyn for a while. They talk about boys and how Katelyn found out about her cancer when she passed out in school once. She was lucky and they found it early. Her immune system is so weak when she's on chemo she has to stay in the hospital.

"I have to go visit some of the others now," Ryan says, patting Katelyn's knee. "But I wanted you to know I'm so inspired by how resilient you are. Whenever you're healthy again, we'll have to get you to a show or something, okay?"

Zoe pulls out her phone and makes a note of the promise.

"Maybe I could come to the Radiance tour! It looks so cool from my friend's pictures."

I can see Ryan bite her lip, not wanting to disappoint the girl, but there are only so many shows left and she might not be healthy enough to get to one. "How about the next time I release an album, you can come to the listening party?"

If Katelyn's squeal is anything to go by, she's highly agreeable to this alternative. They hug once more, Ryan hugging Kathy as well, and we leave the room, Maxine pulling the door closed behind Ryan.

"Did you get that?" Ryan asks Zoe, the businesswoman fully in control.

"Yes. I'll get their address for the invitation."

"Great. Make sure to ask the hospital for all everyone's billing accounts and whatnot, too."

"Already done," Zoe says with a knowing smirk.

We move off to the next room and repeat the process. I turn to Zoe while Ryan chats with the family.

"What does she mean about the billing stuff?" I whisper.

Her eyes slide to me for a moment before settling back on her boss, waiting for her cue with the guitar or on any notes she needs to take. "She'll cover anyone's bills that can't afford them."

I look around the floor and count twenty rooms. "That has to be millions of dollars," I say, making a guess.

"So? Ryan makes in one concert what she needs to do this." She turns and gives me her full attention. "Something you should get used to is Ryan gives with both hands. You'd think she's trying to go broke with how much money she gives away. Her investment team is the best at what they do, and they make it all back for her. Trust me, she's fine. Whatever you think she has? It's a drop in the bucket of what she has."

"Zoe?" Ryan calls. "Could I get my guitar?"

Zoe breaks away from our conversation immediately, going to her boss and coming back to me.

"I don't want her to get taken advantage of," I tell her.

"And you think these people are doing that?" Her voice takes on a tone of anger I've never heard from her before, and I see the woman Ryan trusts to manage her empire. "Not a single person on this floor is going to know she did this for them. There will be anonymous benefactors and bills insurance suddenly 'covers.' We have this down to a science. By the time it's all said and done, these people won't tie Ryan to their paid-off balances. Being wealthy, truly wealthy, has different rules than being a regular person. She has so many non-profits to funnel gifts through for things like this, your mind would be blown. You might be her boyfriend, but you have a lot to learn about what it is for her to be Ryan Jade. No matter how much money you make."

Shocked, I realize she's right.

A professional athlete might make a few hundred million in their careers, tops.

But Ryan? The top of what she could earn isn't fathomable to me.

We move from room to room. Some Ryan sings, some she doesn't. She plays video games, board games, tells stories. Listens.

Whatever the kid needs or wants is what she gives them.

It takes a couple hours to go through all the rooms. She never wavers even though I know she's dead tired. Every interaction gets all her enthusiasm. All of her attention and focus. I love being here with her. I love getting to see this side of her.

I look around while Ryan greets the second to last patient. Inside a glass room is a little boy we haven't talked to yet sitting on a beanbag chair, video game controller in his hand. He looks around sadly, but when he sees me watching him, he perks up. He waves to me, calling me in. I look back at the room and see Ryan deep in an interaction. Knowing I won't be missed, I make my way into the glass room.

"Do you know how to play *Kingdom Come III*?" he asks, no preamble, holding up another controller with a hopeful look on his face.

"As a matter of fact, I do," I tell him, thinking of the hours I've played this game with the guys during downtime at training camp, sitting in the beanbag chair next to him. I take the proffered controller and he hits the start button.

We fight dragons and collect treasure, trying to make our way to the castle's keep to save the royal family. He's better than I expect him to be, and he laughs as the remaining dragon bites off my head, blood spurting along the walls.

"Oh, man!" I cry, my body falling limply to the floor 'Loser' flashing on my half of the screen.

The boy runs in while the dragon is distracted with eating me, and snags the invisibility potion we'll need in future levels. His avatar jumps as the screen moves to the next level, but he saves the game and turns it off.

I turn to check on my group and they have moved to the last room.

"Which room do you belong to?" I ask him.

"That one," he says, pointing to the one Ryan is walking into. "My sister is in there. She's dying."

I'm not sure what to say. If I should offer my condolences. If I should say nothing and just let him talk. And then I think of Anya.

"I have a sister, too," I tell him.

"Yeah, I know."

"You know?"

"Yeah. You're Dominic Reynier. You're one of my favorite players on the Thunderhawks. I didn't want to say anything in case you wouldn't play with me. Mom says we have to give celebrities their space and stuff. Privacy," he says, rolling his eyes like he thinks it's ridiculous she thinks he wouldn't already know that.

"Yeah, well, I'm not a celebrity. I'm just a football player."

"You're a celebrity. Even my sister knows who you are now you're dating Ryan Jade and she doesn't even like football," he says with a scoff. "Sucks about the Super Bowl. Do you think you guys will win it this year?"

"We are sure going to try."

"My dad said you need to get your head out of your ass and catch the ball, but I told him you're still one of my favorites even if you did drop it."

His defense of me is touching, even if his honesty is brutal. I appreciate it, regardless. His dad isn't wrong. "Are you supposed to say 'ass'? How old are you?"

He puffs up his chest. "I'm twelve. I'm a man. I even have a girlfriend. She let me hold her hand on the bus once."

I stifle my laughter, remembering my first girlfriend and being equally as excited for such a small thing.

"That's really cool, man. You better treat her right. Be nice and listen when she talks."

He nods. "Yeah. I bought her some candy the other day. It was her favorite and she gave me a flower she picked from the playground. Mom dried it for me so I could keep it. She put it in this photo album thing. She has a dried flower from all the ones my dad brings her. And she has some from when my grandma died. She'll put some more in there when my sister dies, too." His voice gets small and he looks down at his shoes, but I can see the tears lining his eyes.

"I bet it's hard having your sister sick. Mine's my best friend. It'd make me sad if something were to happen to her."

He sniffles and I see his shoulders start to shake. I wrap my arms around him and he clutches onto my shirt, his tears pouring out in great gasping sobs. A few tears roll down my face at his sadness and my inability to do anything to fix the problem. When he calms down, he pulls away, swiping at his eyes.

"Sorry," he mumbles.

"You don't have anything to be sorry about. It's good to cry every once in a while."

He looks up at me, his eyes wet. "Do you cry sometimes?"

"Yeah, I cry."

"Well, if you cry, then I guess it's okay if I cry," he says in a determined way and I feel like I helped him just a little.

Ryan comes out of his sister's room and we both watch her.

"My girlfriend has yellow hair, too. She's pretty. Not as pretty as your girlfriend, but she's pretty. She's the prettiest girl in my class."

"I bet she's beautiful."

"Do you love your girlfriend?"

Ryan catches sight of me and she waves as we lock eyes. "Yeah, I do."

"I think I might love my girlfriend, too."

"What's your name?" I ask, realizing I've spent the last forty-five minutes with the kid without knowing his name.

"Arthur but my friends call me Art."

"Thanks for letting me play that game with you, Art."

We both stand and walk to the doorway. He gives me a hug before dashing away to his sister's room. Ryan walks up and wraps her hand around my bicep.

"Who was that?"

"Art. He's the brother from the last room you were in."

Her eyes go sad. "Ah. Looked like he was pretty happy."

"Yeah, we played a game together and talked girlfriends."

She gets a twinkle of amusement in her eyes, wiping away the sadness. "Did you now?"

"We did."

"Did he give you some good tips for having a girlfriend?"

"You'll have to wait and find out," I joke and she laughs, shrugging off the sadness from the last room.

We walk to the room where Ryan's stuff sits so she can get back into disguise and we can leave. Before she closes the door, she stops and turns to me.

"I need you to know how much I love music. It's something I can't live without. Performing, all of it. I *love* it. When it gets to feeling like it's too much, when all the privacy invasions and the crowds and photographers and all the issues start to feel too heavy, I do things like this.

"This is why I keep going. None of the bad will ever outweigh the joy I feel knowing what I do can bring a little bit of happiness to people's days. In a cancer ward. On their drive to work. Wherever they are. If their day is better because of something I made, something I created...well, everything else doesn't matter."

She shuts the door gently and my shirt sticks to my skin with Art's tears and I know she's right.

# CHAPTER TWENTY-SEVEN

## RYAN

Dominic is sitting on the couch with his tablet. His brow furrows as he watches the slowed down video of some play. For some reason, I never thought about how much work goes into being a professional football player outside of practice and games. He goes to team workouts, has sessions with personal trainers, and studies so. Much. Footage.

I guess it's not too much different from me getting ready for a tour, it's just surprising how often I find him scribbling notes to himself.

"Good morning, sleepyhead," he says, without looking at me.

'Morning' is a bit of a stretch since it's past eleven and I just woke up. "Morning. So, Sebastian texted."

He pauses the game and puts the tablet down, giving me his full attention. "Why?"

"He wants to have dinner with us?" His eyes bore into me so deeply I feel the urge to shift from side to side in order to expel my nervous energy.

"Do you want to go?"

Five words.

Not a complex sentence and yet, those five words have rendered me speechless and my mind a barren wasteland of thought. Do I want to go? Or do I feel like I should? Is it, that I want to see he's actually doing well so I can finally say, 'See? Aren't you glad you gave him that money? He was able to get his life together.'

My mouth opens a time or two, but no words come out.

"Ry? Do you want to go to dinner?" I pour all the confusion, longing, anger, and need that has built up for my father into my face. "Dinner it is, then. Tonight? After the recording studio?"

Tears well up in my eyes at his easy acceptance and understanding of what I need but can't say. Three little words almost fall from my lips then, but I don't let them. Afraid it'll ruin this perfect thing we have going. Afraid he'll see how desperate I am to hear him say it back to me. How much I need to be loved.

My fans filled that void for years. I gave everything I had to them and they returned the favor.

It was never enough.

"Yes," I whisper.

"Sounds good. I think I'll order the shrimp."

I laugh and swipe at the tear that fell. "I think I want to have it here."

"Can there be shrimp?"

I shrug. "Probably."

"I'll eat that, then." He goes back to his game and I'm left standing there with no way to tell him how much it means to me how easy this was.

Cash always told me if I wanted him to know what I was thinking, then I'd have to tell him. This man gets me. He *sees* me in a way no one else has or does.

"Okay. We have to leave for the studio in twenty," I say, and go to leave the room but Dom's voice stops me.

"Anya dropped off some pastries this morning. She was trying some new recipes last night and figured she'd share. They are in the kitchen if you want anything."

"Your sister being a baker is my favorite thing." His laugh follows me into the kitchen where I select a croissant. The raspberry, lemon, and cheese flavor makes me moan. I go to our bedroom and pull my phone out of my pocket, calling Mom, shoving the last bite in my mouth, crumbs all over my shirt.

"There's my girl!" Dad says stealing the phone from Mom before she can even say hello.

"Hi, Dad. What are you two doing today?"

"Well, you know us. We have Monday BINGO down at the bar and then, if you can imagine, your mom has a sex toy party!"

"What?" I yell, laughing hysterically as Mom wrestles Dad for control of the phone. I hear a loud 'omph' and then Mom's red face appears on screen.

"Honey, don't listen to your father. He's being silly."

"I didn't want to listen to him about your dildo party, Mom, but unfortunately I have ears!"

"Well, now, Ryan. Your father and I aren't dead."

Much like Anya did at the football game, I slap my hands over my ears, dropping the phone to the bed. "I don't want to hear this! I am *begging* you to stop talking."

She huffs. "Why are you calling?"

Why am I calling? Because any time I talk to Sebastian, all I want is my mom.

"Just missing you," I tell her, not wanting to ruin her good mood.

"Aw, I miss you too, sweetie! How's Dominic?"

I can't keep the smile off my face. "He's good. Just studying up for the game on Sunday."

Mom smiles at me in return. "I just love seeing you in love."

Clearing my throat, I shift. "I'm not in love, yet, Mom."

She rolls her eyes. "You sure about that?" she says. "It's been clear as day to me since Thanksiving. You both wouldn't stop making goo goo eyes at each other. And then, not to be indelicate, but we heard some noises coming from the room when we wanted some late-night pie. We weren't spying! And we left quickly! But those aren't the noises of people just fooling around."

"This is my nightmare." I grab Dom's pillow and put it over my face trying to suffocate the life from my body.

"Honey, don't be embarrassed. Your father and I used to participate in very vigorous lovemaking! And on one spontaneous weekend, we even went to a swingers' party."

"Okay, welp. Glad we had this talk, I'm hanging up now. I love you both. Bye!"

I press the 'End Call' button before she can get another word out and sigh. That was the phone call from hell. Dom's footsteps move closer and the door opens.

"Do your parents use vibrators?" I ask him and his eyes go wide.

"Ryan. Please. Whatever this is, there's not enough brain bleach in the world to erase the images trying *so hard* to implant themselves into my mind right now. If you have any love for me in your heart, you'll take the sharpest left turn out of this conversation. I have a game on Sunday, and I'm not going to be able to study thinking about parents and vibrators."

His reaction makes me giggle and I sit up straighter on the bed.

"If I have to know it, you have to know it. They also used to have athletic sex and tried swinging. Oh! And they heard us having sex at their house."

"My God."

"Yeah, so now whenever I look at them, I'm going to know they know how I sound when I come with your dick in my ass."

"You know what? I can see this is a bad time and I'm going to go get a lobotomy or something."

He turns and walks out of the room.

"Ask if they'll do a two for one special!" I call out to his retreating back.

Cash sits in the chair at the mixing board, his head bopping to the song playing. Subconsciously, I rewrite the lyrics, slowing the tempo down, adding a melancholy tune. His longtime producer, Steven spots me, giving me a nod.

I've watched him work with Cash many times and while his style isn't my preferred sound, I can admit he's incredibly talented. He worked on the song that got Cash his first Grammy nomination.

The current song ends and Cash turns.

"There she is," he says, pulling me in for a hug. "What did you think of that one? It's going to be my next single."

"It'll be a hit. Good beat to it."

I reach behind me, touching Dom's hand.

"I'm sure you could punch up the lyrics. You always write the best ones in my songs," he says, smiling at me in the way that used to make my stomach flop. Now there's nothing. No flop. No butterflies.

"This is my boyfriend, Dominic." I pull him forward, in the small space, pretty much throwing him between me and Cash.

"Hey, man. Thanks for letting me borrow her for this song. I just can't seem to get the words right, and there's no one better in the business," he says, shaking Dom's hand and I want to groan. You'd think we'd all be past pissing matches by now, but apparently not.

Then again, next to Dom, Cash seems almost tiny.

I choke on the laugh wanting to escape at the thought of them both whipping their dicks out and measuring. Dom is bigger. By a lot.

In fact, all the fans who would happily go to bed with Cash would be greatly disappointed by what he's packing. I didn't mind. He was perfectly adequate in the bedroom, focusing on me long enough to get me off half the time. Now I've had Dom? I can never go back.

"If she wants to do something, who am I to stop her?" Dom says, a serene smile on his face.

"Yeah, I remember it always being the Ryan show when we were dating, too," he chuckles. "But she's the best muse I've ever had and I can't let her go."

Hurt flashes through me, leaving an embarrassed blush in its wake. No matter how I tried to shrink myself when I was with Cash, it was never enough. The day a headline read "Ryan Jade's

Boyfriend" instead of using his name, I thought he was going to have a fit.

That was the first time he kissed someone else despite us being together.

"It's the best show, if you ask me," Dom remarks, placing his hand on my lower back.

"Are you ready to get to work? I don't have a lot of time," I interject, crossing my arms over my chest.

"Steven, pull up the track?" Cash says to his producer. He pulls out his phone, showing me the lyrics he has in mind.

Calling it a love song is a little misleading. The woman begs the man to come be with her, while the man is dating around, unsure if he wants to settle down. By the last verse, he walks away, choosing his career over her.

I cock an eyebrow at him, annoyed he wrote our relationship into a song and then asked me to help him finish it.

"What do you think?"

"It's good. I think there is potential for a few rewrites," I say, pulling a notepad to me and getting to work.

Paige sets the takeout containers down, and I begin spooning everything onto the serving platters I had her buy today while we were recording. The restaurant is one Sebastian and I have been to before back when I was sixteen and in town for a concert. It was when I was an opener and he was sober. It lasted eleven months that time. Normally I'm a jittery bag of nerves when I see him, this time, with

Dominic at my back and being emotionally tired from the successful writing session, I'm as calm as I've ever been.

The doorbell rings and I drop the metal spoon.

"I've got it!" I yell out, Paige taking over my task and getting everything to the table before disappearing.

Ripping open the door, my heart is in my chest. No matter how many times I tell myself not to get my hopes up, the moment I see Sebastian, they soar through the roof. Dom stands behind me. Ready.

A silent guardian.

"Hi there, pumpkin!" Sebastian says, the moment I have the door open, pulling me in for a hug that I resist.

"Hi. This is Dominic."

"It's a pleasure to meet you, sir," he says, taking my father's hand.

"Donald. It's great to finally meet you."

"Dominic."

"Sorry, son. I'm not the best with names. I'm sure I'll get it eventually."

"Welcome to our home," I tell him, waving him in.

Sebastian whistles, looking around the house. "Nice digs, baby girl."

I don't correct him, knowing the ownership of the house is a bit of a sore spot. Dom decided not to list it once he calmed down, yet I still don't want to push it in his face I lied to him in the first place.

Leading the way into the dining room, we all take our seats, talking about small things.

"Before we get started, do you mind if I wash my hands, kiddo?"

"Bathroom is down the hall. Second door on the left," Dominic says pointing, and Sebastian nods. I pick at my nails beneath the table.

"He seems good, yeah? Doesn't he seem good?" I ask Dom in a hushed whisper. He's not putting on the gregarious personality of Sebastian Slate. He feels like a normal, every day *dad*. "I think he's doing good."

The fact he's here at all is something. I can't count how many times I've agreed to plans only for him to cancel them last minute.

"It'll all be okay. I'm right here with you," Dom whispers and I try to relax until Sebastian takes his seat once more.

"How was rehab? It looks like it's working," I tell him, snagging a shrimp off Dom's plate.

"It was great. I think it's going to stick this time. The money you gave me has been helpful. I was hoping you'd be able to slide me a few thousand more. I'm working on a new record and I need to pay for the production."

My forks freezes halfway to my mouth, hopes dashed against the craggy rocks of reality.

Of *course* this meeting is about money. He's never shown up for anything unless he was getting something out of it. Why would this time be any different?

Why do I do this to myself every time?

My fragile heart shatters as my last hope of ever having a relationship with my father dies. I can't keep doing this. It's not about the money. If I knew giving him every last penny right this second would mean he'd be clean and sober and we could *finally* have the father/daughter relationship I always wanted, I'd clean out my bank account.

It'll never be enough. There's nothing I can do, nothing I can be, that'll make him want me. It doesn't matter I share his love of music. No matter how big of a star I become, it'll never be enough.

Because it was never about me. It's always been about him and his lack, not mine.

After Cash's crack at the music studio about it always being the 'Ryan Jade show' and now this, my already frayed emotions snap, anger taking hold.

"Where the hell is the previous money I gave you? Or the money before that? Hmm? Or the money before that? This is un-fucking-believeable."

"Ry," Dom says, gently, resting a hand on mine, trying to get me to calm down.

Sebastian's face turns stormy, his mask falling like it did when I would ask him to read me a bedtime story when he was trying to write a song. Like my very existence is nothing more than a nuisance to him.

"You owe me your career, *daughter*," he spits over his half-filled plate "You think you would have gotten anywhere without me? Who do you think got you your first recording contract? Huh? You think my own label didn't know you were my daughter? They only wanted you because of me."

His words feel like a slap across the face. Trying to claim my success for his own.

"If that's true, then why didn't they tell everyone you were my dad? I'll tell you why. They didn't want my name tied to a washed-up drug addict alcoholic that almost OD'd and couldn't even walk straight, let alone sing. You are never going to get another penny from me. I'm done. I have my real mom and dad and I don't need you coming around anymore."

"You ungrateful little—"

"Do not finish that sentence," Dom growls.

"Don't tell me how to talk to my kid," he snaps back.

"I think it's time for you to go."

"I'll leave when I get my money."

Dom watches him for a second and then leaps, grabbing him up by the collar and pulling him from his chair. Bradford jumps into the room from the kitchen, ready to step in, but Dom stops him with a look.

"You're getting nothing from Ryan. It's time for you to go now. Don't call her. Don't text her. Don't even think about her. Your problems are your own."

Sebastian pulls out of Dom's grip, straightening his shirt with a rough tug. "I never wanted you anyway," he spits at me, the kill shot to my heart, before turning on his heel and leaving, slamming the door with finality.

"Baby, are you okay?" Dom asks, kneeling on the floor in front of my chair, my hands tight in his grip.

I feel my face crumple. Years of sadness break the levee walls, flooding my heart with all the hurt and disappointment I've hidden from throughout the years At the first tear falls, Dom bundles me into his arms, holding me through the torrent of emotion.

With a hiccup, I pull back, wiping my eyes.

"I'm sorry," I say, wetly.

"Ry, there is nothing for you to apologize for. Okay?" I nod but his eyes don't leave my face. "I want you," he whispers.

"What?"

"I want you. I want you so much. He might not be able to see how amazing you are, but I do. You're amazing. Don't let him tell you otherwise."

I press a soft kiss to his lips, his words wrapping around me. A phone rings in the kitchen and I hear Bradford's clipped replies.

Stepping into the dining room, his words become clear.

"Got it. Call them." Hanging up the phone, he looks at Dom with a grim set to his mouth. "Someone broke into your old house. The police are being called now. We have to go meet them."

This night keeps getting better and better.

# CHAPTER TWENTY-EIGHT

## DOMINIC

R ED AND BLUE LIGHTS bounce off the house and I stand there, unsure what else to do. Once the pictures were taken, I was led through everything to tell them what was missing.

The entire house was ransacked. Holes that look like they were punched and kicked through the sheetrock. The couch is in tatters, the knife from my own chopping block left stabbed into one of the cushions. Curtains are pulled from walls. Bedding is ripped and torn and thrown about the bedrooms. Beds lean off of their bases, resting on floors.

It didn't seem like they were even looking for anything, everything was still there from what I could tell.

It seems like this was done for fun.

That is, if you ignore the big, huge, glaring sign painted on the living room wall in dripping red paint.

*She's mine or she'll be no one's*

All the horror movies I've seen play through my mind. How the people in them are tortured and torn apart by their captors.

How that could have been Ryan. We could've been here. Although Brad and his team are highly trained professionals, who's to say the stalker wouldn't have been able to sneak in. They aren't infallible. And by the time it was noticed, it could have been too late.

Ryan opens her mouth to respond, but snaps it shut. A man in slacks and a dress shirt walks up, a woman by his side in a similar outfit.

"Mr. Reynier, I'm Detective Donaldson and this is Detective Davies. We need to ask you a few questions," the woman says.

I look to Ryan's lawyer who showed up mere moments after we did and she nods.

"When was the last time you were at this residence?" the man asks, flipping open his notebook that had appeared in his hand.

"Oh, um." I look at Ryan trying to think. "The day after the season opener? Um, September sometime."

"So you haven't been here for five months, give or take? Why didn't you break the lease when you moved?"

"Correct. The terms of the lease were very strict. I could only terminate early if I moved to another state to play for a different team. I guess the owners had been burned a few times with people renting the house and then buying something shortly after and leaving."

"Do you have anyone check on the place for you?"

"The security company we work with comes over on a bi-weekly basis to make sure everything is in order. You'll have to check with my head of security. I believe the schedule is Tuesdays and Saturdays," Ryan says.

"We'll verify that information. It was shared with us, Miss Jade, you have a pretty serious stalker. Is that correct?"

"Miss Jade's team has shared any information regarding her stalker with the police department and they decided no action would be taken," the lawyer interjects, but the detective is not thrown off.

"Of course, ma'am. As I'm sure you understand, we are just covering our bases. Mr. Reynier, did anyone else have a key to this house? A housekeeper or a friend, perhaps?"

"My family all have keys. The security team. Some assistants," I tell him.

"Pretty long list then. We'll need to get all of their names and information so we can make sure they weren't involved."

"Involved? Why would any of them be involved?"

"Again, just covering our bases."

The lawyer cuts in abruptly. "That'll be all for tonight. My clients have had a shocking evening. If you have any further questions, you can direct them to my office." She hands them both cards, which they pocket. They say their goodbyes and move back toward the house, walking through the wide open front door.

Ryan looks around the street for a second before moving to stand in front of me, grabbing my face and forcing me to focus on her.

"Hey, there's nothing we can do here now. Let's go home, okay?"

"Sure," I say, no emotion in my voice. She calls out to Bradford who's talking to a cop and waves him over.

"We need to get out of here," she tells him and he nods, touching his earpiece and instructing the driver to get back to start the car.

Neighbors have come out of their houses to see what all the commotion is about. Phones are pointed at us, recording, as we climb into the car, but the tint is dark enough to hide us.

"Babe? Are you okay?" Ryan asks, stroking my arm, reversing our positions from earlier.

"Why didn't you tell me?" I ask her, avoiding the question, not knowing the answer. "You made it sound like no big deal."

"I didn't want to scare you away."

"I deserved to know how serious it was."

Am I mad she didn't tell me the true extent of the situation? Sure. That's not the only reason for all the emotions churning deep within my chest. I look at her, concern bright in her teal-blue eyes.

There was a violent threat against us. And it scared me. I think about how Ryan is basically a hermit when she's not on the road. Maybe part of it is enjoying being home since she has such a busy schedule, but that's obviously not the whole of it.

"I'm sorry," I tell her, resting my hand on her thigh, gripping it tightly because I'm so relieved she's here with me. Safe.

"What for?"

"I think I didn't want to admit how serious it was. The stalker. Even after he spray painted my car it didn't click. Until now. Every time you leave the house, you put your life on the line. Any stranger you meet could be this guy. Hell, they could be a security guard at a venue you work at that could have access to you. And I never took it seriously. I saw the crowds and the screaming and it was intense, but I never considered it could be violent and that was stupid of me.

"You hear about this sort of thing, but I've never had it happen to anyone I know, so I didn't realize how scary it must be to live with it.

The fact you go on tour, hell, even leave the *house*, shows how brave you are. I'm sorry."

She gives me a sad smile. Taking my hand but not removing it from her thigh. "It's okay. It's not an easy thing to accept, I understand that."

"I love you." If someone placed Ryan in the Lourve on a pedestal and told patrons she's a statute, no one would bat an eye. That's how still she is. So, I panic. "You don't have to say anything. I'm not going to pressure you. If something had happened to me, or God forbid you, and I hadn't said that? I'd never forgive myself. I think I loved you when I met you dropping off that cake for your parents.

"And then again when you gave me a second chance after not calling you. And again when you met my parents. And when I met yours. I think I've loved you every day since you shook my hand. I think I even loved you the first time I saw you on stage. I'm sure it was just me hoping and wanting it to be true, but we locked eyes when I came to see your concert before we met. You winked at me and I think I loved you then."

"Dom—"

I can't stop now that it's coming out.

"Then you sang that song. You sang that song and if there was any piece of my heart that wasn't yours yet, it was then. I love you, Ryan Jade. With everything I am and I was scared, before. Scared that I wouldn't be enough, that I was too small for such an amazingly talented, caring, beautiful powerhouse of a woman. No matter what this crazy world throws at you, at us, I want to handle it together. I want you. There's nothing about your life that can make me run. Because I love you and if I run, that won't change, and then Anya would have to drown me because apparently I'm a moper when I'm sad—"

She raises a hand up and covers my mouth, stopping my tirade. Saving us both from a world of embarrassment while I continue to ramble and tell this woman, who has not responded at all, how I love her. Ryan's mouth opens, and every inch of my body breaks out in a cold sweat.

There's no way she's not going to break up with me after that ridiculous diatribe, no matter how true the words I said were.

Including the bit about being a sad moper.

Anya's not wrong about that.

"If you both wanted to continue this conversation inside...we're home." our driver says, stopping Ryan from responding.

I flush with embarrassment that there was a witness to my stupidity.

"Yes. Yup. In the house. Yes. Good, good idea, Bradford."

"It's Justin, actually."

"I knew that. Sorry. Stay here and let me get your door." I almost fall from the car onto the garage floor. Stopping by the trunk, I put my hands on my head and try to catch my breath. "I don't think that could have gone any worse." My feet carry me to her door and I open it, holding out a hand to help her. "Mi'lady."

*Shoot me in the fucking face.* I think the only way I could make this more awkward is if I honked her boob or something else truly, deeply moronic. If she broke up with me right now and ran as far away from me as she could go, I'd understand.

Anya would mock me mercilessly. I'd have to change my name and fake my own death.

Her skin on mine stops me from planning my fake funeral. She steps from the car and looks up at me and begins walking into the house, dragging me behind her.

But I don't mind.

I'd follow her anywhere she wants me to go.

# CHAPTER TWENTY-NINE

## RYAN

My car waits in a line outside the venue. Sequins cut into my legs where the mini dress meets my skin. I twist the diamond butterfly ring on my finger with nerves, Dom's confession of love still playing in my ears.

And my deafening silence, even a week later.

It's not that I'm not falling in love with him. I'd be stupid not to. But Sebastian's final words and the spray painted threat echoed in my head and tied my tongue. Why would he want to love someone who brings all of this into his life?

I saw the lingering fear on his face over the destroyed house and I couldn't bring myself to say it back in the moment. I didn't want to pour out my heart to him on a night tainted by Sebastian and the stalker. I want the moment, like our first kiss, to be just ours.

After the exhausting evening, we went to bed, kissing gently in our room until we fell asleep wrapped up in each other's arms.

"Ryan? Did you hear me?" Zoe asks, cutting into my thoughts. The fans outside the car scream as someone ahead of us begins walking the red carpet, their voices muted by the car.

"Sorry, what did you say?" I ask her, my earrings dancing when I turn my head toward her.

"I said Cash is in the car in front of us. You both will take some shots alone, and then they want you to take some together."

"Is it not enough we are presenting together?" As the reigning Best Female and Best Male Artists, the awards show wanted us to present both awards together this year. Maybe I should have said no, but I try my best to always celebrate the accomplishments of my fellow artists. Dom said he didn't mind I'd be missing his game on one of the few Sundays I don't have a show, but I could see in his eyes I hurt him.

Especially after my silence.

"Ryan," Zoe says, a touch of annoyance in her tone and I focus on her again. "Hey, I know you've got a lot going on right now, but I need you to focus up. You can't be distracted when you step out of this car."

"I got it," I tell her, an equal bite to my words.

Thinking and worrying about Dom isn't a distraction.

Well, it is, but not a normal distraction. I care about this man. It makes sense my thoughts are going to be taken up by him.

Zoe opens her mouth, but our car moves to the front of the line and one of the attendants for the show is opening my door before she can say another word.

"Miss Jade," he says, holding his hand out.

I take it, pulling myself from the car and, with the first flashbulb, I'm on. The fans in the seats surrounding the carpet stand and scream for me.

I wave.

I smile.

I blow kisses.

I pose.

I'm the perfect pop star. Photographers scream my name, demanding I look their way, hoping for a shot where I'm making eye contact with their camera. The flashes are blinding.

I wish Dom was by my side. He would be here. Even though I know he wouldn't necessarily enjoy all the screaming and the pictures, and the guaranteed camera on us during the entire show, there's no doubt in my mind he'd have been here for me if he could've been.

"Cash, get in there with Ryan," one of the photographers yells out and I remember Zoe's instructions in the car.

Cash looks amazing in that nonchalant rock star way he has. I realize how much he reminds me of Sebastian in the pictures I always saw of him growing up. The easy confidence and swagger come naturally to men like him. The way he feels most comfortable when eyes are on him.

And when they aren't on him, how he was always scheming to get them on him again.

His strong arms wrap around me, lifting me off the ground and spinning me around.

Despite myself, I laugh, remembering all the times he did that when we were together. He puts me down and for a moment, I'm staring into his arresting eyes.

"I've been missing you, Ryan. I know I fucked up, but I'm different now. I've changed." His ringed hand reaches up and tucks a stray hair behind my ear. "You always made me feel wanted. I want that again."

He's changed. How many times did Sebastian tell me that? How many times did he promise this time would be different? Hell, how many times did Cash himself promise me he'd be different?

And they never were.

They never will be.

He didn't even say he wanted *me*, the person, just that he wanted to feel wanted again. He wants me for how I make him feel.

"Kiss her!" a photographer yells and it's like I've been dumped in a frozen lake.

"I'm with Dom," I hiss at Cash, trying to push him away, but his arms band around me.

"Don't cause a scene," he whispers harshly and I still. "You'll come crawling back to me, eventually. He's not made for this life."

Turning in his arms, I give my best fake smile at the cameras, tomorrow's headlines going through my mind.

*Is there trouble in paradise for Ryan Jade and the newest in a long line of boyfriends?*

*Another casualty in Ryan Jade's never ending quest for love?*

*Why can't Ryan Jade keep a man? A look back at Ryan Jade's exes including the newest, Dominic Reynier.*

Figuring I've given the photographers enough chances to snap a shot, I break free of Cash and walk into the theater, swallowing down my tears.

The show goes to commercial break and I check my phone one last time. In desperation, I texted Dom, begging him to understand the pictures that are no doubt circulating of me and Cash mean *nothing*. That there's not a single part of me that wants him back.

His game should be ending soon, so I keep holding out hope he'll respond before I make it out on the stage for the first award. It's too late when a stagehand is ushering me into place. Zoe snatches my phone from my hand, and one of the production members cues my entrance.

Music pumps through the venue from the live band, and my Ryan Jade persona slips into place like breathing.

Cash walks from the opposite side of the stage, reaching out toward me, but I don't take his hand, no longer caring what other people think. I'm with Dominic.

Someone who has been so consistent and unwavering.

Stepping up to the mic, I read the words on the teleprompter.

"This year has been full of amazing female artists. Covering every genre, they made us laugh and cry and dance with their music."

Cash steps up to the microphone, pushing his arm against mine, but I take a step away, putting space between us.

"They've left music forever changed and I'm honored to announce the nominees." He runs through the list of six names and I clap for each one, remembering my first awards show and what a magical night it was.

I step up to the mic once more. "And the winner is," I say, breaking the seal on the card. "Rose Monroe."

Rose makes her way to the stage and I can feel her shaking as I hug her. "Congratulations," I tell her, genuine excitement for the young rapper.

"I grew up listening to your records. I wouldn't be here without you," she tells me before turning to the microphone to thank everyone who made her win possible. My expression feels a little more real after her words, mending a piece of my heart Sebastian left shattered.

We all walk off the stage. Rose is immediately surrounded with people directing her for different photo shoots as a newly minted Top Female Artist. Dancers dash out onto the stage, one of the nominees of the night performing a song.

Looking around, Zoe seems to have disappeared during my first presentation. I wish I could check my phone before the next one. Craning my neck, standing on tiptoes trying to find her, Cash walks up to me.

"Ryan, you never answered me on the carpet," he says, stepping into my personal space.

He's always crowded me, when we were together. I used to think it was romantic, but now I'm just annoyed.

"Yes, I did. I'm with Dom. That's not going to change."

"Tell me you didn't feel anything when we wrote that song together. There's no way you didn't!"

By the time we were done with the song in the studio, I had rewritten almost all the lyrics. Cash believes the beat is where the magic of a song resides. I couldn't disagree more.

The heart of a song is the lyrics.

My heart lives in the lyrics. Every beat writing the song of my life.

Sitting on that studio floor, leaning against Dom's legs, I wrote everything I felt. Not for Cash, but for Dominic. I thought I loved Cash when we were together. That the push and pull of our relationship was what passion was supposed to feel like. Burning. Scorching. Consuming.

In this moment, I realize why I could never fully let Cash go. Why he could always pull me in no matter what he had done to me, promises of better.

I was so used to chasing after Sebastian, begging him to love me, giving him everything he asked for on the hope he'd finally want me, *love* me. That's what I've always thought love was. It was never giving up on someone.

Never letting them go.

Maybe that's not what love is, though. Dom's smiling face enters my mind, all the times he's taken care of me. When he's been there without my asking. I never doubted he would be.

Maybe love doesn't have to mean letting people break promises to you and forgiving them.

Dom has shown me, maybe I do deserve more, and not because of what I can do for people. He wants me for me. I haven't told him I love him with my words, but it's written in every beat of my heart. I stand there, looking at Cash, and I know Dom is the one I want by my side through it all.

"I'm done, Cash. I've moved on. You should, too."

"You'll miss me one day," Cash hisses, as Zoe appears out of nowhere, handing me my phone.

**Dom: Can you bring that dress home with you?**

**Dom: All I can think about is taking it off your body with my teeth**

I smile. "No, I don't think I will," I tell Cash.

Handing the device back to my manager and friend, I straighten my shoulders as the performance ends, readying to walk out and present one last award for the night before going home to my man.

# CHAPTER THIRTY

## DOMINIC

MUSIC PUMPS THROUGH THE speakers and my head nods to the beat, but I don't hear the lyrics. I visualize myself making catches, breaking tackles, and scoring touchdowns as I pull up my pants. Any time a thought of Ryan tries to take over, I push it from my mind. Focus is the name of the game today. After I texted her I was at the stadium and to have a good concert tonight, I shut the door on outside distractions.

This game is do or die.

This is where I start to get my redemption for failing us when it really mattered last season and secure my place on this team for the future.

The winner of this game will go on to the Super Bowl. Each week that has passed, our team has dialed in more and more. We're making cleaner passes. Blocking better. Applying pressure better. All of our hard work throughout the session is culminating into a team ready to be on the biggest stage of our sport at the perfect time.

I want a repeat of last year, but this time, with the correct color of confetti falling down around me.

My name in the air pulls me from my mental drills, diverting the focus I'm working so hard to maintain.

It's the way my name is being said that has my head snapping around.

A breathy, female voice fills the locker room as all of the men surrounding me quiet down. They are never quiet. Ever. Even when we lost the Super Bowl they weren't quiet. Promises of retribution and proving ourselves the next year kept the silence at bay.

I'm frozen in shock.

*"Dominic, I'm going to come. I'm going to come. I'm—"* Ryan's moan and my grunted praise break the spell and set me off in a panicked hunt to find the source of the sound.

The guys all shift uncomfortably, getting out of the way like you would jump from the path of a rabid animal. In the back are Tim, Scott, and Dwayne standing in a circle, a phone in the center. I look at the screen and there I am. Fucking Ryan at a brutal pace. Her breasts are bouncing with each thrust and her head is hanging from the bed, ecstasy written on her face.

Video me looks up and it looks like I'm making eye contact with the camera, a smirk on my face as I chase my release.

I grab the phone and hurl it against the wall. Plastic and bits of glass rain down. No one, not even the owner of the phone says anything. My heart is racing so fast, I'm afraid it's about to explode. Cold sweat drenches me.

How many people have seen this? Heard this?

Think I would record and share this?

How did this fucking *happen*?

Tank walks through the crowd and grabs my arms, pulling me behind him. He throws me into an empty office and slams the door behind us.

"I—" I start, but he interrupts me.

"Shut up and listen. Reynier, there is nothing you can do about this right now. I promise you, Ryan's lawyers are all over it, working to get it taken down and to find out how this happened. I know you want to run and deal with it, I get it. I've been there. There is *nothing* you can do. Nothing. It's out there. The sick fucks that did this won this round. It'll be out there forever.

"How you move forward, though, *right now* is what matters. You have to show them they didn't win. Even if you have to fake it. We have a game on the line and your brothers need you."

"I have to call her. I need to make sure she's okay."

My mind might be spinning out, but my heart is pointing toward Ryan and making sure she's okay.

"There's no good that'll come from looking at your phone. I'll tell Lorelei to text her and let her know you're okay and you guys will get through this. You both are professionals. Block it out. Sitting around waiting to find out what happened and to get it taken down isn't going to do anything but make you crazy."

He's not wrong. That doesn't mean I don't want to jump on a plane and go to Ryan. He must understand that with a look at my face.

"She's not going to cancel her concert. You know this. Be stronger than the panic."

I nod and begin pacing around the room, trying to expel the energy and refocus. Ryan's moans keep breaking through my mental walls and I have to start all over. Angry pounding on the door startles me.

"Carlston, Reynier. Get out here," Coach Williamson yells.

Tank looks at me, waiting for my nod before pulling the door open. The team is standing, geared up and ready.

"An attack was made on your brother and his lady tonight. Show them you can't be rattled. Show them how we stand together. Show them we are family. We protect our own. Prove it," Coach says.

There is no chant. No cheer. No hyping.

Everyone streams by, slapping my shoulder in solidarity before leaving the locker room. Once everyone has left, Coach stands in front of me.

"Ready?" I look at him and say nothing. "This is going to be the game of your life. Show you're worthy of the challenge."

The thought of my parents and Anastasia comes to mind and everything they've sacrificed to help get me here. The love they have for me. That they will always have for me.

And I think about Ryan. Everything she's faced in her storied career. All the times they have tried to bring her to her knees and failed. How they will fail this time, too. We aren't going down without a fight.

I put my helmet on and forget everything.

For the next three hours, nothing else matters.

Nothing outside this facility exists.

There's this game, my brothers, and that's it.

My cleats are loud on the concrete as I jog to the tunnel, ready to fight.

For the first time since I've joined the team, the locker room is closed to media. All interviews will happen in the media room or in spaces designated by Geoff. Every outlet is trying to get time with me. It doesn't matter we're the conference champions. They want to talk about the fact the entire world has now seen Ryan orgasm.

We cheer and celebrate our win, popping bottles of champagne and spraying it all over the plastic covered locker room. It's sticky and sweet and a piece of me doesn't care at all. I hate this has been tainted by the video. It's what I've been focused on for the entire season.

It took everything in me to stay in the game. I played every offensive down, the mental load of running plays keeping me in the present. When the defense was on, it was harder. That is, until Tank started grabbing a tablet from one of the support staff on the sideline and going through every play and what the other team was doing so I could better find holes and exploit coverages. He pointed out every time I could have gone left instead of right and been wide open. How I could open up my awareness to better serve my team.

While Tank is a tight end, he has an amazing understanding of the game that goes way beyond his position. Whenever he decides to retire, it'll be a waste of his talent if he's not an offensive coach.

When the final whistle blew, every camera person ran to surround me, but I ignored them and walked into the tunnel without so much as a 'good game' to the other team. I put everything I had into the game, scoring two touchdowns, and I was done. I couldn't ignore my life outside the stadium a second more.

I pick up my phone and I see the texts.

I ignore all that aren't from Ryan or my family.

**Mom: We love you, honey. We have your back.**

**Dad: Those touchdowns were perfect, son. I'm proud to be your dad. Tell Ryan we love you both.**

**Anya: Do you know how awful this is? I can't get away from seeing my brother having sex.**

**Anya: Aren't you glad me and Parker didn't get freaky on the show?**

**Anya: You're welcome for not scarring you.**

**Anya: I'm going to need therapy.**

I almost laugh at Anya's messages. To some people it might seem flippant, but my sister has always known exactly what I needed. I know she's there if I need to talk. I know she'll go to bat for me and tell anyone she can to fuck off if they say anything bad about me and Ryan because of this.

She doesn't have to say it.

The singular text from Ryan tells me I made the right choice, letting Tank convince me not to run off and make sure she was okay. I always knew she was strong.

**Ryan: Zoe showed me your touchdowns. Nice dance moves. I see someone has been practicing.**

After both of my touchdowns, I did some of Ryan's choreography instead of my normal touchdown celebrations. The first one, I was alone, in the end zone, my brothers not knowing what to do.

On the second one, everyone joined in.

And I don't mean only my brothers.

The fans as well.

I like to believe every person in that stadium danced with us as the song I pulled the choreo from was played over the speakers.

They showed me they were there for me. That they loved me. That they loved Ryan. It touched me in a way, that simple show of solidarity and support, that will never be replicated.

And I hope her fans did the same for her.

# CHAPTER THIRTY-ONE

## RYAN

Sky: We need a lunch date soon, ladies. It's been too long. Plus, Ryan needs to give us an update on her two boyfriends

Ryan: Cash and I aren't together

Karter: That's not what it looked like to me

Taylor: I'll have some free time in a few weeks. Ryan, your dress looked gorgeous at the show the last week.

Shaking my head, I ignore the messages. I pace the green room for a few minutes, mindlessly scrolling social media, going through a few last-minute vocal warm ups.

Then I see it.

The headlines, accompanied by my face frozen in orgasm plastered across every site for the entire world. My hand shakes, thumb hovering over the link trying to decide if I want to click it or not.

If I want to verify my privacy has been obliterated in the most unforgiving of ways.

Zoe comes bursting through the doors and grabs my phone from my hand.

"We're already working on getting it taken down," she says, grabbing my hand. "Do you want to cancel the show?"

I'm frozen, my stomach turning in waves of sickness, threatening to overtake me. This is real. One of my worst nightmares come to life.

"I can't cancel," I tell her. "I don't cancel concerts."

"Ryan, they would understand." Her eyes are sympathetic.

I want to run to Dom, but I can't let this coward beat us by canceling my concert. The moment I stepped into the spotlight all those years ago, I knew privacy was only an illusion from then on. It shouldn't be this way.

It shouldn't be acceptable to share my intimate moments without my consent.

"No. I won't let them break me. The show goes on."

She nods and leaves the room, I'm sure to talk to my lawyers and anyone else needed to handle this and I sit on the floor of my dressing room and breathe until my heart is no longer racing.

Before I can blink, it's time.

I'm pulled from my room and readied for everything that stands before me. They won't win. I won't let them break me.

My platform rises and I force myself to focus on nothing but the music. I move through the choreography automatically, thankful muscle memory is a thing. The song and energy from the crowd loosen me up with each passing second.

As the song ends, I notice something…weird. The crowd quiets. Even in my monitors I can barely hear them, which isn't normal. I look to my dancers as I circle, getting ready for the second number, raising my eyebrow in question. All they do is shrug in confusion.

I turn, striking my pose, and freeze.

"First verse in three, two, one," the mechanical voice says. I don't start singing.

Seventy thousand people stand there, quiet, raising their phones. It takes a second to register what's happening.

They are making a rainbow. A rainbow for me. To support me.

At the top of the stadium in the seats farthest from me starts the purple. It cascades down into blues and greens and yellows and oranges until I notice, immediately next to the stage is the red.

I don't know how they managed it in such a short time. The amount of organization that went into this is incredible. All the communication. The dedication.

For me.

I wonder how many of them have experienced something similar. How many have had their privacy shredded like that? And without the means to do anything about it. I have an entire team working to get the video down. Even though it will live on the internet forever, the gossip rag that posted it doesn't deserve to make a profit off it.

I know it wasn't Dom who sold that video. He would never record me without my consent. I don't think we have more than a handful of pictures together not taken by paparazzi, in fact, because it's not something we think of when we're together, too busy in the moment together.

Holding my hand over my heart, I bow to the crowd. My gratitude is limitless for this display. Knowing they have my back, I vow to put it from my mind and give them everything I have.

"Restarting 'Lipstick Lies' in three, two, one," my technical team tells me through my monitors and I strike my pose once more.

The rest of the concert goes on without a hitch. I know I'm giving the best performance of my life. These people deserve it. And I deserve it. I deserve to enjoy these few hours with the people who gave me the life I love so much by supporting my music.

Everything else, I'll deal with later. The embarrassment. The shame. All of it.

For the duration of the show, all I felt was love.

"I love you all so much! Thank you for being an amazing crowd. Good night!" I say at the end.

Confetti rains down as my dancers and I take our final bows. I move around, happiness written on my face, waving as the fans continue to cheer. They pour every ounce of love into me they can, like they have all night. Tonight, it feels like being wrapped in a cocoon and I feel safe.

Cared for.

I wanted to cancel tonight and go to him. But above all things, I'm a professional and so is he. And like I knew he would, he stayed strong. I couldn't be more in love with him.

Being here, though, was everything I needed to face what is going to be waiting for us on the other side. Making my way offstage, I wave to the crowd until, finally, I'm hidden from view. Zoe swoops in, her face finally filled with color again.

When she walked into my dressing room to tell me the news, she could have been a ghost for how pale she was.

"Dom scored some touchdowns," she says, handing me her phone. I watch the plays. On the second one, my brow furrows and I have to watch it again.

At the end, I see it.

My dance moves with a side of Dominic flare. Then I notice his teammates. And their fans. Everyone is doing the dance and my eyes water again. Seeing the support from his teammates and their fans, not only to him but me as well, touches something in me.

We fly to my dressing room, the last quarter of the game playing on Zoe's phone. The Thunderhawks are ahead by twenty-four, so I'm not concerned about their winning.

"I need to get home," I tell Zoe as I shoot Dom a text about the dancing.

"I already have the plane ready," she tells me, and I'm so glad I hired her all those years ago.

A few raindrops splatter on my forehead as I rush from the plane to the awaiting SUV, but it doesn't matter. All I care about is getting to Dom. Even though it's just after midnight. He told me he was putting his phone on airplane mode and going to bed two hours ago, after the sweep for any more cameras was done.

By the time we pull into the garage, the rain is coming down much harder.

"Good night, everyone!" I tell the security team as I run into the house, making a mental note to grab my bag from the car in the morning.

I race up the stairs and slow outside of Dom's room, the floor creaking slightly. On quiet feet, I push the door open, and make my way inside. Laying on his stomach, the covers are tangled around his legs, one naked ass cheeked bared to the cool air.

My mouth waters at the sight. No matter what's happening, a naked Dom is always going to demand all of my attention. I strip out of my clothes, leaving them on the floor by the footboard before crawling onto the bed. He mumbles in his sleep as I jostle him but is pulled back under.

Leaning over him, I press kisses to his muscular back. His breathing changes, gets deeper with a soft purr. A strong arm snakes out, wrapping me up and pulling my body partially under his as he shifts. Dom throws a leg over mine, trapping me, his erection pressing into my hipbone and his face is buried in my hair.

"Missed you," he mumbles.

"I missed you, too," I tell him, stroking his arm.

"Sex?" he asks, and I laugh.

"I think you'd have to wake up for that," I tell him, kissing whatever piece of him I can reach.

"No," he mumbles, a bit of a whine to his voice, as he begins humping my hip.

"Move your leg." He shakes his head and I chuckle again. "If you move your leg, I can spread mine."

His leg moves immediately and I reverse our positions, throwing my leg over his hip. I grab onto his dick, pressing it against my entrance, and shift myself down until he's fully seated inside me. The stretch burns, but I love the bite of pain.

I move my hips back and forth slowly. It only withdraws him by a few inches, but it's enough. The angle makes him hit the spot deep within me and my body begins tightening.

"Does this feel good, baby?" I ask him, squeezing my pussy as I tilt my hips backward. He moans his response, his breathing picking up.

I ride him gently. Eventually, he starts thrusting. There's no real power behind it. I love our regular, aggressive pace, but this slow, almost lazy form is amazing too. Pinching my nipple, I feel my release nearing.

"Are you going to come with me, Dom?" I pant in his ear, my pace picking up.

"Yes," he says into my hair, not having moved his face.

"Yeah? You're going to fill me up?"

"Fuck, yes. You're mine." His voice is sleepy but no less intoxicating.

"I'm so close," I tell him, just like I did in the video, but I push the thought from my mind. All of my muscles tighten and I begin moving even faster, chasing the building release. "Three more strokes, baby. Come with me. Please come with me."

He grunts as I stroke him. In and out. In and out. My jaw drops as I shift backwards once more and as I come back to him, hard, I shatter.

His dick pulses deep inside me as I squeeze him for every drop, my body shaking with the power of my orgasm. We lay there, connected as his dick deflates, and I know we're going to be able to get through this.

Walking downstairs, one of Dom's Thunderhawk t-shirts hanging from my frame and some soft sleep shorts, I pause mid-stride at the dining room.

"What's all this?" I ask a still shirtless Dom as he adds two pancakes to a plate already loaded down with eggs and bacon. My mouth waters. All my mouth seems to do around Dom is water. It's not something I'm ever going to get sick of.

"This"—he says, putting the plate down at the chair across from him—"is your breakfast."

"My breakfast?" I say, surprised.

"Yup." He places a single daisy in a glass of water before turning to me and smiling. "Yesterday was awful. For both of us. And I know it's going to be hard for both of us going forward. I want the hard with you, Ryan. I want everything with you. This is something we have to get through. I know we will. There's nothing I'm more sure of."

He hasn't said 'I love you' again since I didn't say it back to him after the hospital, but that's okay. Because this said it.

Him being here is saying it.

And that's enough.

I walk to him and press a kiss to his lips. "I'm sure of it, too." I move around the table and take my seat. "This looks amazing."

The bacon crunches, perfectly crispy, and I hum in appreciation.

"Zoe called me. She said the cops looking into the break-in at my old house want to come and talk to us."

"Was there a break in the case?" I ask, shoveling eggs in my mouth.

"She didn't say. They'll be here in an hour, though."

I nod, pulling one of my legs up, setting my foot on the seat of my chair. "I think we need to talk about what we are going to say. This is an attack I'm not willing to let go without a response."

He nods, wiping his mouth with one of the cloth napkins he set the table with. I love how at home he is in the space and it gives me hope we can keep this house. It's my favorite I've ever bought.

"I have some thoughts about that. We can talk about it once the cops leave."

"Sounds good," I say. And it does.

All of this has been a shock, painful. I've felt embarrassed at having such a private moment shared with the world against my will, but surprisingly, I've not felt an ounce of shame. Because this was something done *to* us. Why should we feel shame at the actions of a coward?

No, all I've felt since the news broke is love and support from the people around me.

And mind numbing anger at the person who did this.

# CHAPTER THIRTY-TWO

## DOMINIC

DETECTIVE DAVIES IS SITTING across from us and I have to fight to keep my body from fidgeting. It feels like the time in high school my friends and I threw some bottle rockets at passing cars, one of them happening to be a cop car. They took each of us home, sitting us down with our parents and making sure we knew how dangerous it was. I thought Dad's head was going to explode. I'm sure every kid that's been taken home by cops thinks that, but his face was so red, I was sure we'd be cleaning blood splatters off the wall.

But I survived the grounding.

Barely.

Now whenever a cop is sitting across from me, I feel like I'm in trouble.

"Miss Ryan, Mr. Reynier. Thank you for meeting with me. I needed to ask you a few questions."

"Sure," Ryan says, her hands tucked between her knees. Her, well, I guess our lawyer is sitting in the chair next to the cop and she watches him with sharp eyes, ready to jump in the second she needs to.

"We are aware there was a video leaked of your intimate activities, and I have to ask, Mr. Reynier, did you release that video?"

I want to be angry they'd even ask, but after catching the one frame where it seemed like I was looking at the camera, I don't blame them.

"Absolutely not. I wouldn't betray Ryan like that. And anyway, recording isn't my thing." I grab Ryan's hand, linking our fingers together.

"Do you know of anyone in your life who would release such a tape?"

"Of course not! Why would someone even do that?" I ask, outraged. I love the people in my life and they would never do something like this.

"According to a source we were able to find at the publication that released the footage, they paid five million dollars for it. I'd say that's a pretty good reason to do it."

Ryan jumps in. "The people in our lives make plenty of money or are married to people that make plenty of money. The financial gain wouldn't be a driving factor."

That's not entirely true. Her father doesn't have access to a lot of money. In fact, he's been hitting up his daughter because of his lack of funds. She must feel my hesitancy because she looks over at me.

"What is it?"

I look between everyone before settling on her again. "What about your dad?"

"Sebastian? He would never do something like this."

"Sebastian? We have that your father is Matthew Sampson," the detective says, confused. Ryan looks to her lawyer.

"Detective, my client is willing to share information with you to support the investigation, however, we need guarantees the information will not be become public."

"This entire investigation is highly controlled. Other than myself, my partner, and my boss, no one can get into the files." We all sit there, but no one speaks. He rolls his eyes. "I'll look into it myself and if nothing comes from the information, I don't see why it needs to even be in the report."

Ryan looks at her lawyer who nods.

"My father, my biological father, is Sebastian Slate. He recently was released from a rehab center. He would do anything for money, including selling videos of me."

The cop's pen scribbles across his pad of paper with this new information. When Ryan stops talking, he looks up.

"Wait, he wasn't in Mr. Reynier's other residence?"

"The old house?" I ask.

He looks between us both. "Have you actually watched the video that was released?"

Ryan's face flushes immediately. I clear my throat. "Um, I saw some of it. I was more focused on me and Ryan. Not any of the details in the background or anything. I don't think Ryan's seen it at all?"

She shakes her head emphatically.

"I see. The video was taken in Mr. Reynier's old home. We believe the break-in at your previous residence was to retrieve the recording device as we did not find any such equipment after the break-in."

My ears heard the words, but my brain doesn't want to process them and what they could mean. The implications.

Ryan freezes on my side.

"We only had se—" She stops herself. I know what she was going to say.

We only had sex at that house one time. The night before the world knew about us.

Sebastian has never been to it.

Which means the camera was planted there before September. And the only time people have been in my house that weren't my family or Ryan or Zoe was the Fourth of July party.

Someone I invited into my home put a camera in my bedroom.

How, the *fuck*, did they happen to have a camera ready?

Because I told everyone Ryan would be there and to make sure their guests would be cool.

"This is my fault," I tell her, my heart breaking. "I wanted to make sure no one was invited that'd bother you. That opened up the chance for this. It had to have been one of the friends someone brought. Ry, I'm so sorry." Tears choke my voice.

Here I was, upset her job had invaded my life, but I let someone invade hers in the worst way imaginable. Her small hands bracket my face, forcing me to look at her.

"This is *not* your fault. This is the fault of the person who took advantage of your welcoming heart. How would you know they would sneak a camera in?"

"I should've known. Anything you touch is worth money. I should've known. I should've asked Bradford to sweep for cameras."

A solitary tear runs down my cheek, but she stops it.

"Mr. Reynier, I understand the guilt you're feeling right now. Unfortunately, I do have to ask you to write me a list of all the people at the party and I'm going to have to interview them," Detective Davies says, holding out his notepad.

Ryan lets go of my face, the feeling of her hands lingering. I take the paper from the detective and begin writing out my friends' names. Friends who might have sold a video of my girlfriend and I to the highest bidder.

We sit in my living room alone, cop and lawyer finally gone. A numbness has taken over while I mentally run through the list of names I gave the detective over and over again, trying to figure out which person is the one that did all of this.

"We should hold a press conference and release our statement. We don't want to be quiet for too much longer," Ryan says, breaking the quiet that had fallen over us for the past twenty minutes.

"No."

"What?"

"No press conference. No curated statement." There's nothing I want less in this moment than to read someone else's words to talk about this entire situation.

"Dom, we have to say something."

I look at her, *really* look at her. She's exhausted and afraid. To-morrow, she goes to her next city for three more concerts, and instead of spending quality time together, we're sitting here trying to unravel the mess brought into our lives.

That I brought into our lives.

"I'm not saying don't say anything, but this was an invasion of our privacy, of our private lives, and I don't want it to sound like we are talking to a board of directors or something. I want *us* to make a statement."

Her eyes get big and round, her bare mouth gaping open and closed and I wonder how long it's been since she's made a statement that wasn't written and approved before she made it. All these years, everything she's released has been calculated in the name of the business that is Ryan Jade. She doesn't go off the cuff. The most raw thing she's done was sing that song to me in the middle of her set.

It must be scary, to be faced with this. Even despite standing in front of huge crowds of thousands, every word and step she takes is pre-planned. Choreographed.

"Hey, I know this feels like a lot. You can do this. You do this all the time, putting your feelings down to music. It's no different here," I tell her, tucking a loose strand of hair behind her ear.

"It is different! Do you know how many versions of those songs I've written? Tons! Every word is specifically picked."

"Ryan, you can do this. It's not going to be perfect, and I know that can be hard to accept, but they need to hear from us."

I can see the moment she chooses to trust me.

"Okay." It's easy. Simple. It means everything to me.

"Okay."

Taking her phone, I lean it against some geometric knick-knack on the table and open the first social media app I find.

"This is going to be a terrible angle for me," Ryan says, and I can hear her shifting around on the couch.

I laugh. The woman doesn't have a bad angle. It's almost inhuman how beautiful and perfect she is.

"Ready?" I ask, looking back at her, my finger hovering over the live button.

"Ready."

A countdown from five appears on the screen when I press the button. Just long enough for me to get back to the couch and grab Ryan's hand.

The comments are immediate as people join.

"Hey, everyone, it's Dom and Ryan. We wanted to get on here to address everything that has happened in the past few days. As many of you know, a recording of us has been posted for everyone to see. What you might not be aware of is, not only was the release of the video done without our consent, the recording was taken illegally," I say.

I look at Ryan and give her a nod of encouragement.

"I've been in this industry for two-thirds of my life. It has been a privilege to create art you all love. That look into my life is on my terms. Having such an intimate, private moment leaked for the entire world to see has hurt us beyond measure," she says, tears in her voice.

"Obviously, we can't stop everyone from watching it, but if you're a fan of Ryan's or mine, we ask you to refrain from sharing, viewing, or even talking about the video. Let's pretend it's not out there at all. We can't erase what was done. We *can* refuse to give the people trying to profit off of us against our will what they want, with your help. Your attention, even when you're defending us, is what they want. It doesn't matter if engagement is bad, it's still engagement.

"I also want to take a moment to talk to the people in the crowds the night the video was released, both at the Radiance tour and my game. Your support and love meant the world to us. To watch you all embrace my girlfriend in her time of need when I couldn't be there...it lifted a weight from my shoulders."

Ryan smiles at me and I lean in to kiss her, not for the audience, but because we are making it through all of this together. I couldn't do this without her. I thought I hated all the scrutiny that came with her life. All the fans. That night changed everything for me. Watching her audience care for her, changed how I feel about all the craziness.

How could they not love her?

"Watching everyone dance with Dom to my song was amazing. From the bottom of my heart, thank you for taking care of him for me."

"We are going to come out of this stronger than ever. I love this woman, and there's nothing that can take her away from me."

The comments are coming so fast they are a blur as I get up and stop the live session. Ryan exhales behind me.

"That wasn't so bad," she says, a touch of surprise in her voice.

"No, it wasn't bad at all."

"You realize you told the world you love me, right? There's no way that video isn't going to be posted everywhere."

"At least it's a video I'm okay with being posted everywhere. I wanted the person who did this to know they didn't win."

It feels good to take back control. Geoff or Zoe would have written something better, but I'm glad we let our words come from the heart.

"So, what now?" Ryan asks, leaning her head against the back of the couch.

"Maybe we should go hide in bed," I tell her, rubbing my hand up her thigh. She looks at me, smirking.

"Oh yeah?"

"Yeah."

"Well then, take me to bed."

I get my arms under the back of her knees and around her back and then stand. She squeals in my ear as I run up the stairs to hide away from the world and be in the moment with her.

# CHAPTER THIRTY-THREE

## RYAN

T HE SOUND OF THE blender echoes in the house, reaching me from the kitchen, pulling me from the light doze I've been in. Dom has been up for an hour getting ready for the team workout. With only ten days until the Super Bowl, his days have been even more filled than normal.

It has amazed me how consistent his schedule is every week. Team meetings, workouts, practices, run throughs of the game plan. It's all organized to almost a military precision, something my career has never had. The only time my schedule is similarly regimented is when I'm on tour. This week it all changed, with the Thunderhawks doubling their focus, readying for the big game.

Dom's spirits have been much higher after they won the conference championship, Dom scoring the first touchdown that started an unanswered forty-point run.

With a yawn, I sit up, grabbing the pile of mail from my night-stand I had dropped there last night. A thin envelope falls to the floor, grabbing my attention first. Picking it up from the floor with my fingertips, I look at the return address of my business management firm. One thing I was adamant about when I first started my team was I'd be kept abreast of everything happening through summary reports. There are too many horror stories of someone trusting the wrong person and then finding out when the IRS or someone comes knocking, everything they worked for is gone.

This envelope is much smaller than my normal packet I receive.

Sliding my finger under the flap, I break the seal and pull out the thick, cream paper.

*My love —*

*How many times have I told you my patience was coming to an end? You know I don't like it when you ignore my instructions. It makes me angry, Ryan, when you do not submit to me the way you should. I only have your best interests at heart. We are destined to be together, husband and wife!*

*You must learn your lesson. Only your submission will save you, Ryan.*

*Luckily for you, I have a teacher's heart.*

*I thought sharing the video of you laying with the man currently leading you to ruination would bring you back to the path of light. Your desires are dark and depraved. The way you opened your legs like a wanton whore allowing him to taint your purity with his seed, the way you begged for his filthy hands on your body, should have made you recoil as it did me.*

*But you begged for more. For him to continue rutting into your body like an animal. My body.*

*This pantomime of a relationship shows that I must take matters into my own hands. I know now you are too far gone to return to me on your own. He has you under his spell and it must come to an end so we can be together as we are meant to be. I will have to bring you back by force. To cleanse you.*

*To wash the filth from your skin.*

*It is my cock and my seed that will bring you to the light. My love will burn away the darkness within. I will save your soul, or you will die in the attempt.*

*I will see you soon, my love.*

*Yours, forever.*

The signature. My brain almost can't comprehend what I'm seeing, sure it couldn't possibly be blood. I stare at the paper, stomach roiling. Hurling myself from the bed, I barely make it to the toilet in time, my entire body clenching with every violent heave. Breathing in through my nose and out through my mouth, the cool tile against my legs helps me focus.

Paper crinkles and I see it, the letter crushed in my hand.

A scream crawls up my throat, but my panic holds it inside, afraid to make a noise.

"Ryan? Are you okay?" Dom asks through the door, startling me.

My eyes are glued to the paper ball as I answer. "I'm fine, babe. Just wasn't feeling good. Maybe I caught a bug or something from one of the dancers."

"Do you want me to get you something? A washcloth or some water?" The doorknob jiggles, but luckily in my dash I locked it.

"No, that's okay. Zoe should be here soon and I don't want to get you sick or anything. You should get going. You're going to be late."

"Text me if you need anything, okay?" Guilt rises at the worry in his voice. I refuse to distract him with the newest letter.

"I will."

"I love you," he says, and he pauses, waiting for me to say it back I'm sure. And I want to. But I can't. Not so long as being with me puts his life in danger. He turns from the door and leaves, his footsteps getting quieter the further he moves away from me until I can't hear him at all.

Shifting over, the wood of the vanity is hard against my back. I sit there until my ass goes numb, wondering what I should do.

"Ryan? Dom told me you're sick. What's going on?" Zoe asks through the door. Standing on unsteady legs, I turn the lock, letting my longtime friend in. "Sweetie, you don't look so good. Do I need to call the doctor?"

Bile rises in my throat, burning. "I need to call my mom." My phone sits abandoned on the bedside table. Stilted steps carry me toward the device, my sanity hanging on by a thread.

"Are you pregnant?" Zoe asks abruptly, blocking the doorway, forcing me to look at her. "You're rarely sick. I know this tour has been crazy and with everything else going on, I know you've been all over the place. You *never* throw up. Ever."

"I'm not pregnant," I tell her, my brain unable to even comprehend such a thing right now. Especially with a psycho stalker on the loose.

"It's okay, if you are. You only have this last week of tour and you're not showing." Her eyes fall to my stomach and my arms cross over it in reflex. "We could easily keep it quiet and once the tour is over, you don't even have to leave the house if you don't want. I think we could hide it for your entire pregnancy if that's what you want. Or we could hire a photographer and announce it ourselves. We'll have to up the security team, though. The fee for a picture of you with a baby bump will go for top dollar, so there will be even more paparazzi following you around. I'm sure we can get a private OB-GYN."

The Zoe that's my friend is gone. This Zoe is my publicist and manager. I've received a death threat, one that, after everything I think is pretty credible, and she's worried I'm pregnant.

"Stop! Get out, please," I beg, pushing past her, snatching up my phone. "I need my mom," I say, more to myself than her, dialing the number.

"Sure. I'll be downstairs if you need anything."

She walks out of the room, shutting the door behind herself. I count my breaths, the only thing keeping me together.

Until Mom's face appears on my screen.

"Favorite daughter, how are you, sweetie?"

My lip trembles. "I—" That's as far as I get before tears pour down my cheeks. Muscles burning, sobs grip me. Mom whispers to me in soothing tones. The words are beyond my hearing. She could be reading me her grocery list for all I know. She's not here and fissures are racing through my heart, breaking me beneath the weight of the life I've chosen. Gradually, my sobs turn to crying, then to sniffles. Exhaustion blankets me.

"What's going on, Ryan?" Mom asks, once I've returned after washing my face.

"I got a letter today. From the stalker."

Her eyes sharpen. "What did it say?"

"He said he has to cleanse me, even if it kills me. He's the one who released the video."

She barely moves. I can see her protectiveness settle over her like armor, ready to go to battle to save her daughter. "Have you shared it with the police and Bradford yet?"

My hair falls into my eyes as I shake my head. "Not yet."

"What are you waiting for?"

"To stop puking and sobbing, for one," I say, more bite to my tone than I intend.

"Of course, I'm sorry. I can't imagine what this must feel like. What did Dominic say?"

On the wall by the door is a piece of art from one of my other houses that I had shipped here. It's one of my favorites despite its simplicity. A golden sun sits in the corner of an otherwise blank canvas. The paint on one of the rays runs down, dripping off the bottom. It's that single line of paint that makes me feel sad. Like the sun is crying. My eyes are locked on the painting when I answer the question.

"I didn't tell him." Silence is golden, they say. But it's not the gold of the sun I'm looking at. It's tarnished. Dull. Aged. A few chords play in my head, trying to pull me from the moment into my safe haven of creation. Finally, I can't take the golden silence any longer, and I look in the eyes of the woman who has loved me every day of my life. "I think I should break up with Dom."

There it is.

The thing I haven't said but needed to be put out into the universe. Not because I want to leave Dom, but because it's an option that could lead to de-escalation. Even though I hate it, I have to consider it.

"And you think he'd accept that?"

"It doesn't matter if he accepts it, he can't force me to stay."

She sighs. "Sweetie, all that would do is add another stalker to your life, and I think one is already too many."

"He wouldn't stalk me," I scoff. Her eyebrow raises and I feel thirteen again, caught in a lie about how no boys would be at a birthday party. I wanted my seven minutes in heaven. All she had to do was raise that eyebrow and the truth came tumbling from my lips like an avalanche. "Okay, so maybe I would end up with another stalker. At least I know he wouldn't be threatening to kill me."

"That's a point in his favor," she jokes and I laugh as she intended. "I know you've had to handle so many things on your own. There are very few people that can understand the life you've led. And you have to protect yourself more than most, but if you can't share this burden with Dom, if he wouldn't want to help you carry it, then he's not the guy for you. But if he would be there for you, like I suspect, baby girl, you have to give him a chance. Let him prove to you that you're not alone in this."

"And if he gets killed because I was selfish and didn't push him away?"

Her eyes soften with sympathy. "Letting him love you isn't selfish. Love isn't running away from someone to protect them. And it's not buying them houses without telling them." I shift on the bed. "It's not hiding the messy, hard, dangerous parts of your life. You deserve to be loved as you are. You deserve to have someone love all of you and that includes your job and everything it comes with. Your father and all those stupid friends made you believe you weren't worth anything unless you were useful and that's not true. You're worth everything because you're *you* and Dom knows and he loves you for it. And he's not going to walk away from you without a fight. This isn't forever. He's going to be caught, Ryan. Don't let him steal your life away from you without laying a finger on you."

"I can't risk it," I whisper, my eyes filling with tears. How there are any tears left, I don't know.

"It's Dominic's choice. He can walk away if he thinks that's for the best, but you can't make that decision for him. Let him love you, Ryan."

Cash and Sebastian enter my mind, and all the times they walked away from me, and I realize, for the first time, nothing I could have done would have changed either of those outcomes. No matter how perfect I tried to be, no matter what I did for them, I couldn't force them to be what I needed.

I couldn't force Sebastian to be sober and to want to be a dad.

I couldn't force Cash to be faithful to me.

And I can't force Dom to stay by not telling him everything. If his reaction to finding out I bought this house taught me anything, it's that hiding things from him will be what breaks us. He doesn't need me to be perfect.

He needs me to be *me*.

I nod. "You're right. I'm going to tell him everything."

"Your father and I could come to your last show. If you need us."

"No, that's okay. I don't need to add anyone I care about to the line of fire. I love you."

"I love you, too. Always have, always will. Call me tomorrow."

I blow her a kiss and hang up the phone. Throwing the blankets off me, I stand, more in control than I have been since I opened the letter. *The letter*. Grabbing the paper by the corner, I hold it out from my body, walking downstairs to the living room where I know Zoe and Bradford are waiting for me.

"This needs to go to the police," I tell Brad. He scrambles to get a plastic bag from a drawer, and I drop the letter inside. "And I need the loudest alarm money can buy."

He zips the bag and looks at me, solemn. "I know just the one."

# CHAPTER THIRTY-FOUR

## DOMINIC

RYAN'S BREATHING IS DEEP, a barely noticeable snore with each inhale. The night light in the bathroom, that wasn't there when I went to work this morning, helps me see the outline of her face. Dinner tonight was…weird. It was almost like a Ryan robot was in the house.

She made dinner herself.

Her smile never faltered.

And she refused to talk about whatever was wrong this morning. I was so worried, I called Anya. She guessed Ryan was pregnant and was worried about my reaction. I never planned on having kids without being married first, but I love Ryan. And she's amazing with children. Would it be so bad?

We haven't been using protection and IUDs aren't one hundred percent effective. Maybe she's freaking out because she's on tour? We could hide the pregnancy. She only has a few shows left.

Blaring noise startles me, and Ryan's eyes snap open.

"He's here," she yells, but I can barely hear it above the alarm. Ryan grabs my hand, pulling me. She scrambles from the bed, blankets falling to the floor in her haste.

She shoves me into the closet, pulling the doors shut, and locking them from the inside.

"Wait, when did you put locks on the inside of my closet?" I yell. She doesn't hear me. Wide, glazed eyes stare at the door. Her hands tremble against her chest. "Baby?"

Reaching out to her, cold skin meets my fingers.

"Ryan? Who's here?" She trembles and I don't know what to do.

The sudden silence is almost as deafening as the alarm. Or it might be the residual ringing in my ears. Banging rattles the closet doors and Ryan screams a scream directly out of a horror movie.

I slap my hands over my ears, the sound piercing.

"It's Bradford. We're clear out here," he says. It's like she lost her voice the screaming ends so suddenly. I turn, flipping the lock on the closet door.

"Let's get out of here," I say, turning back to grab Ryan, but no one is standing where she was five seconds earlier. "Ry?"

Some of the clothes on the bottom rack move. Crawling over to her, the carpet is soft beneath my knees. Separating the clothes, I find Ryan, arms around her legs, rocking back and forth.

"Babe?" I say, my voice controlled. Reaching out to her, she shrinks back into my clothes, shattering my heart with her jerky movements. "Ryan. It's okay. Bradford said the coast is clear."

"No. It's a trick. He found me. He's going to kill us. We can't leave," she says in a small voice.

"Ryan, you're safe. It was a false alarm or something. An animal most likely tripped the alarm."

Not that I had an alarm before the day started. That's a different problem for a different time. She shakes her head vigorously, tears starting to trail down her face.

"He promised. He promised he was going to kill me if I didn't break up with you. And I didn't. Now he's going to kill me."

Confusion at her words wars with my need to protect her. Unsure what to do, I look at the closet doors. "Okay. I'm going to go talk to Bradford and then I'll be back, okay? I'll come back for you."

Standing, I move toward the door.

"No!" she yells, her nails scraping down my arm as she hurls herself at me. "Don't go out there! He'll kill you, too."

My heart breaks. Pulling her off me, I squat, pushing her hair behind her ears.

"I'll be right back, okay? Why don't you go hide?"

She nods, crawling back toward the clothes. I swipe the tear leaking from my eye away, knowing I have to deal with this for her so she can feel safe.

Bradford is waiting outside the door, gun holstered. "Is she okay?" he asks.

"No, I think she's having a nervous breakdown. I've never seen her like this. What the fuck happened?"

"Someone tried to break in. They got away. We think the alarm scared them off. But they definitely got too close for comfort."

Sweat covers my body.

"Is there anything to tell us who it was?"

"They were wearing a mask. And they drove a Honda without license plates. The most common car in existence. There won't be any finding them. All we can do is step up our game."

My nails cut the palms of my fists. "And what does stepping up our game mean this time? Huh? I have a panicking girlfriend hiding behind some clothes in my closet crying about how a guy is going to kill her! What the fuck are we doing?"

"We are doing the best we can, Dominic."

"Yeah? Well, it's not good enough." I storm back into the closet, pausing before I go back to Ryan. My anger is not going to help this situation.

Taking a deep breath, I hold it for five seconds before releasing it. On the sixth repetition, my muscles finally relax, and I make my way back to Ryan.

Moving the clothes, I crawl in next to her. Her breathing is less ragged. I grab her hand, linking our fingers together, and wait.

"I've been lying to you," she admits to my shirts. "About how scared I am of this stalker. I've been pushing it down, not thinking about it, because if I thought about it, it became real, and if it became real, I couldn't breathe. So I didn't think about it. I told myself it wasn't a big deal. I pretended like everything was okay, perfect. Like always."

Understanding dawns. The *he* she was talking about was her stalker. I blame my brain being scrambled by the alarm and trying to calm Ryan for not making the connection earlier.

"Will you tell me now?" I ask. I want to hear it. I want to hear everything about how this woman is feeling. I want to be there for her, but you can't be there for someone if they don't tell you what's going on.

And maybe it's on me for not pushing her more.

"The letters started about a year ago. It was funny to me, at first, how he swore we had a connection. It always confuses me a little when people say things like that. You'd think they'd understand who I am on stage isn't all of me." She rolls her eyes. "Then they started getting more direct. 'I want to take you out.' 'We would be perfect together.' 'You're going to be my wife one day.'"

She sniffles, and I think about the day I met her and how I told my sister I was going to marry her. I hadn't known anything about her, yet I was so sure I'd met the woman of my dreams. Am I as bad as her stalker? Or is it different because I *had* met her in person? They always say when you know, you know. Does that count when you meet a celebrity you've "known" for years through their art?

She continues, stopping my downward spiral without even knowing.

"There were never any threats, so the cops couldn't do anything. When you came into my life, we had such a connection, even when we first met, and everything changed. Once we went public, the letters started becoming more and more serious. The one I received this morning was the first one where he finally threatened me. He said he'd cleanse me by assaulting me and if that didn't work, he'd kill me, kill *us,* to end my separation from him. It was signed in blood. That's why I was sick this morning. Not only did it say all of that, it was addressed from one of the various managers I have.

"Many pieces of my life are well known and easy to track down. Some things we have layers upon layers to keep things hidden. The letter was sent through the one that's not public knowledge. He found information that's not readily accessible and used it to terrorize me. I had Bradford install the alarm so we wouldn't be caught unaware.

"I'm scared, Dominic. I'm really scared."

I'm scared, too, but I hold it together, wanting to be strong for her. I kiss the back of her hand, the skin there finally warm once more.

"What can I do to help? Do we need to move again?"

"You would do that?" she asks, looking at me with red-rimmed eyes.

"I would do anything for you. Don't you know that by now?"

"Don't you know it goes both ways? I don't want anything to happen to you," she says, squeezing my fingers.

"Are you ready to get out of this closet?"

She nods and I pull her to her feet. My arm wraps around her shoulders and I guide her downstairs.

"I don't think that alarm was loud enough. I almost slept through it," I joke, trying to get her to stop shaking.

A watery laugh.

That's the only thing she gives me. For now, it's enough.

Bradford is standing in the middle of the living room, talking to other members of the security team. Everyone is dressed in all black. If I didn't realize how imposing they all were to begin with, I definitely would now.

"I'll be bringing on another firm to assist us until this threat is under control. I know them all personally and I would trust them with my life. Any time Ms. Jade and Mr. Reynier are in residence, there will be guards at every point of entry on the first floor with roamers watching the second floor. Luckily, there are not a million windows on this house like there are on some of Ms. Jade's other residences."

The men chuckle at that. He's not wrong. Ryan has a deep affinity for windows, which is a little surprising due to the army of rabid fans.

"Those on shift tonight, I will be talking to each of you individually about what went wrong. Consider yourselves all on probation."

"Hold on, Bradford, I don't think that's necessary," Ryan chimes in, her soft heart wanting to take care of the team she's known for so long.

He turns to look at her, arms crossed over his broad chest.

"Ms. Jade, an armed intruder almost got into the house tonight. Being on probation is the least of their worries." His tone is sure as they have a stare-down. When she refuses to back down, he softens. "Ryan, he dropped his bag going over the fence. There was tape, ropes, and tasers. I'm assuming he had other weapons on his person. He didn't come to say hi and get your autograph. He was prepared and he was coming for you."

Other than a small shiver, she stands strong. I'm much more of a mess. Someone is coming for my girlfriend and no matter what the professionals around us do, it's not enough. And I'm useless to stop it. Sure, I'm a big guy and I hit people professionally, but it's not like I have training against an armed intruder. Maybe I need to work with Bradford on how to protect myself and Ryan in case we are in public and something were to ever happen.

"Good thing we got the alarm then," she says, backing down.

"I would like you to wear this at all times going forward." Bradford holds out a simple looking bracelet and Ryan takes it from him without remark, slipping it on over her hand.

"What's that for?" I whisper as Bradford continues talking to the team.

"Panic button and locator."

I nod. "Are you okay?"

"No."

"Why don't we try and go back to bed?" I ask her, worried about the dark circles under her eyes.

"No, I think I'm going to write a little bit."

"Want some company?" I kiss her shoulder, hoping.

"That's okay. You should try to get some sleep. I'll be up in a bit."

She kisses me and I keep it short despite the desire to pull her close to prove to both of us she's okay. "Write a number one record."

"I always do," she smiles and walks away.

When I hear the door to the media room close, I follow her. The floor outside the room is hard against my ass. It doesn't faze me. I can't leave her alone right now. Not when I came so close to losing her. So I give her the illusion of privacy and listen to the faint music coming through the door.

# CHAPTER THIRTY-FIVE

## RYAN

THE RESTAURANT COULDN'T BE more pretentious if it tried. Sky picked it, begging me to get us in last minute, so I wasn't expecting anything less. It feels weird trying to pretend like everything is okay, but I can't show the cracks in public. Yet it's almost nice, faking like everything is fine and letting go of all the stress and panic for a few hours.

"Ryan, *finally*, it's been so long since you've joined us," Sky says, kissing both my cheeks.

I refrain from rolling my eyes. "It's been a crazy year," I tell her, moving to plant the customary kisses on Karter's cheeks.

"I don't know, you didn't have trouble getting together with us at the beginning of the tour. Now, with that sexy boyfriend of yours, you don't have any time for us," Karter says.

"If I had a boyfriend that looked like that, I'd never spend time with you all either," Taylor says, giving me a hug. She's never been one for the kisses the others require.

"I'm pretty sure you disappeared for six months and wouldn't answer your phone, let alone show up in person when you were talking to that diamond mine heir," I say, my tone joking, but the words make Karter's eyes narrow.

I give her my fake smile and I realize, she might not know it's not my real one and that makes me a little sad. I've been friends with these ladies for so much of my life and other than Taylor, I'm not sure we're really friends.

Not like Dom is with his teammates or his sister.

Maybe he's right. Maybe they've been using me this whole time.

"Do you think we should get a bottle of Dom Perignon?" Sky asks, picking up the alcohol menu first, as always.

"What about one of the Bollinger's? Change it up a bit?" Karter asks.

"I'm going to get a pomegranate martini," Taylor says, tucking her sleek, chocolate brown hair behind her ears. "Ryan? What about you?"

"Some tea and honey, I think," I say, wanting to take care of my voice for my show tomorrow night. I catch Karter's eye roll and ignore it. For someone who's never had a job in her life, she can be pretty judgmental about the things I have to do for mine.

If she can't understand that level of devotion, then I almost feel sorry for her. Without drive and passion for something, life can be very boring, even with endless money. There are only so many yacht trips and parties and things you can go to before they all start blending together.

Maybe that's why Dom and I get along so well. The dedication and drive needed to become a professional football player is the same thing required from me.

A job I love with every fiber of my being. *Stalker be damned*, I think to myself and I almost laugh with the realization. I will not let this man take everything I've worked for, everything I love, from me. Feeling stronger than I have since I opened the letter, my brain starts working on how we can try and draw the stalker out.

Once we give the server our food and drink orders, I turn to Taylor.

"How's everything with the foundation?"

Her smile is blinding and pulls one from me. "It's amazing. We just fit some new lower leg prosthetics for a firefighter. A beam fell in a fire and crushed them."

"I think I saw that on the news. He was very attractive," I say and her cheeks turn almost as pink as the blazer she's wearing today. It's one of her favorites and complements her beautifully.

"I don't notice things like that. It would be inappropriate for me to be attracted to one of our recipients." She grabs her martini from the server's hand, taking a big gulp, finishing it in one go. A tiny belch leaves, her hand flying up to cover her lips. "Oops. Can I get another one, please?" She asks, handing the glass back to our server who disappears once more.

I raise my eyebrow, taking a sip of my honeyed tea. The other girls don't take notice of how flustered Taylor is, but she whispers anyway.

"He's asked me out a few times."

"And you've said no? If I'd met him before Dom, I'm not sure I would've had the strength," I joke, more to get a rise out of her than anything.

"It wouldn't be ethical." She looks up at the server dropping off her new drink. "Thank you."

One thing I love about Taylor is how kind she is. Unlike Sky and Karter, she always treats people well.

"You're not his doctor," I tell her as the other girls laugh loudly at whatever they're discussing.

"I know. You know how brutal the media can be, though. If anyone thinks there's a hint of impropriety, I'm fucked."

"There's nothing improper, Tay. Take the chance. You never know what could happen. I never thought I'd meet someone like Dom setting up for my parent's vow renewal. I almost didn't give him my card and I think I would've regretted it for the rest of my life."

Our server drops our food off and quickly disappears, leaving us to our conversations once more.

"How's everything going with him, by the way? Talk about shitty news coverage with the tape and everything."

"Oh my God, Ryan! Out of everyone to release a sex tape, I never would've included you on the list. Props to you though! You definitely looked hot," Sky says, sipping from her glass of champagne.

"*She* didn't release it, Sky. Didn't you see her and Dominic's livestream?" Taylor says, disgust written on her face.

"I was in Majorca, Taylor," Sky sneers.

"She was busy promoting that music festival, remember?" Karter interjects. "Speaking of which, Ryan, do you think we can borrow your plane next month? There's a red carpet for a film release in

New York that we want to walk. I've been flirting with the lead in my DMs."

*"I can buy a plane ticket, babe. You don't have to rent me a whole ass jet. It's only me,"* Dom's voice says inside my head.

A switch flips and I realize, I can't do this anymore. I can't pretend like my friendships with Sky and Karter are real. They are exactly like Sebastian and even Cash, to an extent, and I'm done. If my career ended tomorrow and I lost everything, I know in my heart I'd never hear from Sky and Karter again.

And I deserve better.

I turn to Taylor. "Want to get out of here?"

"I thought you'd never ask." She drops her napkin on the table and pushes her chair back.

"What the fuck? You're leaving?" Sky says, flabbergasted.

"Don't pretend like you care. The only thing you care about is what my name can get you. Feel free to delete my number."

We start to walk out, Karter yelling at us across the dining room. "Aren't you going to pay for your food?"

I turn back and grin. "Considering all the trips and dinners and everything I've paid for, for both of you, I think you can get this one."

Their mouths drop open and I link my arm through Taylor's and we walk into the beautiful day.

Once Bradford has us safely tucked into the car, I let her see my imperfections. I tell her everything about me and Dom and the stalker. She hugs me, telling me how it'll all be okay. And I believe it.

Safely home, we head out to the backyard and sit by the pool, four guards posted around the yard.

Super normal.

"What are you going to do?" she asks after I tell her of the latest letter I received.

"I don't know. We have to catch the guy and I don't have any idea who he is."

"How's Dom dealing with all of this?"

"Amazing, all things considered." No matter how well he's taking everything in stride, I want to protect him.

And until this guy is caught, neither of us are safe.

"What if you fake break up?" Taylor asks, looking out at the pool.

"Like, just in public?"

"Yeah! You could release a statement to the press 'Our schedules weren't working' or whatever to get the heat off you for a bit."

I consider the idea, knowing exactly who I could call to release such a story. The sliding glass door sounds on the tracks, stopping my response, and we look back, my lips parting at Dom's wet, tousled hair.

"Hi, sorry to interrupt. I wanted to let you know I'm home." He comes over and gives me a kiss before holding his hand out to my friend who stands to shake his. "I'm Dominic. It's nice to meet you."

"Taylor Neuman. Sorry for invading your house."

"No apologies necessary. Ryan can invite whomever she'd like into our home."

*Our* home. I glow at that.

"Taylor is in charge of AeroFlex Prosthetics."

He looks at my friend with interest. "Wow, that's amazing! My sister did the desserts for your most recent gala."

"We met at one of your games, actually, and with Ryan vouching for her, I knew I had to hire her. The cake she made for us was a huge hit. Anastasia is amazing!" she says.

"I agree, but I'm biased. Babe, can I talk to you for a second?"

"Of course!" I say, jumping up from my chair.

"It was nice meeting you," he says, turning toward the house. Following him, I close the door behind me. "What time are you leaving tonight? Or have you decided to fly tomorrow morning?"

"I'm leaving tonight. All of my stuff is in the car. I didn't want to leave before you got home from practice."

His arms come around my waist pulling me to him. I can feel him starting to harden behind his jeans. "I know how I can make sure you miss me when you're gone," he says, lighting my insides on fire.

"I think we should break up," I blurt and his eyes go wide.

# CHAPTER THIRTY-SIX

## DOMINIC

M Y ARMS FALL AWAY from her and my eyes begin filling with tears. I've never cried at the end of a relationship before, yet the thought of never seeing or talking to Ryan again, never tasting her, I can hardly bear it.

"You want to break up?"

"What I meant to say was I think we should break up as far as the world is concerned. A fake break up. Taylor mentioned it and I think it's a good idea. Maybe I could do an interview and try to lure him out? Or get him to back off if he thinks I'm single again? I didn't mean to scare you, I'm sorry."

She grabs my face, pressing gentle kisses to my lips.

"I think my heart stopped. You can't go blurting out you want to break up, Ryan!"

"Baby, I'm sorry! Of course, I don't want to break up with you. I don't think I can imagine my life without you. We have to do *something* to try and get all this scary crap to end. There are four bodyguards in the backyard right now and like six more in here guarding all the doors and windows. Don't you think that's insane?"

"Yes, it's insane! It's all been insane. But it's what we had to do."

"Exactly. We had to do it. What if we have to do this? You have the Super Bowl in a little over a week. I have shows for the next three nights and then the last three shows next weekend. I can go stay at one of my other houses between cities. This way, you can focus on football and we can try to bring an end to this."

I shift around, not liking the option. Even though I can see the logic behind it.

"But I'll miss you," I say, almost whining. I've gotten way too used to her being here whenever she doesn't have concerts.

"I'll miss you, too. And we can talk. We just won't be able to see each other in person."

"I don't like this. We have all the security systems here and then we'll be splitting the team. Have you talked to Bradford about this?"

She grabs my face, thumbs rubbing my temples. "I wanted to get you on board first and if you agree, we can talk to him together. You need to decide soon so we can get everything in place before I leave tonight. Luckily, we already knew I was going to be gone. This is only extending the plan already in place."

Nodding, I move away from her, pacing a little. Trying to get my thoughts in order. Wanting this to finally be over, and not having any other ideas, I decide to go along with this plan.

"Fine. We can break up. Just know, I'm not happy about it, even if it is fake."

An email dings on my phone and I smile. The package I got for Ryan was delivered. Checking the time, I calculate she only has forty-five minutes until she leaves for the venue. Taking the stairs two at a time, I video call her. It's only been forty-eight hours without her and I'm over it.

"Babe, a package should be there from me. Go get it," I tell her when she picks up, hair already pressed straight.

"What kind of package?" she asks, giddy.

"The fun kind." I hear the front door open and close. "Take it to your bedroom."

"Did you send me a sex doll?" she jokes, following my instructions.

"Something like that."

The room is fairly nondescript. It's beautiful, of course, like all the rooms she stays in are. It just lacks any personality or individualism, a rental property through and through.

She rips the box open and pulls out a smaller red one.

"What the hell is this?" she asks, her eyebrows drawn down in confusion as she reads it. I grin, waiting for her to get it. "Wait, you're going to fuck me with this?"

"Yup! Listen, I know it's been crazy lately and we haven't had a chance to connect in that way with all the stress and now the fake breakup. I want to make you feel good before you go out on the stage. You in?"

"Fuck, yes. What do I need to do?"

My dick hardens instantly.

"Get on the bed. Set some pillows up and lean the phone against them. Then get in front of the camera and open your robe." I can already see the wetness between her legs. "Perfect, now take it out of its package."

While she grabs hers, I pull up the app on my phone as well as the piece I need. The silicone is soft and feels similar to a person. It'll never feel as good as having Ryan herself, but we have to work with what we have.

"Now what?" she asks, her eyes focused on the ribbed cock in her hand.

"Turn it on, then pull up your phone. I put an app in there. It's called 'LoveUrself.' It came preloaded with the toy." I turn mine on, the blue light indicating it's paired. "Good. Now put it in your pussy."

She reaches between her legs and follows my instructions, my mouth watering as I watch the toy stretch her.

Sticking my dick at the opening of my toy, I pull it down roughly, the silicone stretching to accommodate my size. Ryan's eyes go wide and her body jumps. "Do you feel that?"

"Holy shit! Yes!"

I slowly pull out before thrusting in again and she moans, her eyes closing. "Dom, holy *shit*, this is the best toy."

"Open your eyes and look at me, baby."

Her teal eyes are filled with lust, her chest heaving. My hand starts pumping the sleeve faster and faster, her legs fall open.

"Where was this—" she cuts off with a groan, her back arching off the bed as I switch angles. "Where was this on all the weekends we were separated?"

"Does it feel good, baby? Me fucking you like this?" I say through gritted teeth, my orgasm careening toward me.

"Dom, I'm going to come. Don't stop. Don't stop. Don't—" I watch as her entire body tightens, mouth dropping open.

Her orgasm breaks over her, legs pulsing with it. I don't stop, fucking her through her entire release until she lays in a boneless heap against the pillows. My dick is as hard as a diamond and I keep taking her, enjoying watching her in the aftershock of pleasure, until I come with a groan.

I check the clock on my phone.

"Babe, you need to get going."

"Huh?" she mumbles, partially asleep and I laugh.

"Your concert."

She awakens with a start. "Fuck! I have to go!" She grabs the toy and pulls it from her pussy, her wetness glistening there.

Scrambling off the bed, she pauses, leaning in front of the camera. "I'll call you tomorrow," she says, blowing me a kiss.

"Have a good show," I say right before the picture cuts out.

I climb off the bed and move to the bathroom to clean myself and the toy. Best money I've ever spent.

# CHAPTER THIRTY-SEVEN

## RYAN

IT'S BEEN SEVEN DAYS since Dom and I decided fake breaking up would be the best way to try and draw my stalker out of the shadows. When I was standing in front of my boyfriend, I was sure, positive even, I could handle it and I'd do anything to end this.

Standing in the middle of an empty stadium at sound check, I feel differently.

The ocean of empty seats stretching out before me could have a killer in one of them within the next twelve hours. When Dom and I announced via spokespeople about our separation, the news exploded across the world.

Even though it's fake, I hate everyone thinking I don't want to be with him.

There are guards everywhere and it'll be much harder to get to me here than, say, when I'm getting on my plane after this weekend.

Dom's playing in the Super Bowl in two nights and, caught stalker or not, I want to be there for him. He quickly forbade it though, saying if we don't catch him, it'll show we were lying if I'm at the game.

Logically, his argument makes sense.

Emotionally, his argument is shit and I hate it.

The music cuts out and I realize I've been standing, staring at the seats for the past few minutes. My dancers circle around me.

"Boss? You alright?" June, my lead dancer, asks, breathing heavily. Normally they don't do sound checks with me by this point in the tour, but I asked them to be here with me to give me support.

And since they are amazing people, they easily agreed.

"Sorry, I was off in my own little world right there." I put my mouth up to my microphone. "Can we take it from the top?"

The electronic voice in my monitors starts the countdown for the song again and we all hustle to our spots. I strike a pose and try not to think about my stalker for thirty more minutes.


Once sound check is over, I hustle back to my rental house for a video call with the lead detective back in Los Angeles to confirm what's going to happen tonight. They've been working tirelessly sharing information with the police local to my concert, trying to keep me and my Jade Stones safe.

"This conversation will be an hour. Then we have the interview set. Marline is already at the house. Security is watching her closely, so don't worry," Zoe says, running through her ever-present list.

"I'm not worried. I trust Marline."

Marline Washington has been a constant in my career. Whenever I want to share something with the public on camera, I go to Marline.

We pull into the driveway and I'm quickly ushered into the house. The gated community is private. Not as private as the one I live in with Dominic, however, most people wouldn't expect Ryan Jade to be hiding out in a retirement community, so we've been unbothered since we landed. Different from the normal places I'd stay, we hoped we could fly under the radar.

"Miss Jade, the head of S.W.A.T. is in the living room," a uniformed officer says, opening the door for us before we even reach it.

"Thank you," I say, moving past him at a quick clip, ready to get this over with.

Pulling out my phone, I video call Dominic.

"Ry," he says in greeting, his voice firm.

"Ready?" I ask, and he nods, turning his phone to the head of the investigation.

"Hello. For those of you who don't know me, I'm Detective Davies of the LAPD. Lieutenant Smith, would you like to run through your plans for everyone?" he asks the S.W.A.T commander.

"Sure. In one hour at nine hundred hours, Miss Jade is going to make a statement to the press calling out her stalker by leaving veiled messages for him throughout the interview. It will air at eleven hundred hours. Ms. Washington will ask specific questions to allow Miss Jade to give the answers as provided by myself.

"At twelve hundred hours, Mr. Reynier will go to the stadium for practice. While we do not think he is the primary target, we will be on the look out. At fifteen hundred hours, Miss Jade and her team will head to the stadium to prepare for her concert. Once there, her normal routine will be followed. I have provided the list of activities to all of my personally vetted officers. You will not be alone for a second," he says, directing the last bit to me. All I can do is nod.

"Great. Let's go through the plan if he should show," the detective on the phone says, and we run through the plan again.

All of these things were communicated to me via email which I've read like a bedtime story every night, but hearing them aloud again allows for me to mentally run through them one more time. A mentor once told me being prepared mentally and visualizing success can be as important as any other preparation.

Exactly an hour after the meeting began, we end. I take my phone back from the commander and smile at Dom.

"Are you going to score a touchdown for me today?"

His smile doesn't reach his stern eyes. "It's only practice, babe."

"Dom, it's practice for one of the biggest games of your entire career! You should be excited and promising your girlfriend you'll score for her. That way you're prepared to score for me on Sunday!"

"You're right," he says, dragging a hand down his face. "I'm just worried. Yes, every time I touch the ball, it's for you. We'll celebrate once all this is over. I miss you."

"I miss you, too."

"Go to your interview. You're going to do great. I'll be able to watch most of it before I have to leave. I love you."

My response is on the tip of my tongue, trapped behind my teeth. I don't want the first time I tell him I love him to be when we are hundreds of miles apart.

"Go kick ass," I tell him, blowing him a kiss and hanging up the phone once he's sent me one in return.

"This way," Zoe says, stepping up to my elbow, leading me to the screened in back patio where Marline waits.

Olive skin glowing beneath the lights, her red nails tap on her phone screen. Perking up when I enter, we smile at each other.

"Ryan, you look amazing. You always do." She kisses one of my cheeks in greeting and I return the gesture.

"I saw your girlfriend finally proposed. Congratulations. Let me see the ring." Obliging, she holds her hand out, showing off a showstopper of a ring, the intricate filigree around the main stone, catching my eye. "It's gorgeous. I never had any doubt. She's always had such amazing taste."

"Especially in fiances," she says, sitting back down. "Off the record, how are you doing?"

I take a deep breath and relax. This is why I love Marline. She thinks of me as a human first, second, and third, and a pop star fourth. "I'm scared. At the same time though, I hope it works."

"Not that you asked, but I love you and Dominic together. You seem like you fit together."

"He's it for me," I tell her and her eyes well. Not because she's sad she can't use the quote, but because she knows what it means for me.

"Well then. Let's get this guy thrown in jail so we can get your happily ever after."

The countdown begins and we both slip into our professional personas, the red light flaring to life.

"In a few hours, Ryan Jade is going to perform one of her last shows for the Radiance tour. This morning, we are sitting down with her, reflecting on the last eighteen months of her life and her most recent heartbreak," Marline says talking directly to the camera before turning to me. "Thank you so much for talking with us this morning, Ryan. And congratulations on the crowning achievement the Radiance tour has turned into."

"I'm so happy to be here with you, Marline. It's a little bittersweet. I don't know what I'm going to do with all my free time." We both laugh on cue. "This has been the tour of my life to this point. It has been amazing to share it with all my Jade Stones and the special people in my life."

This was my cue to her to start getting into my relationship status. Her face turns to practiced sadness.

"Speaking of special people, let's talk about you and Dominic Reynier. You met, fell in love, and then decided you didn't like football? What happened?"

I actually give a genuine laugh. "Oh, no. I love football. Things with Dominic just weren't the same after the sex tape leaking. I realized all the deviant desires he was awakening inside of me were wrong and shameful. I didn't want to have to keep pretending it was okay. He brought me the greatest pleasure I've ever had, but it was all too much."

Marline leans in, engaged. "Ryan, tell us the truth. Did Dominic record the two of you having an intimate relationship without your knowledge or consent?"

Here's where it gets tricky. We think it would play well to the stalker if it seems like I'm covering for them and their misdeeds, but I don't want to throw Dominic under the bus. No matter that we will be walking all of this interview back once the stalker is caught, there are going to be people who believe Dom was the perpetrator.

"I'm saying we broke up for a reason and I'm going to be patient next time and make sure I pick the right person. I'm ready to be a wife." I turn toward the camera, picturing the stalker on the other side, listening. "I want to make sure the next person I'm with wants to be my husband," I tell him.

"Let's pause there for a second," Marline instructs the camera operator. The red light indicating he's recording goes off. "That was amazing, Ryan. Do you think it'll work?" She pulls her compact out of her purse, dusting her nose with powder. When we do these interviews normally, our makeup teams would be off to the side, ready to rush in and fix any perceived imperfection the second we needed a touch up.

This time, it's just us and the cameraperson.

"I hope so. I'm ready to get back to Dom."

She reaches over, grabbing my hands. "You'll be together soon enough. Once this is over, it'll all be worth it. You'll be safe and together and you can put this all behind you."

I link our fingers together, missing having Dom's physical touch as comfort. It's not the same with Marline, but it feels nice.

"I hope you're right."

She signals to the cameraperson and they start counting us down and we separate, once more ready to be recorded. When the red light turns back on, Marline smiles and I wonder if I've done enough.

# CHAPTER THIRTY-EIGHT

## DOMINIC

THE BALL BOUNCES OFF my helmet and everyone groans. If this were any other week, I'd be running suicides until I was puking my guts up. With less than forty-eight hours until the Super Bowl, the coaches are going a little more lenient on us.

Then again, maybe running some suicides until I couldn't run anymore would finally get my head off of Ryan, her stalker, and how badly this could all go.

Whistles blowing, the wide receiver coach comes over, grabbing my face mask.

"What the fuck is wrong with you, Reynier? Your little girlfriend broke up with you and now you can't catch the ball? Get your head out of your ass before I trade you and make you watch the Super Bowl from the sidelines, crying!" he yells into my face, spittle flying.

"Yes, sir," I say, knowing there's nothing that can dig me out of this hole except my undivided focus.

Every time I try to focus and run my route, the thought of Ryan bleeding out on the ground pops up and it's all I can do to keep myself upright.

"Run it again!" he yells, blowing his whistle, my ear ringing from the proximity.

Jogging back in place, I draw my attention inside my body.

Muscles tensed, ready to run.

Heart pounding.

Lungs billowing.

The ball is snapped, and I'm off in a dead sprint down the sideline. Logan rears back and hurls it, a perfect spiral. My hands cradle the contours of the ball, pulling it into my stomach in a tight grip. The defense comes at me from the left, shoving me with two hands just enough to throw me off balance and out of bounds.

"Fucking, finally! Nice of you to join us, Reynier!" Coach yells before calling the next play.

Seventeen plays later, practice is finally done. Sweat runs down my body as I walk into the locker room.

"Dominic, meet me in my office," Coach Williamson says, walking off to talk to one of the training staff.

When the head coach wants to see you after a shitty practice, it's not normally good news. Sighing heavily, I make my way to his door and wait.

"Come in, son," he says, clapping me on the back, pushing his door open. "Shut the door."

I stay standing as he moved around his desk, sitting down and leaning back in his chair. His bushy mustache twitches.

"Ryan's security team briefed me and the head of security here on the situation. How are you doing?"

"I've had better days. Either way, I'm sorry for my inattention today at practice."

He swivels back and forth in his chair. I think about standing beneath the lights last year and how badly I wanted to win. Now, this chance at redemption is here, and I might get benched all because I lost focus.

I trained my entire life to be a Super Bowl champion, but I can't find it in myself to care.

Because Ryan matters more.

Ryan matters most.

"When the pressure is on, are you going to be able to focus?"

Standing up straight, I want to give him the 'yes' I know he's looking for. Instead, I settle on the truth.

"I'll do everything in my power to do so."

He waves me out of the room without a word.

Guys laughing and talking assaults my ears as I walk over to the lockers. Tim's towel is wrapped around his waist, water dripping off his hair.

"How was the meeting with Coach?" he asks, pulling his boxer briefs out and putting them on beneath the towel. "Are you getting benched?"

"I don't know, man," I say, taking off my jersey and pads and dropping them on the floor. "He wasn't exactly thrilled with my performance today."

"I'm sure the breakup has been hard, it seemed like you really liked her. Maybe it's for the best? Now you can both be with someone who won't hold you back from your dreams. I had to break up with

Paige because she was too busy following Ryan Jade around. Pretty sure she was half in love with her, too. It was always 'Ryan this' and 'Ryan that.'"

The statement shocks me. I hadn't realized they were dating, but my focus had been solely on Ryan.

"Yeah, it's for the best." My voice is monotoned but he doesn't notice, pulling his shirt over his head. Deciding to shower at home, I throw on my clothes and head out of the facility.

Reporters yell my name and questions at me from behind the barricade as I walk to the car with my security team. I ignore them.

Slamming the car door shut behind me, I pray Ryan's stalker is caught tonight so I can stop worrying about her safety and start worrying about salvaging my dreams.

The air conditioner awoke with a shake and clang. Every hour and twelve minutes, the noise would start, air blowing into the hotel room. Despite the rare occurrence that our city is hosting the Super Bowl this year, *and* we are playing in it, we still stayed in a hotel so we could focus.

Not that focusing, let alone sleep, has been easy with the air conditioner from hell.

And knowing Ryan's stalker is still free in the world.

He hasn't sent Ryan any more letters, which is good, but he also hasn't shown up like we were hoping, but there's one more chance.

Minutes tick by on the clock, my alarm blaring when it flips to eight. Ten hours from now, I'll be playing in the Super Bowl.

I pick up my phone intending to call Ryan, her face flashing on the screen.

"I was getting ready to call you," I tell her, propping the phone up against the pillow next to me, turning to lay on my side, matching her position.

"I must be a pretty good girlfriend to be able to read your mind like that."

"You're the best one in my book. I can almost let all the others go, that's how great you are," I joke, smiling as she frowns.

"Saying I'm one of many, huh? You realize I could have a ripped, beautiful man here in twenty minutes, ready to take care of me?" she asks, playing along.

"Nuh huh. I'm farther than twenty minutes away and there's no one that compares."

"I see someone's feeling cocky today. Are you ready for the game?"

The freckles on her nose enchant me as she sniffs, wiggling down further into her blankets. My eyes trace the sweep of her cheek. Her puffy lips begging to be kissed.

"I'm more worried about you than the game," I tell her, softly. "The night of the break-in really scared me and I want you to be okay."

"I know, love. This has been the hardest thing I've ever experienced, but it's going to be okay. There will be more security than I've ever had. The stage is huge. If they show up, they aren't getting close to me before they get caught," she reassures me, and I think, reassures herself a little.

In her speech, I didn't miss the fact she called me 'Love.' I want to smile, almost tease her for the slip, but I don't. I'll never pressure her to tell me she loves me, even though I'm pretty sure she does.

"Kick him hard in the nuts if he gets close to you. Better yet, aim at him with those killer spikes on your heels. Those will do some damage."

She laughs, her face brightening and for a moment, all I know is how much I care about this girl.

"I'll make sure to give him a good kick, heel or no."

"Good. I miss my amazing, best I've ever had, girlfriend being in my bed."

"I miss my blanket hog of a boyfriend," she jokes, giving me her slightly imperfect, completely real smile.

A calendar reminder scrolls across the top of my phone and I dismiss it with a flick of a finger.

"Baby, I have to go. Team breakfast."

"Good luck tonight! I told Zoe to get me a TV or something for under the stage so I can watch during costume changes. Score me a touchdown."

"I'll score you two, just because I like ya."

We blow each other kisses and I hang up, smiling at the black screen, throwing the blankets off. That conversation did more for me than ten hours of sleep ever could.

Breakfast is a large buffet made specific to our team dietitian's requirements. Bacon, eggs, pancakes, yogurt, and fruit as far as the eye can see.

"My bed smelled like feet. I'm pretty sure they forgot to change the sheets," Tim says, shoveling eggs onto his plate, a slight hitch to his step.

"My AC unit had a personal vendetta against me or something. I couldn't sleep through the racket," I say, following behind him, filling up my plate with twice as many eggs. We'll eat again before the game, but I prefer to keep myself fueled throughout the day so I don't overeat at any one meal.

We move over to the tables in the ballroom, silverware already at each place, as well as a glass of water, orange juice, and a carafe of coffee. Tim tucks into his eggs, wrinkles his nose, and grabs the salt and pepper from the middle of the table, dumping what feels like half the shaker out.

Picking up a pancake from my plate, I put two slices of bacon, a heap of eggs, and a dollop of syrup on top before folding it like a taco and biting in. Tank sits down at our table, taking a deep drink of coffee before mumbling what I believe is good morning.

"You going to actually catch the ball today? Don't need a sleepless night losing us points," Tim says, a bite to his tone, nerves probably getting the best of him.

Tank cocks an eyebrow, looking between us. "What's your field goal percentage this season, again?"

Tim scowls at him and I jump in, not wanting there to be any riffs on the team during such a big day. "I promised Ryan I'd get a touchdown for her, so I have to catch it."

"I thought you two broke up?" Tim asks.

Fuck.

Fuck.

*Fuck.*

"Oh, yeah, we did," I lie, sticking to our plan of not telling a soul the breakup is fake. "She called this morning, though. Wanted to wish me good luck. She's a good person, like that. There aren't any hard feelings."

He looks at me, taking a bite of pancake, and chews without breaking eye contact. "Sounds like she's still hung up on you, bro."

"Maybe a little."

"You hung up on her?"

I take a drink of orange juice, washing my breakfast down past the lump forming in my throat. "Maybe a little."

We both focus on our plates once more. The room fills out as people take their seats. While it's the Super Bowl, this feels exactly like every other start to a game day we've had throughout the season. Maybe that's a good thing. Letting the pressure go and settling into the routine of football.

Maybe the routine can help me let go of the stalker distraction and get my mind ready for what's ahead.

Ryan's right. We've done everything we can to protect her. It has to be enough.

Our last media engagement before the game is a circus. It was crazy last year, but the number of people this time is easily double, if not triple. Geoff stands off to the side, ready to step in as needed. I'm sandwiched by Logan and Coach Williamson.

Last year, no one cared about talking to me.

This year, thanks to Ryan, I'm a main draw.

"Dominic!" one reporter shouts, raising her hand, butt almost leaving the chair in her excitement. I point to her and everyone quiets. "How are you doing since the breakup? Is your mind focused on the game or the loss of your girlfriend?"

I look to Geoff and he nods. We prepared for this question, and many like it, in the days leading up.

"Any time I'm on the field, my focus is on my brothers and our opponents. Everything I have will be focused on the biggest stage in this game, and I'll be laying it all out on the field like I know every other person will."

Logan nods, leaning toward his microphone. "This is part of being a professional athlete. To compete at the highest level, you have to be able to compartmentalize. There's no way to be here and not be mentally tough. Reynier is focused on the job at hand."

When it's obvious we are done answering the question, everyone's hands go up again. Coach Williamson points to one.

"What does it mean for you and your team to be playing this game in your home stadium?" the guy asks, pen poised.

"Thunderhawk fans are the best in the country. To be home with them during this game, it brings a level of energy and excitement you don't get in other cities," Coach says.

"How does it feel to be back here a second year in a row?" one of the reports calls out before we can pick someone else.

I jump in to answer.

"It feels like there's still work to be done."

Coach claps me on the back as Geoff steps up to the front. "Our time with Logan and Dominic is over. Tank Carlston and Tim Blankenship will take over."

We stand, smiling and waving as we walk off the stage. Walk through is quick, and there's just enough time for me to go back up to my room and take a short nap. By the time I wake up, the sun hangs low in the sky. Checking my phone, I shoot off a text to Ryan, wishing her luck on her last concert. Turning it off, I tuck it into my pocket and head downstairs to get on the bus.

The guys are quiet. It's almost eerie. I can feel the concentration radiating from them. Squeezing past our backup kicker, talking in hushed whispers to his coach, I slide into the seat next to Tank. He holds up his fist, and I tap my knuckles against his. My brain plays snap cadences, running through every play in our playbook, visualizing myself scoring touchdowns. I'm so deeply in the zone, it's almost a surprise when I'm standing in the tunnel, ready to go.

This year, my ankle is taped perfectly.

"Men. Tonight is the night we prove the haters wrong. Show them we deserve to be here. Show them what happens when they come to our house. Team on three. One. Two. Three," Logan yells.

"Team!" we respond.

Turning toward the opening of the tunnel, we head out into the lights, my mouth stretched wide in a smile.

# CHAPTER THIRTY-NINE

## RYAN

**M**Y HANDS ARE SHAKING. I'm about to take the stage for the last time on this tour, hoping my stalker makes his presence known. The last two nights were uneventful, but there's still time. Looking at my phone that's sitting face up on the couch in my dressing room, I smile at Dom's message.

**Dom: Kill it out there**

**Dom: Every touchdown is for you**

**Dom: I love you**

We've talked constantly, and yet there's a cloud hanging over all of our conversations. Not knowing when we'll be able to be seen together again is wearing us both thin. After tonight, we both have time off.

We need to take a vacation.

To a private island.

Alone.

I take a deep breath and let it out to the count of ten, trying to get my heart to stop racing. Zoe's knock at the door is right on time and yet, it feels like it's too early. She pushes the door open and I turn to her.

"Do you have the game on under the stage?" I ask her, caring only about Dom.

"We could only get it on a tablet this time. You'll be able to see it anytime you're changing costumes." When I instructed them to figure out how to keep me updated on the Super Bowl, Zoe gave me an exasperated look. Like how could I not know she'd already have taken care of it. Especially since I had a pretty bad breakdown at the fact I wouldn't be able to attend the game until this guy is caught.

"And the cops?"

"Everyone is prepared. It's all going to be fine. Trust me."

"I do," I tell her, following her out to the golf cart, surrounded by what feels like an army.

My leg bounces as we drive. Zoe, tapping away on her phone, presses her hand to my knee in silent command.

Dancers and stagehands run around backstage, the cops standing vigil, eyes scanning the crowd. Rumors have been circulating the past few days about the increased level of security. I haven't confirmed anything for the team beyond telling them to follow any and all instructions given to them no matter what's going on.

They looked nervous, but they're professionals. And the show must go on.

I crawl through the darkness, seeing the tablet as I pass, the national anthem playing.

Crouching down on my platform, the voices in my monitors start counting down as I begin to rise.

For the last time, I raise the microphone to my mouth and sing.

*Pulse of the party, with a groove so sweet,*
*Catching dreams like confetti, dancing on our feet.*

The crowd is possessed.

In all my years in this business, I've never once seen a crowd like this.

Tears stream down faces. Screaming themselves hoarse. They're so loud even my monitors almost can't block them out. My team and I are feeding off their energy and giving it all back to them plus some.

I hold my pose as I'm lowered beneath the stage, one of my longer costume changes. A bottle of water is held out to me, which I chug as costumers pull at my shoes and zippers. Eyes glued to the tiny tablet, I watch the game, stepping out of my clothes automatically.

*"Dominic Reynier has been on a tear today. Already received ten passes for over a hundred yards. Samuels and Reynier are on fire. But the Thunderhawks have had some costly mistakes on defense and that missed field goal might be the difference here tonight,"* the announcer says, via closed caption.

Before the next play can start, I'm rushing to my spot, jumping onto the platform that's already rising.

Three more songs, the concert is halfway over, and I notice movement to the side of the stage as I spin around. More and more audience members start looking over to the side. At the pause between songs, I look at Zoe on the floor to the left of the stage, her face ashen as she watches something happening in the wings. Before I get confirmation of whether it's my stalker or not, the next song starts.

# CHAPTER FORTY

I FLY OFF THE stage as confetti rains down. Normally, the last show of a tour would be bittersweet and I'd take my time soaking it in. This time, I want to get to my dressing room and watch the rest of Dom's game. The third quarter just started and there's no time for nostalgia right now. I might regret my hasty retreat tomorrow, but tonight? Tonight is for supporting the man I love.

Zoe is by my side the moment I'm off stage, my parents already tucked away back at the rental, waiting. They'll have to wait a little longer.

"Was it him?" I ask, hustling through the tunnel and toward my dressing room.

"No. It was a fan that had a sign to hold up asking for your autograph," she says, switching between a walk and light jog to keep up with me. I'm disappointed, without letting it distract me.

"Is the game on?"

"Yes, it's all ready for you. I sent Paige to grab some food for you. She'll be back in a minute. I'm going to check in with Bradford and then I'll be back."

"Thanks," I say, pulling the door open for my dressing room, rushing in, security posting up on each side of the door.

The tablet sits on the table. Rushing toward it, I wake up the screen and check the score, bouncing in excitement at our lead. Setting it back down, I reach under my arm and grab the zipper on my last outfit, cold metal against my temple stopping me.

"Don't scream, or you die," a voice says behind me. Turning slowly, shaking, I look into Tim's eyes. "Hello, Ryan," he says, serene. "I've come to take you home."

If he didn't have a gun pointed at me, you'd think he asked me how my concert went for how calm he looks. The crowd cheers for something happening and the moment feels surreal.

"Why aren't you at the game?" I need to press the button on my bracelet, but I'm scared if I move, he'll pull that trigger.

"This was more important. You see, Reynier told me you called him today. Wished him luck." His brow turns down, a bite of anger edging into his voice. "You disobeyed me *again*. It was bad enough having to watch you give your body over to Reynier, but to know you tried deceiving me? I knew our lessons couldn't wait any longer." He takes a step toward me and I back up automatically. "I told you not to move."

"How did you get in here?" I ask, trying to distract him long enough for Paige to bring me my food or for someone to come and check on me. "There's security all over the place."

"Do you know how many employees it takes to run these stadiums? No one here knows everyone. It took a security jacket and a concession employee running late for their shift to get in the door. And since your team was focused on protecting you wherever you were, no one was worried about an empty dressing room or the backdoor seemingly blocked by equipment in the middle of a concert. Now stand up. We have a plane to catch."

"I'm not going anywhere with you," I tell him. His hand tightens, finger dancing on the trigger. I look up into his face, anger dripping off every plane. Something inside me shifts, settles. I feel a smile light my face, the performance of a lifetime starting. "I'm sorry. That wasn't very nice. Would you mind if I changed before we left? This dress could attract attention."

Tension releases from his shoulders and the corners of his lips lift. He steps back, putting space between us, the gun still pointing at me.

"Good idea. But make it quick."

The handle on the door turns. "Ryan? I was able to get some food left over from craft services," Paige says, trying to push the door open.

Time slows. Tim spins around, aiming the gun at the door. Making a split-second decision, I throw my body into the back of his legs, wrapping my arms around him in a tackle I hope would make Dominic proud. The gun goes off. Paige is screaming, but I can't look and make sure she's okay as Tim and I fall to the floor, the gun jostling from his hand as we land. I reach up, grabbing one arm with all my might, keeping him from grabbing the gun.

Security bursts through the door as Tim breaks my hold, Bradford shooting him in the arm with a taser. Tim flops around on the floor, electrical current racing through his body.

"You're okay?" he asks me, moving to the groaning Tim, flipping him over and zip tying his hands behind his back.

"I'm okay," I say, shaking taking over my body. Moving over to Paige, I kneel in the scattered food, hugging her to me.

"Tell me you weren't hit," I demand into her hair.

"It missed me."

Zoe comes in. Tears choke me as we make eye contact. She drops to the floor, hugging Paige and I and the dam holding back my emotions breaks.

"It's over," she says and I can hardly believe it.

She lets me cry for a moment before pulling back and drying my tears. "You should go to the game."

"I can't leave, Paige."

"Yes, you can," Paige says. "Please, go to the game. I'm begging."

Searching her eyes, I see her conviction. "Okay."

Zoe pulls me to my feet. "Brad. I'm taking her. Have the cops call me. She'll give her statement in the air and be back tomorrow, if needed. We have a game to get to."

He looks up at us and gives a thumbs up, pausing the conversation on the phone I didn't realize he was having.

"Better get a move on," he says, pointing to two of my normal guards, indicating they should go with us.

With Zoe steady beside me, her arm around my waist, we run.

# CHAPTER FORTY-ONE

## DOMINIC

"Killing it tonight, Reynier," Coach says, slapping my shoulders. His words go in one ear and out the other. My eyes haven't left the game since the first whistle blew.

My game has been perfect. I've carried the offense every moment we needed someone to step up.

Needed a first down? I got open.

Needed someone for a trick play? I gave an Oscar worthy performance, pulling defenders out of coverage.

Needed someone with sure hands for a touchdown? It was like I slathered my gloves in glue.

One more quarter.

Fifteen minutes is all that stands between me and that trophy.

My dream.

The defense is putting the weight of the game on offense's shoulders, and we are rising to the occasion. Our lead is slim, but it doesn't matter. So long as we have one more point than them at the end of the game, we'll be hoisting the trophy.

Hopefully, the missed field goal by our backup kicker won't keep red and gold confetti falling from the rafters tonight.

The coaching staff didn't say why Tim is missing the game. I assume something happened during warm-ups. Like he snapped his kicking leg in half or something. That's the only thing I can think that'd keep him from this field tonight.

The other team snaps the ball and their quarterback is sacked, making them go three and out. Grabbing my helmet off the dryer, I pull it down onto my head once more, determined to show every person in this stadium why we are here.

I line up opposite a defender, watching for the silent count.

"Hey, Reynier! Do you think after this I could get Ryan's number? I'll make sure not to fumble her like you did."

The words barely even register in my ear, let alone my brain. Really, the only one that does is 'Ryan.'

A part of me has been worrying about her since we hung up the phone this morning. I want to know how her concert went, if the stalker ever showed up.

Shaking my head, I focus back on the game. She would never want to distract me. So, I don't let her. My mind wraps the thoughts of her and tucks them off to the side, their presence a warm glow pushing me forward. Logan hikes his knee and I count for a heartbeat before breaking off the line. Slapping my opponent's shoulder, I leave him on the ground behind me, the ball making contact with my hands a fraction of a second later for the first down.

We march down the field. Play after play. Touchdown after touchdown.

With six seconds left on the clock, we are down by one.

Unlike last year, though, I know it doesn't matter.

"Gentlemen, this is it. They're going to be on Reynier like he owes them money. Let's have some fun with it. Sticky icky on three. Break," Logan says, clapping his hands.

Logan lines up in shotgun and I move to the right, along with two other wide receivers.

"Ready," Logan yells out, reading the coverage and smiling. "Cover two. Hut, hut, hut."

The ball is snapped and Logan fakes the hand off to the left and I set up a screen on the right, selling it until the defense commits. Heart racing, I break, running for the open back corner in the end zone.

A hush falls over the crowd. Logan releases the ball and it sails, a perfect spiral, landing in my arms. Hugging the ball tight to my chest, I drag my feet, falling to the ground out of bounds.

Whistles scream and the crowd goes wild, TOUCHDOWN THUNDERHAWKS flashing around the stadium. Red and gold confetti rains down around me.

All I see is her.

Ryan stands in the mouth of the tunnel, screaming and jumping with tears streaming down her face. She didn't even change out of her concert outfit.

Dropping the ball that should be going in my trophy case, I rip my helmet off and run to her, lifting her in the air. Our lips collide in fiery, searing passion until we are forced to break apart or die from lack of oxygen.

"Mr. Overachiever getting three touchdowns after promising me two," she says, her voice reverent. "I'm so proud of you."

"I couldn't have done it without you."

"I love you, Dominic Reynier. I'll always be here by your side, for as long as you'll have me."

My heart bursts and I spin her around, laughing. I don't think I could be any happier in this moment, right here with her.

"How does forever sound?" I ask when I set her back down. It's not a proposal, only because I don't have a ring. And like with our first kiss, I want it to be the two of us. But I need her to know, I'm not letting her go.

"It sounds like an amazing beginning."

I kiss her again, setting her down on her feet readying to head to the center of the field where the trophy presentation is being set up. I pause.

"Was he there? What happened at the concert."

She presses a kiss to my cheek, love in her eyes. "We can talk about it more later, but it was Tim. We caught him."

Fear and worry lifts from me and I kiss her once more, glad we're finally free.

# EPILOGUE

# SIXTEEN MONTHS LATER

## DOMINIC

I HAVE SEEN RYAN in haute couture. I have seen her in nothing but a blush. Every iteration of her is amazing and perfect and everything I could ever want.

Ryan in a wedding dress tops everything. Tank was right. This is better than winning the Super Bowl.

The custom light cream gown is perfectly tailored to her figure, down to the centimeter. There are no embellishments. Just simple satin flowing down her curves.

She takes my breath away.

Then again, she could be wearing the most ill-fitting, ugly gown I've ever seen, and she would still take my breath away.

Her parents flank her as she walks down the rose covered aisle in our backyard. An instrumental version of the first song she ever wrote for me plays out of the speakers and a tear falls down my face.

She could have had an entire live band here, thrilled to play for this moment. Instead, she recorded herself playing every instrument. When I caught her learning to play the violin, I thought she was crazy, but listening to her love for me in melody played by her fingers?

Life changing.

A seven-month pregnant Anastasia stands next me as my best woman. No one else would do. Without Anya, I never would've met my soon to be wife. Our parents and Parker sit in the front row, really the only row. Lorelei and Zoe, next to them, Tank crying already.

Taylor stands on Ryan's side, her dark blue bridesmaid's dress as perfectly tailored to her.

After an eternity, Ryan stands in front of me. Her mother lifts her veil, kissing her cheek, followed by her father. A choking sob breaks free of his throat as he holds a hand out to me.

I take it, holding it tight.

"Take care of my baby girl, Dominic. Give her all your love. She deserves nothing less."

"She has it already, sir. Until the universe burns into nothingness, she'll have it."

He wipes at his eyes, letting my hand go, following his wife to their chairs.

Ryan steps up to me and gives me her imperfectly perfect smile. The one she only gives to those who know her best.

"Hi," she breathes and I almost laugh for its simplicity in such a big moment.

"Hi. Ready for me to become Mr. Ryan Jade?"

"Ready for me to become Mrs. Dominic Reynier?"

"I don't think I could wait one more second."

At my declaration, Tank steps up and moves behind us, looking out at the crowd.

"Please be seated," he says to the seven person congregation. "Welcome, everyone, to this intimate affair where Ryan will finally put Dominic out of his misery and marry him."

We all laugh because it's true. Two months after winning the Super Bowl, I proposed to the love of my life. When I suggested running down to the courthouse that afternoon, she refused, stating we were going to have the perfect wedding.

Sure, this is more romantic, but every month for the last fifteen I've asked her if it was time. Every month, the answer was no.

Until last month, when Tim was sentenced to twenty years in prison.

The day after the Super Bowl, Ryan met with the police via video call and gave her statement of everything that happened in her dressing room, and the Thunderhawks officially cut him from the team. Come to find out, Tim had placed the camera for the video after his and Paige's rendezvous while she was in the bathroom. He continued dating her to get information on Ryan, successfully cloning her phone, which is how he found out who her business managers were and was able to get the last letter into her hands.

Ryan refused Paige's letter of resignation when she tried to quit, tears streaming down her face at the hurt she felt she had caused, instead reassuring her all the blame for everything that happened rested solely on Tim's shoulders. They both started therapy over the situation and were able to find some healing and closure.

But the real closure came during the trial, when Ryan told her story from start to finish, one last time. I sat in the gallery, silent tears streaming at all she went through. In the car after the sentencing,

Ryan asked how soon we could be married and three seemingly endless weeks later, we stand before the people we love.

Other than those surrounding us, no one else knows about this wedding.

Ryan never wore her ring in public.

We always evaded any questions about when we would get engaged on every red carpet and in every interview. We might never tell the world we got married.

This might be a secret we keep to ourselves until one of us accidentally slips.

It's not because I'm not dying to tell everyone this smart, talented, funny, beautiful human has decided to let me stand by her side until we die but because the truth of our relationship is just ours. To share or hide as we see fit.

"Having a front seat to Ryan and Dominic's love has been both deeply entertaining and touching. There have been struggles and strife. There have been the highest of highs. Every day, they chose each other and this love. Now it's time to tie these two together.

"Dominic and Ryan have written their own vows. Dominic, would you like to go first?" Tank asks.

"Well, I definitely can't go after a professional songwriter, can I?" I joke, winking at my bride. "Ryan, I told my sister when we met I was going to marry you. First, I want to thank you for not making me a liar. Second, I want to thank you for the honor of being your husband.

"You make me a better man. Not only for the things you bring into my life like laughter and love, you also push me to heights I never thought possible. Without you, I'd never be the man standing before you. Your drive and passion bring out the best in those around you, including me.

"I want to be better for you because, like your dad said, you deserve nothing less. We won't always have happy times, but I vow to stand beside you no matter what. There is nothing about you or your life that could pull me from your side. *You* are worth everything. I promise to spend the rest of my life working to deserve you. Working to lift you up. To give our lives every drop of happiness we can squeeze from this world."

Ryan leans forward and presses a soft kiss to my lips, her red lipstick perfect when she pulls away.

"I love you," she whispers just for me. It doesn't matter everyone here can hear us without microphones, the declaration is ours only.

"That was beautiful, Dom. Not a dry eye in the place," Tank jokes and we all laugh again. It's perfect. The exact right amount of levity. "Ryan? Would you like to put my teammate to shame and show him what vows really sound like?"

"I would," she says with a laugh and I feel a knot in my throat. "Dom. I have a lived a blessed life. Everything I've ever wanted I've gotten, except in love. I threw myself into relationships and gave them everything I had, yet I always felt like I came up short. Like I wasn't enough.

"Until you. You assuaged my fears. You loved me even when your life was on the line. I was selfish, wishing for you, my soul mate, when I had already gotten my biggest dream. But I don't care. I'll be selfish and take every day as your wife I can get. Thank you for showing me how I deserved to be loved.

"I would go through everything that came before this a thousand times over so long as you are waiting for me at the end. Your love has healed me. It has lifted me up. It has kept me safe. It has been the lighthouse in the storm. Your love is my favorite song and I can't wait to listen to it for the rest of my life."

I squeeze her hands, trying to release some of the pressure in my chest.

"Thank you, Ryan. It's now time for the exchanging of the rings." Tank pulls the rings from within his jacket pocket and we both grab up the other's ring. "Ryan, you first. Repeat after me. I, RyanJade Marie Collins, take you, Dominic Reynier, for my forever love. I bind myself to you. For the highest highs and the lowest lows, from this day forward until I cease to exist."

Her teal eyes glitter with unshed tears as she slips my ring on my finger, repeating Tank's words. It feels like it was always meant to be there.

"Now your turn," Tank says, turning to me. Before he can repeat himself, I start.

"I, Dominic Reynier, take you RyanJade Marie Collins as my goddess. I will worship at your feet. I will live my life devoted to you. I will be yours forever."

When the ring settles onto her finger, I know I was right when I first met her. We were always supposed to be here.

The air becomes charged, anticipation thick.

"Dom, Ryan. With the exchanging of your rings and promises to each other, I now pronounce you husband and wife. You may now kiss each other," Tank says and our guests cheer, the sound fading into the background.

A single tear falls down Ryan's face. Reaching up, I wipe it away before pressing a kiss to her soft lips.

"You're my wife," I whisper when I pull away, in awe at the words.

"You're my husband."

"Forever?"

"Forever," she says, and we turn, hand in hand, to face all life can throw at us.

# ACKNOWLEDGEMENTS

And thus ends the Cameras & Chemistry series. This has been such an amazing ride over the past few years and I'm truly so excited you came on this journey with me that started with a literal dream about a couple in a reality TV show. I couldn't think of a better way to end this series than on Dom and Ryan's story.

I want to thank my uncle for letting me pick his brain about how the Thunderhawks would support Dom and Ryan's relationship and other WAGs. If there are any inaccuracies in this book, they are mine alone. He did his best to impart his decades of experience to help House of Devotion be as accurate as possible.

To Christie. For naming Dominic James.

As always, to Courtney Parker. For giving your name and likeness to this story. And for giving me your friendship. The only reason I continue is because of your encouragement and willingness to listen to twenty minute long voice memos.

Thank you to my friend Taylor who allowed me to use her name and likeness as inspiration for the one good friend Ryan has in this book and for being a good friend to me.

Kayla, thank you for buying House of Deceit so we could become friends. I'm glad you were one of the first to ever read this book.

Dani. My beloved critique partner. I love you. There's nothing else I can say except I'd be lost without you.

Paige, Emily, and Amber, thank you for all the emotional support you give me on a daily basis. And for all the conversations that are impossible to finish because we get distracted.

To Carley, Jess, and the amazing Happy Endings book club hosted by Under the Cover. I have had so much fun over the past year talking about books I never found time to read. Thank you for picking House of Deceit to be one of them while I was writing this book. Y'all being my first ever "author interview" was a moving experience and made me feel more like an author than anything else I've done has. I appreciate for y'all letting me be me in our monthly meetings.

Beth Stedman. You have an amazing ability to see what is missing in every story I write. They are better for your keen eye and Marco Polo messages.

Makenna Albert. Four books down. I hope hundreds more to go.

Lucy. Thank you for making such amazing covers for this series! They are so amazing and I loved working with you over the past few years on them.

Sarah Lamb. Thank you for your eye for details since I will make the same grammar mistakes forever and ever. Without you, this book would be riddled with them.

Even though this book is dedicated to her, I want to thank my older sister Jessi. I haven't lived a day on this Earth without her. She is my best friend and the person I couldn't live without. I'll follow you wherever you go for eternity. Even though I hate moving.

## About the Author

N.E. Butcher was born and raised in a suburb of Kansas City, MO. Recently returned home after 13 years away, she's enjoying putting down roots while spending time with her loved ones. When not daydreaming up stories, you'll find her engrossed in a gripping book, knitting gifts for loved ones, or embracing her creative side with home DIY projects.

An unabashed Taylor Swift enthusiast, N.E. Butcher finds inspiration in the singer's lyrics and melodies and always has her music playing in the house that she shares with a lovable dog and an adorable cat.

Join her on a romantic journey as she delves into tales of love, heartbreak, and second chances, captivating your heart with every turn of the page.